DYE. RUN. DON'T DIE

A LOVE STORY

GladEye Press

Brian: "Do you always carry this much shit in your bag?

Allison: "Yeah, I always carry this much shit in my bag—you never know when you may have to jam."

—*The Breakfast Club*

Prologue

BANG, bang, BANG, the metallic sound of Winnie's cowgirl boot hammering out a slow, metrical beat against the faded pink side of the Fold 'n Fluff washing machine on which she was perched bounced off the walls of the deserted laundromat. The place was as seedy as laundromats go—old, dented up dryers lining the back wall, washers lined up in similar neglected fashion in the center of the room; an eerily glowing fluorescent ceiling light making an irritating high-pitched buzzing noise as it flickered on off, on off like a scene in a bad horror flick.

She didn't want to be here, but it was the only time she could do a load of clothes—not that she had a lot of clothes—but working the 6:30 a.m. to 5:00 p.m. shift at the diner left her scant time for running errands and doing chores like laundry.

Good thing no one was around except her, but why would there be? Nobody went to the laundromat at midnight in Hooker ("It's a location, not a vocation" was the town's motto), Oklahoma, pop. 1,918, 1,919 if you counted Mrs. Toomy's visiting niece from Oskaloosa. 1,920 if you counted Winnie, but more than anything, she didn't want to be counted. Although Hooker wasn't her destination of choice, she hadn't had time to choose a particular location; getting away quickly was the goal, any old place would do.

Seven weeks ago, she sat at the kitchen table in their southern California apartment, scissors in hand, and cut off her honey blond locks, dyed her short uneven hair jet black, dashed off a quick goodbye note to Jimmy, grabbed her camera, of course, and enough stuff to stow in a small suitcase, and walked, no ran, out the front door. She'd ended up here in the Oklahoma panhandle, a new girl with a new name: Jenny Jet Jones.

Winnie picked up a ragged and outdated copy of *People* magazine from the table and tried to focus on the banal lives of celebs to pass the time, but quickly found herself slipping into California memories, home, her life there, and the day she ran. She had been panicked that day, for sure, and in a hurry, but instinct told her to do what her mother would do. Heading straight for the cupboard in the bathroom she pulled out a box of hair color stashed on the shelf. As weird as having multiple boxes of hair color might seem, for Winnie, it made complete sense. If you've ever, as she had, experienced having your hair dyed leaning over a dirty sink in some gas station bathroom because your mom has once again whisked you away in a hurry from another bad situation, you know that it is something that is best done at home. In your own bathroom, where it's clean.

Like the character Allison in *The Breakfast Club* who boldly proclaimed, "You never know when you might have to jam," Winnie had learned to be prepared, yet, for all her experience with leaving places in a hurry, she still couldn't claim that she was any good under pressure. Realizing she'd wasted precious time with the hair coloring/cutting business, she had hastily grabbed a few things and impulsively jumped on the first Greyhound out of town. It wasn't until somewhere down the road, after sinking deep into the well-worn bus seat, that she had time to think things through. Any more delays could potentially get her killed, but certain things had to be addressed, like money, for instance. It was a good thing that she had held on to the financial aid money she'd received for her last term at UC Irvine.

There was enough in her personal savings account to pay next month's rent on the apartment—it was the least she could do for Jimmy, considering the abrupt departure she was making from his life—purchase another bus ticket, and then keep her going for a little while until she could find a safe place to lie low for a while and maybe find a job doing something menial and low-key.

Before pulling out the battery and SIM card from her beloved smart phone, Winnie transferred funds for the rent to her and Jimmy's shared account. At the ATM in the Riverside bus station, Winnie took out as much cash as she could get from her personal account, which effectively closed it. All hail online banking! Yay technology! It saved precious time not having to take a detour to physically visit her brick-and-mortar bank. Two hours and 15 minutes after fleeing their apartment in Orange County, Winnie boarded the 5:15 p.m. bus in Riverside, bound for New Mexico.

Anyone who has ever taken a bus anywhere can tell you that the journey is never a pleasant one. Her mother had dragged her onto a number of buses during their forays into disappearing over the years, so at least she knew what to expect.

For three straight days, Winnie endured the sounds of near constant flushing as well as an array of nasty odors that emanated from the bathroom at the back of the bus where she had the misfortune of being situated because the bus had been full. Day and night, a parade of passengers traipsed by her to do their business, opening and shutting the door, allowing the offending odors to escape. Despite the forced air from the ceiling vents, the taint of sweat and urine and other bad smells hung in the air like a gaseous cloud as people went yet another day on this bus without bathing.

She attempted sleep, but it was seriously an act of futility. The first night, a young couple, hormones raging, had bounced onto the bus, raced to the back and sprawled out on the two seats directly behind her, tickling each other and erupting into fits of nonstop giggling, which then turned into loud sloppy, smacking making out sounds followed by what seemed like hours of deep-throated moaning and groaning. Winnie dared not peek around the seat to verify what was probably a clear violation of Greyhound bus passenger protocol. And although, thankfully, the couple debarked the next morning, she never could get comfortable, and other than a catnap here and there, deep sleep mostly eluded her.

She remembered dreaming about Jimmy. He was yelling about it being dark out here and banging on the front door. As the dream dissipated, she realized an angry, disheveled man with a purple/pink Mohawk and an enormous nose ring was just yelling and banging on the door to the bathroom. She wondered now if she'd left the lights on in the apartment but forgotten to turn on the porch light. She always forgot and Jimmy hated coming home and fumbling in the dark with the dead-bolt locks.

Jimmy. Sure, he could be arrogant and insufferable at times; for instance, insisting that she remember to turn on the porch light, despite the fact that rather than walking the two steps over to the hamper, he never failed to carelessly deposit his dirty socks and underwear on the floor by the bed. When she called him out on his nonsense, he'd say something flippant like, "just another one of my endearing quirks, babe."

As much as it infuriated her to no end, she accepted it as part of their polar opposite upbringings—he growing up in a stable household with mother and father present, siblings, and pets, versus her chaotic, nomadic life with Missy, picking up and moving every few months. She dared not form relationships, learning early that nothing was permanent, predictable. At first, when she was very young, she had tried to make friends, but quickly realized that at any given time, she could be ripped away, squirreled off into the night on another crazy midnight move to some new town with a new round of issues that her mother couldn't cope with. By the time they finally landed in Orange County when she was 12, Winnie had built up a fairly substantial wall around herself for protection, a wall that only someone as persistent as Jimmy Carson could penetrate.

He was certainly persistent. Jimmy knew what he wanted and doggedly went after it, whether it was a job, a journalism degree, being first in line to see *Star Wars*, or Winnie. She, on the other hand, was perfectly content to operate behind the scenes; the unseen hand making brilliant corrections as an editor, the creative eye behind the lens, flying quietly under the radar far and away from the limelight.

She was pretty sure she loved him and they'd both assumed that after college they'd probably get married. College, however, had taken a bit longer than they had anticipated, interrupted by a little thing called having to make money to eat, but it didn't matter. Life with Jimmy was comfortable. Even if it wasn't always perfect. For once in her life Winnie felt mostly stable. Since moving in with Jimmy at 18, she had lived in the same place for five consecutive years. Five years. Even though life had sort of stabilized for her during high school when mom inherited grandma's house in Costa Mesa, nothing had changed much in terms of Missy's boyfriend turnovers, a chapter that Winnie was working on forgetting about. So there, in that safe nest she shared with Jimmy, she had finally found her way forward and away. She was a good writer, a good editor, but when she picked up a camera, everything changed.

Indeed, the only saving grace on the bus had been her camera. With her cell phone disabled to prevent any sort of online trace, she wasn't able to check any of her apps or email—probably the first time in years that she had completely disassociated herself from social media. But she discovered that having her camera was a better distraction anyway.

For all her mother's shortcomings and machinations and drama, probably the best thing Missy had ever done for her a daughter was buy her a camera. It wasn't much, just one of those small, cheap 35mm film cameras Missy had picked up used at a thrift shop. It not only gave Winnie something to do that summer, but when she got the developed prints back, she was hooked. They were random—candid shots of Missy with a towel around her head, smoking a cigarette, the little boy down the street, all pudgy toddler legs and hands, picking a dandelion, the sun shining through a flower at the perfect angle; bugs and butterflies and graffiti on the sides of trains. Even Missy was impressed with Winnie's unusual eye for depth and detail.

She loved taking pictures. It was her passion. She didn't want to take studio photos; she wanted to capture life, all of it. From gritty black-and-white street scenes to marching bands and musicians and magicians to athletes and little girls with pigtails jumping rope on the playground—a photojournalist's life. And now she had a degree that said she was proficient at it, although she hadn't received the actual piece of paper, and would never have the experience of shaking the dean's hand in cap and gown, considering that her life had been completely upended over the past few weeks. It made her feel a little sad and angry, but the camera comforted her, and the vast, flat desert landscapes flying by outside the bus window provided a multitude of creative photo ops for capturing all of nature's hidden beauty—something Jimmy never appreciated.

Jimmy didn't like the flat sameness, as he called it, of Southern California. He loved its sandy beaches and sunny days and the ocean, but she could tell when he talked about visiting his grandma in Oregon that he sometimes pined for the mountains and forests and rugged coastlines of the northwest. In fact, just a few days before she left he had flown to Portland to interview for an editorial position on a weekly alternative newspaper. According to him, he was a shoo-in for the job, and that would mean that he would expect to drag her up there with him. She would have gone with him, too—in a heartbeat—if only things were different; if only her dad, the real one, hadn't called and knocked a hole in her life as big as the Grand Canyon.

The washer buzzed, dispersing the daydream and Winnie sighed, sliding off the washer to move the clothes into a dryer. Once she had it going, she hopped onto the empty washer again and returned to another string of memories when running had been a normal part of her existence.

The earliest escapes and arrivals were all in Canada, a seemingly endless parade of small, cold, and rural towns. Missy named Winnie after the town she was born in, Winnipeg, Canada, a place she scarcely remembered other than the white, silent, flat expanse of snow-covered plains, so deep you could get lost in a drift and never be found. Then, only distant memories of a family of three moving away to the states, of a dad disappearing, never to return. And after that, the beginning of their long, strange odyssey. A rapid stream of people and places, where a procession of potential replacement daddy's—some nice, sure; some not so nice, would parade in and out of their lives. After each breakup, Winnie knew that once Missy's tears had dried, they would start packing. Again. Another move. Another town. Her mother's neediness knew no bounds.

To a child, one place was pretty much the same as another. The people changed, but not the types of people she met. The schools changed, but not really in important ways—they were all filled with strangers only a little curious about the "new girl" that dressed a bit funny and had strange and slightly scary markings on the parts of her arm that showed.

Winnie was not a pretty girl, at least according to her mother. She tried to soften the blow by telling her that she had nice features, which was Missy's not so veiled way of masking her own embarrassment. For even if Winnie been a ravaging beauty, her mother had pointed out more than once that nothing, even a pretty face, could hide the huge purple colored birthmark that splayed halfway across Winnie's back and chest and all the way down her left arm. Missy loved to tell the story of her birth, how when they'd placed the newborn Winnie in her arms she'd shrieked, "What the fuck?" and nearly dropped her. She said that God had given her a flawed child as punishment for drinking too much cheap wine when she was pregnant. The truth was that Winnie was one of three in 1,000 babies born with a port-wine stain or *nevus flammeus*, also commonly called a firemark.

Missy did her best to camouflage Winnie's firemark with clothing—she only dressed her daughter in long-sleeved shirts with collars and turtleneck sweaters. Fortunately, the weather in Canada was cold, but in the summer, Missy would insist that Winnie cover up, often forcing her to wear the uncomfortable long sleeves even in hot, muggy weather. It was a good thing she was smart, although she kept that hidden too.

When her grandmother, who Winnie couldn't remember meeting, died and left her house to Missy, they moved to Costa Mesa in Orange County, California—the OC. Winnie was 11 and had lived in more than a dozen houses that she could recall. She had been surprised to discover that both she and her mother were US citizens, it had never occurred to her that they "belonged" anywhere.

Never much of a fan of clothes to begin with, sunny Southern California was clearly where Missy belonged, but for Winnie, it came at a price, which was the endless embarrassment of having a mother that dressed like a teenager. Her mother's wardrobe consisted of an assortment of multicolored variations of tank/string/tube tops and several versions of short shorts. She seemed oblivious to the fact that she was getting older and short shorts were starting to look really silly. She'd made the point, often and loudly, that even being tied down with an embarrassing, freakish daughter, at least she wasn't in boring, frigid Canada anymore, and well, in a few years, Winnie would be someone else's problem.

Still, despite Missy's proclivity for leaving her unattended and other gross errors in parental judgment, to little Winnie, her mother seemed grown-up and glamorous. However, when she herself began to reach puberty at around 12, she began to understand that her mother was actually competing with her.

Missy needn't have worried. Winnie preferred books to boys, but that hadn't stopped Missy from trying to encourage her daughter to make friends. Winnie had once made the mistake of inviting a male school friend over—more to appease her mother than anything else. Like something out of a bad summer hijinks comedy, Missy had behaved badly, as expected. Fueled by alcohol, she showed off her cleavage and legs and engaged in inappropriate slightly over-the-top flirtatiousness in her role as the clichéd fading ingénue. Missy loved the attention, as did the misguided 13-year-old boy, who thought Missy was the coolest mom ever.

Yet, as flighty and irresponsible and unmindful of the needs of her daughter, she still possessed an unwavering optimism that seemed to keep them both going.

Winnie quickly learned that her mom would rather believe that things would just get better than to put any effort into making them so, Winnie couldn't help but sometimes admire and secretly hope that she might one day possess that spunky resilient streak too. But she feared it wasn't to be. Back then she had her mother at least and a misguided sense that they were somehow in this together, but now she was all alone and scared, on the run, missing Jimmy, and fighting to tamp down the overpowering fears of what might lie ahead.

Goddammit!" Winnie left the lights on in the apartment, but not the porch light—again! Fumbling with his keys, Jimmy found the one for the dead bolt, then, after a few miscues, the one for the main lock. "What idiot installs mismatched locks on a rental?" He fumed for about the thousandth time. Finally opening the door, he savagely slammed the outside light switch up.

He didn't always come home in such a foul mood. Most of the time, he was merely irritated by the dark porch light and the double key locks. Usually, the smell of dinner calmed him down, and sometimes Winnie apologized about the light (but forgot again the next day), but there was no cooking smell, and the house was silent. He'd talked to Winnie earlier today from Portland before he caught the flight home. She knew he was coming home tonight.

Dropping his suitcases by the door, he did a quick survey of the small place. Winnie must have run out for something, maybe dinner. Another thing that annoyed him—Winnie's classes were all early and his were all late afternoon and into the evening. It was backwards. He was the early bird, the one that liked to be home in the afternoon, the one that liked to cook. Winnie was a bit of a night owl and although a dutiful cook, she was neither good at it, nor did she care much. Maybe she was out getting take-out to celebrate his return, even if he'd only been gone a couple days.

Thinking she may have left a note, he looked back on the table and there it was. It wasn't the simple be-right-back note he expected. "Jimmy, I've got to go. Don't look for me. Try to be happy – Winnie"

"What the fuck?" he exclaimed, confused and angry. Yeah, their conflicting schedules and the stress of facing the end of college as they both finished up their degrees had put a stain on the relationship, but he'd have sworn that Winnie had been basically happy, and as devoted to him as he was to her. Besides, no adult person would consider this even approaching an acceptable way to end a live-in arrangement. They'd been together since high school and living together now for five years. This simply couldn't mean what it seemed to say.

Giving the apartment a more careful look only confused and angered him more. He plopped down on the couch to review the situation. She was gone, but she'd left almost everything of hers and all of "theirs" behind. Her backpack and a small carry bag that she kept her cosmetics in were gone. Some clothes had been thrown and left on the bed, but her favorite jeans and a few blouses were gone. Her camera and accessories were gone too, but then, Winnie would hardly go to the store without the camera. All told, she hadn't taken much, barely more than you'd expect if she'd been fleeing a fire, certainly not what you'd take if you were moving out.

He'd gone off to the job interview up in Portland just the other morning. Yeah, there had been some tension before he left. Winnie wasn't sold on moving to the Northwest, convinced it rained every day and that everyone up there was a poseur or a redneck. Still, she knew it was just an interview, he hadn't told her on the phone that they'd made an offer. Additionally, he hadn't really accepted, only told them he needed to check with his fiancé before he accepted. There was no way she'd leave over that, even if she'd somehow found out he'd already decided to accept.

Mind racing, he wondered if somehow, she'd discovered that he'd called her his fiancé. They weren't engaged, he hadn't asked, and she hadn't pressured him at all. He'd just assumed that once they were out of school and established in careers it would just happen. No, Winnie would just laugh and tease him about his presumptuousness, besides, no one in Portland had Winnie's cell number and of course they had no landline—they weren't old people after all.

"Fuck! I'm an idiot" he realized. Digging his cell phone out of his sports coat pocket, he tried to call Winnie's phone. It went immediately to voicemail. Either the phone was off, or the message box full. Ironically, discovering that calling her wasn't the answer made him not feel so stupid. None of it made any sense and he was hungry and emotionally wiped out from the job interview, flying, and now this. The mundane act of fixing some food calmed him down. As he scrambled some eggs and prepared toast, he put together a plan for tomorrow.

It hadn't occurred to him that the nights in the Portland hotel had been the first nights he's slept without Winnie in bed beside him in nearly four years. Somehow, that thought was inescapable now that he was back home in their bed. Everything smelled of her, and he found himself imagining that she would slip into bed any minute. Where he'd slept like a baby in the hotel, he tossed and turned all night in his own bed.

In the morning he set off to find answers in their old neighborhood. They'd grown up only a few houses away from each other and their parents all still lived there. Well, Winnie only had her mother and a procession of random "step-dudes", some creepier than others. It was a short drive away, but during the drive, he got more anxious. If she was at her mother's, then things must really have been seriously bad—Winnie and her mother barely spoke and then, even rarely did their conversations end well. He thought it more likely she'd stopped by his parents' house. Mom always treated Winnie almost like she was the daughter and he the daughter's boyfriend. Partly because Winnie's mom barely acknowledged that he existed, and mostly because he didn't think she'd go there, he went home first.

"No, we haven't heard from her," his mother replied, already concerned. "Maybe she had a family emergency and will be back once it is settled?" she offered, as much an invitation for her son to confess to driving Winnie away as a real suggestion. Defensively, Jimmy pulled the crumpled note out of pocket and shoved it toward his mother.

"Does that sound like she's got a family emergency, or that she intends to come back?" he demanded angrily. "We weren't fighting, everything was fine . . . normal, then she pulls this. You just don't leave a fucking note and walk out the door!" he shouted.

Even as his mom shrank back and tried to change tack, he was up and heading for the door. "Maybe her mom will be more help," he added unfairly as he slammed the door on his way out. He didn't have to think much; heading toward Winnie's childhood house was almost instinct. As he approached, that changed. He'd only been inside the house a handful of times, almost all after they'd begun living together. Generally, Winnie would come out of the house in response to him tossing pebbles at her window. Sometimes he'd knock, but her mom would always say "Winnie can't play now" and then a few minutes later Winnie would sneak out and join him. Never was he invited in, and never was Winnie allowed to come out when he asked.

Despite the well-ingrained lesson that he wasn't welcome, he forced himself to the front of the rundown little house. Knocking on the door, he noticed that aside from the two obviously derelict cars, one in the yard and the other on the street in front, there wasn't a semi functional rambling wreck in the driveway. No one answered the door. Looking past the dirty and slightly torn curtains, he could see a dingy living room with overflowing ashtrays and a surfeit of coffee cups. He noticed too that there were a couple newspapers on the porch. "Damn," he muttered as he turned away, maybe Mom was right about the family emergency.

He'd missed classes to take the trip to Portland, and he was in no mood to go to school today, but he decided to see if anyone there knew anything about Winnie. Although they had both been in the Cal Irvine journalism school for nearly four years, their different career tracks hadn't provided as much crossover as many would assume, especially the last couple years as they each took their upper division classes. Winnie, of course, was in the visual arts section, photojournalism and multimedia while Jimmy was on the quickly diminishing news writing and magazine track. Although they'd talked about working together someday, her shooting images to go with his reporting, there was little opportunity for them to cross paths at school.

Not surprisingly, she wasn't at her classes, and the random people he asked about her seemed a little surprised. Like him, Winnie wasn't very social, trending firmly toward the antisocial. Neither of them had been popular in high school, and although that could have possibly changed in college, they had each other and no interest in cultivating friends. No one seemed to remember when last she'd been in class, it could have been yesterday, maybe not since last week, and a couple people didn't even know her, despite being in fairly small classes with her over the past few years.

Frustrated, he went back to the apartment half expecting that she'd be there, and everything would get straightened out. She wasn't. Once again, Jimmy berated himself, "email"!, he said as he unlocked the double-keyed door. Almost sprinting into the bedroom where they kept their shared laptop. Quickly he booted it up and waited impatiently as it automatically loaded Facebook. Of course, neither of them had many friends, but Facebook was handy for dealing with classmates on shared team assignments. Because it was so handy, they often left messages for each other using Facebook. He always knew when Winnie had probably left him a message, the page would open with her account, otherwise, it would be his. When it finally came up, it was his, and other than a brief message from a professor about an assignment he'd turned in last week and a raft of offers to make his dick harder, bigger, and in every way superior, he had no messages.

Logging in as Winnie (they each knew the other's password), he wasn't that surprised to see the page basically untouched since he'd sent a quick text from his phone when in Portland. "Love you, miss you and see you soon," he'd sent. She'd seen it when he'd sent it, but hadn't replied. Oh well, he hadn't really thought Facebook would help.

Pulling up email was more interesting, but maybe more depressing. Winnie had been on email yesterday. There was a message from the school admin office confirming that she'd graduated and that she'd withdrawn from the other classes. Dang! He hadn't even realized that she already had the credits to graduate, but then, he hadn't told her he had also hit all his credits last term too. "I guess neither of us was ready to move into the "real world," he mused.

There was another message, from the bank. She'd closed her account! Panicked a bit, he shifted to open their linked accounts. The joint account was still open, neither of them could close it without the other cosigning. She'd transferred next month's rent into it from her account, but that was it. As the email said, her private account was closed, but his was still there and no transactions since he'd bought that horrid Cinnabon at PDX before getting on the plane.

Relieved, but further puzzled, "Who pays next month's rent for the guy she dumps?" he thought as he went back to investigating her email. The bank message had more info that he'd overlooked. She'd withdrawn her money and closed the account from a bus depot in Riverside.

That clarified a couple things. Jimmy had the car, although they'd shared it, it was his. He'd parked it at the airport for the trip. He'd kind of assumed she'd taken off with someone, (Why would he assume that? It doesn't seem like she ever gave him any reason and they shared their passwords.) even if he couldn't bring himself to think that a someone might be some dude she'd dumped him for, but really, he'd hoped she was still in town, still in reach. It also showed that she had been in a hurry and hadn't really planned things out. She must have thought of getting cash after she'd gotten on the bus and Riverside was the next stop. She must have got back on the bus—why would anyone stay in Riverside? But, where was she heading?

"Hey, whatcha doin' here so late?"

Winnie flinched and stopped thumping the washing machine with her foot as she turned in the direction of a man's voice. It was just Dallas. They'd met in New Mexico. Winnie knew from the start that he wasn't trustworthy, and she was okay with that.

Dallas slid his thin frame up and onto the washer next to her. She could smell the beer on his breath. He'd left earlier in the day and she'd promised to pick him up later at the bar.

"Aw, just thought I'd get some clothes washed," she said.

"In the middle of the night?" he asked.

"It's quiet," Winnie answered. "I like it when there's nobody around."

Dallas gave her an unconvinced look. "Including me?" he asked.

"You're okay," she said, hiding a wary smile, "I guess."

"Well, all right, then," he said, clicking the heels of his scuffed cowboy boots together and sliding off the washer. "But don't stay out too late," he warned as he peeked around outside the doorway suspiciously. "You never know, there might be some bad guys out there lurking in them thar streets of Hooker."

That one, Dallas, probably not his real name. An odd duck; nothing special to look at, ears that stuck out from his head and a mean scar that snaked across one cheek; not even very smart, but clever, and there was something about him that Winnie rather liked, although she couldn't quite peg it. They had met in Albuquerque.

After getting off the bus from California, she had checked into the closest cheap motel she could find to lie low for a few days, only periodically venturing out of her room to grab a quick snack—a bag of chips, a cup of weak coffee from the 7-Eleven around the corner, and always with her head down and her hoodie up. The room was little more than a place to crash; a double bed, a nightstand with a lamp, a touch-tone phone, standard Gideon's Bible tucked inside the drawer. Obviously, cable was either extra or nonexistent; the 19-inch TV picked up only three local channels. The bathroom, of course, was what you'd expect from a motel of this caliber, something that no amount of Pine-Sol could disguise. And even with the drab, taupe-tinted curtains drawn, it seemed perpetually dark and dank and had a musty, moldy smell. She was probably breathing in asbestos or any number of toxic fumes, but it was all she could afford, so it would have to do. She could only hope that there was no dead prostitute tucked up inside the mattress or that she was sharing the sheets with a colony of bedbugs.

On the bright side, without the distraction of TV, books, or the Internet, she had lots of time to ruminate on things, particularly Jimmy. Winnie was well aware of her "issues"; she had plenty—mommy issues, trust issues, safety issues—all of which spilled over into her relationship with him. Missie wasn't the nurturing type, not the storybook mommy that a child could lean into and feel safe and secure. Heck, she was lucky if Missy noticed her half the time. And without any adult guidance, it was up to Winnie to try to navigate the big bad world on her own. Her mother's parade of surrogate daddies didn't help matters, although most were okay in their own way. For the most part, they were indifferent to Missy's freakish spawn, and besides, they were mostly drawn to Missy and her low-cut, gold lame tops, tight pants, and ridiculously high heels.

There had been one, however, that she rather liked. Dennis was his name. He was nicer to her than the others, probably because he had a son of his own. The son's name was Seth. On weekends, Dennis had visitation with Seth, so usually they were out doing something together, but sometimes Dennis brought him over to their house. Seth was 13, five years older than Winnie and, for the most part, kept to himself, usually playing video games all day, except for the times throughout the day when he'd go into the bathroom, close and lock the door, turn the fan on, and stay in there for a really long time. She didn't know what he did in there, but sometimes she'd press her ear up to the door and hear paper rustling and the sound of heavy breathing. One time she'd spied on him when he was in the back yard lighting matches and leaning over to burn something. When she'd gone out after he'd left, she found a bunch of dead mutilated bugs and snails with burn marks on them.

One time, Missy and Dennis wanted to go out. They hired a neighbor girl to watch Winnie and Seth. Everything went okay. They ate fast food for dinner, watched TV, and Winnie went to bed at around nine o'clock. Then, sometime in the night, she felt something lightly brushing against her inner thigh. She opened her eyes but couldn't make out anything in the dark. She started to turn over when something hard poked into her back and the light brushing turned into fingers that tore away her panties and began probing her in her private part. Startled, Winnie sat up and while pushing the offending appendages away the light from under the door caught Seth's determined face.

"What the hell?" she cried out, "what are you doing? Go away!" He shoved his sweaty hand over her mouth to make her shut up, and whispered menacingly into her ear, "If you tell anybody, freak," he snarled, "you'll be sorry, I'll come back and kill your cat, or your mom, or you." Tears began to roll down Winnie's cheeks, but she kept quiet. A few minutes later, Seth was gone, and she was alone again in her bedroom. She felt something sticky on her thigh but was too afraid to get out of bed to see what it was.

In the morning, something that looked like a trail a slug would leave snaked down her leg. She rushed to the bathroom and quickly washed it off, and she never said a word about what had happened to anyone, but after that night Winnie steered clear of Seth and she started locking her bedroom door at night. The first time she saw him again, he grinned at her and placed his index finger to his lips menacingly indicating that she'd better not tell. After that, whenever they were in the same room together, Winnie avoided eye contact and slinked away. Inevitably, Dennis and Missy broke up and Winnie never saw Seth again.

She realized a few years later that she'd probably dodged a bullet when she recognized his name in the newspaper. He had been arrested for nearly beating his girlfriend to death. But had she dodged a bullet, really? Her childhood scars impacted her life with Jimmy more than she wanted to admit. It was easier to be like Missy and pretend that everything was great rather than ever dealing with anything. She wanted to be closer to Jimmy. She wanted to tell him how she felt. She wanted to trust that she could safely rest in him, but the issues always seemed to get in the way; to hold her back. She sat in the room and vacillated between calling and not calling him; feeling at the same time brave and like a coward until finally convincing herself that maybe Jimmy was better off without her and all her stupid "issues" anyway.

After a few days and growing tired of snacks and rumination, Winnie decided to do some exploring. A little farther down the block, she discovered a place called The Bus Stop, a greasy spoon that looked pretty rundown and mostly deserted. But, it had a newspaper rack outside the door and with her money dwindling Winnie knew she'd need to find a job fast. It was your classic dump. The booth seats were tattered and worn, the plastic slats on the windows were twisted and bent and coated in several layers of dust; the carpet looked like it hadn't seen a vacuum in months. An odoriferous mixture of bacon/fry grease and Lysol wafted from the kitchen. The sign up front said "Seat Yourself," and not wanting to deal with small talk of any kind, she avoided the counter where the lone customer, an elderly gentleman with one visible tooth, sat sipping something liquid from a cup, instead, she chose a booth that was only mildly less ratty than the others, deep in the furthermost corner where she could spread out the classified section of the newspaper.

The waitress—Meg it said on her badge—dressed in standard waitress fluffery and comfortable shoes, poured black coffee into Winnie's upturned cup, pulled out several creamer cups from the pocket of her apron and unceremoniously dropped them on the table next to it, then handed her a laminated menu with faded pictures of food and walked away.

Winnie sipped her coffee and scoured the help wanted columns looking for some sort of work.

Before receiving the call (*people are coming, run!*) Winnie had been working as a paid intern for a trade magazine. She'd hoped it would lead to something permanent. No chance of that now. And as much as she'd love to put that newly acquired degree to work, she knew she needed something surreptitious, something that she could abandon easily without guilt if necessary.

There seemed to be an abundance of barista and fast-food jobs, but Winnie felt overwhelmed by the unfamiliarity of a new city where she had no clue about the locations of things or transportation for getting there. Maybe it was the dirty booth in the crappy diner, but her emotions surged. She felt hopelessly alone and afraid, and she missed Jimmy terribly. Salty tears began to roll down both cheeks, settling on her nose and lips before plop, plopping into her coffee cup. When she saw Meg coming over to the table to take her order, she quickly wiped her eyes with the sleeve of her hoodie.

"What can I getcha?" Meg barked, pen and tablet in hand.

Winnie sniffed. She had forgotten to look at the menu. Picking it up and scanning it quickly, she pointed to the cheapest item on it. "I'll have an English muffin."

"That's it?" Meg asked, rolling her eyes. "An English muffin."

"Yeah."

With an audibly irritated sigh, Meg closed her tablet without writing anything down and turned to head back to her station but stopped and turned back around to look at Winnie. "Are you looking for a job?" she asked matter of fact.

"Ummm, yeah. I am," Meg responded, sniffing again.

The waitress walked back over to the table and said, "How about here?"

"Here?" Winnie asked, surveying the room. Since the old toothless man had left, she was the sole customer left in the place.

Clearly exasperated, Meg placed one hand on her hip and said, "Do you want a job or not?"

"Sure," Winnie managed to say. Meg walked away and returned a few minutes later with a uniform and an apron that she'd grabbed from behind the counter.

"Here," she said, placing them on the table. "Come back tomorrow at 11:30."

Winnie was excited that finding a job had been so easy, yet a little confused about why she'd been offered the job at all. With hardly any customers, it didn't seem like they needed any extra help. And, the uniform, which featured a low-cut collar and short sleeves, created a bit of a dilemma for Winnie. Never having to deal with uniform wearing, she wondered if they'd mind if she wore a sweater to cover up her birthmark. The following day, Winnie arrived on time, and as she feared, Meg asked her to please remove her sweater. She hesitantly took it off and waited for Meg to gasp in horror, but Meg didn't bat an eye. Instead, she took the sweater, hung it up on the coat tree, and sat Winnie down for a quick tutorial on the menu items.

A few customers came in, ate, left. Piece o' cake, Winnie thought. That is, until lunchtime happened. Seemingly out of nowhere, the doors burst forth and a flood of people began pouring into the diner, filling up every available booth and table as well as the counter. For two solid hours, Winnie was on her feet, taking orders, balancing plates of soup and sandwiches and burgers and curly fries and milkshakes and condensation-covered glasses of Coca-Cola. She had no time to think about anything, let alone her birthmark. No one seemed to notice it, other than the one time when a concerned little girl had pointed to her arm and asked if she was hurt and Winnie had leaned in close and whispered, "No, it's my superpower!" The girl grinned, impressed.

When the lunch rush was finally over, Winnie collapsed in one of the now empty booths and Meg explained that because of its proximity to the bus station, the diner was used as a lunch destination for the riders. Duh, now the name The Bus Stop made way more sense.

Every day, Meg explained, the bus arrived, and hordes of hungry bus riders rushed in to grab a quick bite to eat in the allotted time before the bus departed again. It happened three times a day—at 6:30 a.m., noon, and at 5:00 p.m. for the dinner crowd. Two other girls worked the morning and evening shifts, but their lunch waitress had quit suddenly leaving them shorthanded.

After that first day, life began to improve immensely for Winnie. For one thing, she got free food, which as it turns out, was amazing: the best food she'd ever eaten. And underneath her brusque exterior, Meg was actually quite a nice person. It got her out of the shitty motel room for a few hours. And she had met Dallas. He was the diner's cook/busboy. She'd noticed him that first day poking his skinny neck through the window, watching her curiously from afar.

He was a sketchy little dude; lean with a long, blond ponytail that he kept, by law, tucked up under a hairnet and hat; a small goatee jutted outward from his chin. He wasn't much to look at, he seemed a little smarmy, and he talked too much, but he was one of those people that grew on you, and in the kitchen, he was greased lightning. Winnie had never seen anyone flip burgers and eggs and hash browns and any number of items all at once on the grill as fast and effortlessly as Dallas did. It was truly an impressive sight to behold. And together, as it turned out, they made a dynamite duo, matching each other's pace from the start. It turned into a fun game to see how fast they could get an order out. From Winnie taking the order and slipping it into the carousel to Dallas ringing the bell and her carrying it out to the table, their record was under four minutes. The two of them: a well-oiled machine.

That first week, Winnie was so exhausted from being on her feet, she collapsed into the lumpy motel bed, falling into a coma-like sleep almost as soon as she hit the pillow. She sort of wished she'd brought her FitBit along so she could log in how many gazillions of steps she must be taking every day. Alas, it was only one of many things she had left behind. The second week, the soreness in her feet and calves had worn off and now going back alone to the empty motel room and watching *Wheel of Fortune* seemed way too depressing.

She was restless and bored, so instead of heading back to the room after work, she decided to venture out just a little farther in a different direction. Once she got a few blocks away from the bus station, which was located in a semi-industrial part of the city, she rounded a corner and tucked away like a secret city was an entire block with what looked like a magical mixture of bars and funky shops—the kind of shops that you'd never find in Orange County, shops overflowing with interesting curiosities, and odd things, antiques and baubles and velvet bohemian garments. It was shabby and rundown here, but in a good, revitalizing way; you could sense a carefree, youthful vibe.

Inside one of the thrift shops, Winnie tried on a cool worn denim jacket, accessorizing it with a beret and a pair of retro sunglasses. Turning this way and that way in front of the shop's only mirror, the effect was striking. Now that she was technically "on the lam", maybe it was time she shed the nerd she'd become and seriously become badass. She looked the part. The sunglasses and uneven jet-black bangs poking out from under the beret looked pretty radical. If she was holding a gun she may well have passed for Patty Hearst, the wealthy heiress kidnapped by the Symbionese Liberation Army back in the '70s. Cool.

Down the street a ways she wandered into a used bookstore. Now that she was done with textbooks and assigned readings at school, Winnie was excited to escape into a good novel. A voracious reader, Winnie devoured books like candy. She especially liked getting lost in the big, tome-like, complicated period novels filled with maps and charts and graphs that traced family lineages that spanned generations, but she could also get into a good fantasy now and then. Jimmy, also an avid reader, gravitated toward hard science sci-fi. Probably the best thing about readers in general is even when they're not reading they never feel compelled to fill up the silence between each other with small talk, and the same held true for Winnie and Jimmy. And they both loved bookstores, the dustier and messier the better.

He would have loved this one. It was packed floor to ceiling with books of every conceivable genre. On her way over to peruse the fantasy section, she stopped short. Interestingly, considering her current situation, Winnie was feeling drawn to the thriller, crime section. Hmmm, she thought as she ran her fingers along books by such prolific writers of the genre as Robin Cooke, Mary Higgens Clark, and James Patterson. Perhaps she should brush up on the mob. Without her phone or laptop and no Wi-Fi anyway, she would have to do research the old-fashioned way.

Winnie selected a couple of crime novels, a time travel fantasy, and a biography that piqued her interest, about Canada's top mafia boss, Vito Rizzuto. The elderly, white haired lady with glasses at the checkout looked like everyone's vision of grandma. After observing Winnie's all over the map selections, a broad smiled lit up her face giving her kind eyes a bit of a twinkle. "Excellent choices," she said.

"Thanks," said Winnie, digging out a five-dollar bill from her pocket. "I don't like women writers much," the woman continued. "Oh?" Winnie responded. "I like the gritty male authors much better," she said. "Give me a dismembered body in the first chapter and I'm hooked!" She handed Winnie her books in a plastic bag from the supermarket. "Have a nice day," she said sweetly.

As one week turned into three, Winnie found that she was beginning to relax, to blend in. Even though the room at the motel was still a wreck, she now had books to read, and she had taken to going on early morning walks with her camera. She loved the quiet of the morning, the only sound birds squawking back and forth at each other in the trees. In solitude, she walked along the dingy streets, taking pictures of things only she found interesting, the flower that grew from the crack in the sidewalk or the bright, bold colors of the spray-painted graffiti adorning the walls. And even though the place she worked was a dive, she was discovering how nice it was to fit somewhere, to have made friends. When she'd been with Jimmy it had mostly just been she and him. He had a few friends outside of their relationship, but she did not. Perhaps it stemmed from her old insecurities about always having to leave.

Her new work friends may be casual, she thought, but then, they seemed more interested in her than Missy ever had. Sure,

Missy would make a show of putting on a birthday party for her daughter, if she remembered, but she'd only invite her friends from the local bar and whatever man she was dating. Although she thought of Jimmy almost every night and missed him fiercely, she realized that she hadn't even thought of calling her mother once. Oh well, she told herself, the new Winnie has no mother, she decided, reinventing herself, but she does have friends!

It surprised and delighted her too how much she really liked these crazy people, Meg and the other two waitresses Suzanne and Sophie, and Dallas, of course. If her upbringing had taught her anything, Winnie had learned the art of immediately reading people's expressions to finesse a situation. It had been a useful skill when trying to gauge the strange people she and Missy met. These were the type of people she'd grown up around. These were her people, well, her mother's people—gypsies, tramps, and thieves. During her childhood, she'd met con artists and real artists and musicians and bums and hustlers and barflies and druggies and bikers and hippies. When you live that sort of nomadic life you can expect to meet people of all stripes. Some were nice and kind to the little girl with the purple arm; others simply ignored her; some were terrifying, others were just down and out. They were all untrustworthy to a certain degree, but she understood now that when you exist on the fringe of society, to protect yourself, for survival you wear a mask, and you lie.

For the past five years, she'd been cloistered within the walls of academia, the university bubble of elites—professors, grad students, and people, who in general, had dreams and lofty goals. She wasn't complaining at all. This is what she wanted for herself. School and Jimmy had saved her even. And she couldn't say that she didn't appreciate how structured and reliable her life had become. She would never have dreamed that she'd find such stability with someone like Jimmy. Back in high school when they had "found" each other while working side by side on the school newspaper, they knew that theirs wasn't exactly a match made in heaven. He was loud, at times obnoxious, a little overbearing and a know it all. He had a crude obsession with the female anatomy, and she'd seen him treat others badly, but she had also witnessed a hidden sweet and tender side.

They had been assigned to cover the football game. Jimmy was reporting, but they had both taken their cameras out so they could grab more angles. She was shooting from the sidelines back behind the bobble-head cheerleaders. Cheerleaders didn't bother her all that much, a little too perky, but they didn't seem to notice Winnie, although when one of them, Sherrie Smith had asked if she could copy off her history test, Winnie had allowed it, setting a bad precedent that had continued for the rest of the semester.

At any rate, the following Monday when Winnie had met with Jimmy to go through the photos they'd taken, Jimmy had seemed hesitant to share his shots. And when he pulled up the display of uploaded pictures onscreen, she understood why. Nearly all of them were focused on her, not homed in on the cheerleader's bobbing big boobs and shiny perfect hair as she would have expected, but on her. Winnie was dumbstruck. She had no idea Jimmy had even noticed her. She looked at him and he smiled a weak, I've-been-caught kind of smile. She wasn't sure how to react, so she impulsively gave him a hug and he hugged her back. From then on, they became inseparable, Lois Lane to his Jimmy Olsen, ace reporters.

He didn't seem to be embarrassed to be seen with her like her mom did and neither did his parents, who adored her, and she loved them back as if they were her own. In fact, she spent more time at the Carson's home than she did at her own. Missy was rarely home and usually there was nothing in the house to eat. After they graduated, moving in together seemed like the natural progression. It was the beginning of the end of Winnie's life as a wanderer, until now anyway.

After the busy lunch rush, Winnie and Dallas headed out back of the diner where they had taken to spending their breaks together sitting atop the rickety old picnic table; Dallas to smoke a cigarette and Winnie, who had started bringing her camera along with her, was zeroing in to photograph a jittering jaybird that was perched on the tree limb above.

Dallas took a long drag from his cigarette before casually asking, "So Winnie, some guy called at the diner this morning looking for you."

Winnie froze. "What?" she cried, spinning around and nearly dropping her camera. The startled jaybird flew away.

"Yeah, some guy."

Visibly upset, Winnie grilled him, "What did he say? Did he ask for me by name? What did you tell him?"

"I didn't tell him nothin'," Dallas said. "I said I didn't know anybody named Winnie."

"Why would you say that?" she asked, albeit calmer, thankful that for some reason he hadn't told whoever it was that she was there but wondering why he thought to do that.

Dallas ran his hand through the hair on his chin before turning toward Winnie and bluntly asking, "Who you runnin' from, girl?"

Winnie was stunned. How did he know? "I don't know," she managed to answer. That part was sort of true.

"Well, all right," he said, fanning out his fingers, taking it in, thinking. "But is Winnie Jones your real name?"

She nodded, "Yes"

"When you filled out a W4, did you use your social security number?" he asked.

"Yes, why?"

"Oh hell to the no, girl" Dallas said, springing off the table, clearly dismayed. "Please, please, don't tell me you used your real name?"

"Yes, I did," Winnie admitted to him. "Was I not supposed to? I didn't know. I didn't think . . . Will they be able to track me?"

"I don't know who 'they' are, unless you wanna tell me Winnie, but yeah, yeah, someone can track you down if you use your goddamned social security number."

Winnie didn't want to say, but she wanted/desperately needed to confide in someone, so she came clean and told him about the phone call from her dad, how her mother had told her that he was in the witness protection program, and that when he had said bad people were coming and she should run, she believed him.

Dallas' reaction was immediate and alarming. He dropped his cigarette and stomped on it hard with his boot.

"Fuck me. You're in deep shit, girl," he said pausing. "These people . . . whether it's the mob or the FBI, either way, it's bad news for you." Winnie was scared now. Really scared.

"What do I do? I don't know what to do," she blustered as she shook her head and paced back and forth. Dallas grabbed her shoulders to make her stop. "Winnie. Listen. I can help you. I can. I know some people," he said. "And I know a place where we can disappear."

From there things happened quickly. Within a day, she had quit her job at the diner, and sold every trace of her former life—

her "wiped" cell phone, social security card, California driver's license, and student ID—to a couple of bikers who claimed they "dealt in these types of transactions and whatnot." Since the mysterious phone call at the café, she had taken to wearing her beret and sunglasses as a disguise rather than a fashion statement. After they were finished up with the bikers, she caught Dallas staring at her.

"What?" she said cocking her head to one side.

"You look classy-good," he said winking, "like a girl who's ready to jet."

"Oh yeah, like a Jetty Jet?" she asked, unsure where that name came from or why it seemed vaguely familiar.

"Yeah, Dallas said, wagging his index finger at her. "Jetty Jet, I like that. It suits you."

"Okay," Winnie said as she and Dallas loaded their few belongings into the trunk of his beat-up Toyota Tercel and headed east on I-40 to "disappear".

Five hours and 32 minutes later, they arrived a little after midnight in Hooker, Oklahoma. Dallas pulled the Tercel into a darkened garage and parked. They got out and climbed up the steps to a tiny house built on wheels. Even though it was dark, she could see that it was small, but somewhat larger than a trailer with higher ceilings. Dallas turned on a dim lamp illuminating the living area. A tiny staircase that served dual purpose as shelves led up to a small loft bedroom.

"Whose place is this, Dallas?" Winnie asked.

"Friend of mine, Jules," Dallas said as he dumped their bags onto the sofa. "He's in a band. They're out on the road right now. He lets me crash here sometimes when I need to."

"When you need to? What's that even mean?" Winnie asked.

"Stop asking questions, Winnie," Dallas said. "I'll take the couch; you can crash upstairs. Get some rest, we got shit to do tomorrow."

Once he'd determined that there wasn't really anything more he could do to find Winnie, Jimmy careened wildly between contradictory emotions. His parents were concerned, well-meaning, but ultimately their bland suggestions that "everything will work out" just frustrated him.

For the first week, he made the pilgrimage to the old neighborhood where they'd both grown up. The only change he noticed at Winnie's old house was the mail overflowing the mailbox, then one day just gone. Briefly excited, he contacted the post office, but they'd told him nothing other than they'd received a termination notice and no forwarding address. They didn't know, or wouldn't tell him who'd requested the stoppage, or what had happened to the stockpile of bills and ad fliers.

There were times he actually felt pretty good. He'd never lived alone; he and Winnie had gone directly from their respective homes into the apartment. Pizza, burgers, pizza again . . . having the freedom to eat what he wanted, whenever he wanted, surprised him by how much he enjoyed it. Inevitably though, he'd feel guilty at the thought, and he'd wonder what Winnie was eating? Then the loneliness would collide with the slight joy of controlling the TV remote or sprawling across the entire bed.

On Monday of the second week, Jimmy felt he was going stir crazy when the newspaper in Portland called. He had the job if he wanted it, and they wanted him as soon as he could make the move. More out of frustration than certitude, Jimmy told them he'd be there in a few days.

"Mom, Portland isn't 'clear across the country'! It's still the West Coast." Although Dad was somewhat supportive, he could sense their unease with the move. They'd been fine, pleased even, when he'd originally told them about the interview. That had been more than two weeks ago. "This isn't about the distance at all, is it?" he asked petulantly.

"Well, what if Winnie comes back and you aren't here?" his mother asked. His father nodded along, as if the thought was new to him. They'd always liked Winnie, but Jimmy suspected they were just glad he had found a girlfriend. In his mind, and nowhere else, there had been "girlfriends" before Winnie, but he'd never introduced them to his parents—they were the popular girls in high school and they didn't even know he existed, much less that they were his girlfriends.

He had, once during sophomore year, gotten his courage up and asked the captain of the cheer squad, Sherrie Smith, to a dance. The other guys were always talking about her as being easy. He'd heard she'd given lots of guys blow jobs at a party and even gone all the way many times. He figured that if she'd do that with practically anyone, then she'd almost certainly go to a dance with him.

He'd mumbled a bit, but she heard him. "Oh, Tim!" she exclaimed, seeming to be startled that he'd managed to get her alone by her locker. "I don't think so." He hadn't been able to maintain eye contact; she was just too pretty. He found himself trying desperately to tear his gaze from her sweater-covered breasts. Although she hadn't quite got his name right, she'd said no with what was an apologetic (regretful?!?) tone. He was just about to force his eyes up and ask if another time and place would be better, when she shut him down.

"I don't go out with losers, especially ones that stare at my boobs!" and she was gone. By the end of the day, pretty much everyone had heard that Jimmy/Timmy had asked Sherry's boobs to the dance.

The socially awkward kid who'd had the confidence to ask out one of the school's most popular girls had folded in on himself. Although practically everyone had forgotten the incident by the end of the week, Jimmy couldn't let it go. Every night, and often during the day, he'd think about boobs, almost always Sherrie's, and how close they'd been. In these frequent, fevered daydreams, she always noticed him staring at them, but instead of rejecting him, she'd ask him to touch them. After he'd orgasm, he'd realize how pathetic his preoccupation was, but a while later it would happen again. Most of the time, he thought of Sherrie as his secret girlfriend.

Mom and Dad certainly noticed that he'd changed. He still got decent grades, but he never talked about girls and as far as they could tell, he'd simply stopped being interested. Then, in the middle of senior year, he and Winnie became inseparable. He was happy and his parents seemed even happier for him. He had harbored a seed of resentment—why did they prefer Winnie so much over his "first girlfriend"?

Snapping from his reverie, he barked an answer. "Geez guys, she knew I'd probably get the job. She has my cell number, it is only one number different from hers, and she certainly knows where to find you." He hadn't told them that on the last cell phone bill, he'd noticed that data for Winnie's phone was unused.

His Dad was nodding in agreement with him now, and his mom said as she patted his hand, "Of course dear, we'll tell her how to find you and we'll let you know the second she comes back. Go to Portland; get a place all set up for the two of you, and you'll see. Everything is going to work out."

He didn't believe it, and he had already determined that Portland was going to be a fresh start. He missed Winnie, at times it hurt ferociously, but already he'd begun to think about other girls. It had been nearly seven years since his humiliating experience with the cheerleader, maybe in Portland he'd be able to choose a woman and she'd actually say yes.

Once done with his parents, the job of moving was actually a piece of cake. Neither he nor Winnie were much concerned with possessions and even if they had been, student loans didn't cover much above rent and food. The beat-up little Mazda easily held everything he was taking north, including a couple boxes of Winnie's personal items. Her clothes and some other odds and ends were stored in his parent's attic, but somehow, it didn't seem right to pack away her mementos, plus, most of her pictures and little items had meaning to him too.

Portland had been a big surprise when he'd come up for the interview. It certainly wasn't southern California, but it was much more urban than he expected from all the television and hype the city got. Yeah, it wasn't hard to find hipsters in the crowds, but that was pretty much true on campus in Irvine. Rents were high, but he'd found a small apartment outside the trendy areas, and he'd earn plenty to make rent and have some left over.

"Welcome to the Stump," said the editor of the *Stumptown Weekly* when he checked into the office the day after arriving. His desk was pretty much dead center in the middle of the newsroom with low partitions barely higher than the modest desk that seemed barely sufficient to accommodate the older computer and phone. "You'll be working with Dave for a few weeks until you can get the lay of the land."

Jimmy had been paraded through the office and vaguely recalled meeting David Neusbaum, the paper's star reporter and muckraker. Amazingly, the *Stump* had actually won two major national journalism awards, both for stories Dave had written. The guy looked much less impressive than his reputation. He'd been dressed in "hippy formal" attire, a wildly colorful shapeless tunic, probably hemp, cargo shorts, and sandals. His hair, what hadn't abandoned his forehead and crown, was loosely tied up in either a very sloppily braided ponytail, or possibly the worst dreadlock Jimmy had ever seen. Incongruous black Ray Ban spectacles completed the mismatched slacker/stoner/hipster look.

It didn't take long for Jimmy to realize that, at least as far Dave was concerned, he'd been hired to be the hotshot's gopher. It wasn't so much that he was fetching coffee that bothered him, but the sheer tedium of the work thrown his way. He'd expected to write plenty of copy, telling himself that even covering the boring beats would let his competence shine and after a short time of paying his dues, he'd be turned loose to find the more exciting news. The reality was that he found himself buried in stacks of research notes tied to other reporter's stories. Checking name spellings, addresses, and various other trivia. He'd spend hours each day calling police precincts, checking facts "the driver's alcohol level was .12, not the .13 originally reported?", "the officer in this case has been with the department for 21 years?", and "can you confirm the suspect's legal name is Starbeam Bates?"

He did get to write brief two-sentence capsule community news items for the rarely lively online edition. "The 7th Grade class of Jefferson Middle School will be holding a bottle drive this month to earn funds for a zoo field trip. Contact school Principal Doris Finegal at . . ." The most exciting part of the job was actually just browsing the comments section of the *Stump* news site and deleting the obvious spam and letting the editor know whenever there was a real comment that might merit a staff response.

It was demoralizing, and then got worse when the editor brought around a fresh-faced kid even younger than him. "This is Josh, he's our new intern. He'll be working with you and Dave for the next six months." Interns weren't paid at the Stump, but Jimmy was dismayed to discover that they seemed to sit slightly above his position in the pecking order. Not only was Josh given actual byline assignments, granted they were typically sidebar articles running alongside the features the lead reporters produced, but he actually dropped his fact-checking work on Jimmy's desk.

Four weeks into his Portland adventure and Jimmy was almost swallowed up in despair at work. The social scene outside work wasn't going much better. Pizza or burgers every night was still a bright spot, but the sense of freedom was gone. He'd made a friend of sorts from work. Art, the office mail clerk and general maintenance guy, wasn't someone Jimmy would pick as a companion, but he was single, roughly the same age, and he liked to drink and talk crap about the other people in the office.

Art was pretty funny, and Jimmy did enjoy the caustic remarks about their coworkers, but he wasn't a good wingman. Art was scrawny, and chronically underdressed, even by Portland standards, Jimmy was convinced that girls weren't interested in him mostly because he was hanging with Art. It didn't seem to matter that Art regularly hooked up with women and would leave with them. By then, Jimmy was sure all the remaining women in the bar had associated him with the skater-slacker dude and written him off. Jimmy wasn't interested in the women Art went after; they were never the hottest in the bar.

Generally, he'd look for the women that seemed out of place in the "not-quite-trendy" lounge. When he found one, he always imagined she'd recognize he too was slumming a bit and that future dates would be more upscale. He and Art came here because it was inexpensive and because Art and Bill the bartender were friends. Bill would feed them free drinks sometimes, or more often, charge them for a beer while sliding them a top-shelf cocktail. But Jimmy always had to pay full price when sending one of his targets a drink, a strategy that Jimmy was convinced was the only way to begin the process. Art's strategy of making eye contact and usually initiating contact before sending a drink over seemed to be more successful, not to mention more economical, but Jimmy told himself that might work with the "second tier" girls Art pursued, but not with the women Jimmy was interested in.

In fact, on the rare occasions when a woman he was initially interested in made eye contact, or in a couple instances walked over and said hello, he'd suddenly discover that her dress was too short, her perfume annoying, her voice too high, too low, or that she just seemed "needy". He knew, but refused to acknowledge it even to himself, but their biggest problem was that they weren't Winnie.

Once, he had sent a drink to a cute girl in a group and after it was delivered, she'd smiled at him and came over to thank him. She was even prettier up close, and nice. She smiled a lot and asked him questions about himself and seemed genuinely interested in his answers. When he said something vaguely amusing about his move to Portland, she laughed and lightly touched his arm. Then she thanked him again for the drink and went back to her friends. Although he stared at her for the next half hour, she never even glanced at him.

That night he dreamt of Winnie and how they'd become a couple. They both worked on the high school newspaper and yearbook staffs and were covering the homecoming football game. He would write the story, but both of them were carrying cameras to get photos. After the game, they'd been in the newsroom comparing images they'd taken. Jimmy was a bit embarrassed to show his. He'd actually shot almost all of his pics along the sideline—there must have been two-dozen shots of the cheerleaders, specifically Sherrie, kicking, jumping, bouncing, and smiling. It also turned out that Winnie had been stationed at that end of the field as well. He hadn't really noticed her, but when she saw that she was in almost every picture he'd taken that night, she put her arms around him and gave him a big hug.

Winnie wasn't as stunning as Sherrie, he'd thought, but it really, really felt good when she pressed herself against him. It hadn't mattered to him about her birthmark. He knew she was self-conscious of it, that in the past she'd been bullied, the most by her own mother he would learn later, and that's why she always covered it up with clothing. He had jokingly told her it was her "superpower", but she didn't think it was funny and changed the subject.

Before long, he found himself anxious to spend every possible moment near her. He was surprised to discover that he considered her quite beautiful. That never really changed over the years. He'd almost convinced himself that subconsciously, he had meant to take those pictures of her, that Sherrie had photobombed the shots was irrelevant. In the dream, Winnie was there, he was happy, and then a group of generic women came and took her away, scowling at him as he called for her to come back. Somehow, it didn't seem all that strange the next morning when two detectives showed up at his door, asking about Winnie.

"When was the last time you saw Ms. Hooper?" was the first question once they'd made their introductions and sat at his small table with the coffee he'd just brewed. He wrinkled his brow in confusion, they'd said they were looking for Winnie, but her last name was Jensen.

"Um, I think there's a mistake. I don't know a Winnie Hooper . . ." he began. The darker, stockier agent was writing in a notebook, but the other only hesitated for a second. "Ah, right, Hooper is her mother's maiden name. Jensen was the name she was born with. So, when did you last see Ms. Jensen?"

Jimmy told them all he knew, which really wasn't much. As the interview was winding down, the stocky one asked, "Did the two of you ever go to New Mexico?"

Before Jimmy could think to answer the total non sequitur, he continued, "Social Security records show someone with her name and number starting work at a place, um, the Bus Stop, a diner just outside Albuquerque. Know anything about this?"

"Nope, we never traveled much with school and all, and when we talked about going places it was always places like New York or Europe that Winnie wanted to visit."

With that, the men stood up and the taller one handed Jimmy a card with a number on it and the name "Senior Agent Franklin Barlowe". Although they'd never actually said it, Jimmy had assumed they were with the FBI, or maybe some California police agency, but the card had no logo, no address, nothing but the name and number. Well, he thought, maybe that is what the

FBI did. He let it go without another thought and led them to the door having already begun pondering why Winnie would run to New Mexico. If he'd followed the men out, he'd have seen them get into a late model Corvette rather than anything typical police or FBI agents would be issued.

Already a bit late for work, he scrambled into the office, and then may as well have stayed home for all the work he got done. He did manage to find a couple pictures of The Bus Stop online, as well as the address. It looked as shabby as the name implied and Jimmy simply couldn't imagine Winnie working in such a dive. By the end of the day, without ever really deciding anything, Jimmy knew he was heading for New Mexico.

"So, you think he knows anything?" asked the stockier of two "agents" as he settled in behind the wheel of the Vette.

His partner snorted and shook his head. "Nah, but I'll bet he's on the way to New Mexico by this weekend. We'd better let Walter know that he needs to be ready for a road trip."

The driver grunted in agreement. They'd been sent to talk to the guy in case he did know something, but no one really expected he would. The old lady had said that the girl was scared and hadn't even stuck around long enough to tell her sad-sack boyfriend good-bye.

Mario probably could have tracked the girl down himself, in fact, it was he who'd tracked her to New Mexico through her social security number. She obviously wasn't that good at hiding out. But, Mario had never seen the girl, and unbelievably, her mother hadn't had a single photo of her daughter that wasn't more than 10 years old!

"Yeah, that doofus will lead Walter right to her, but I don't get why we can't just pick her up ourselves and take her to the meeting site," complained the driver, obviously not for the first time.

"Because we've got one job to do. It doesn't matter to Walter if people see him with the girl. He'll be back in Philly making sure people see him once he gives us our money. He has an alibi and no one can connect us to the girl. Geez, we've been over this a billion times!"

The driver just grunted. It seemed like a bunch of fancy thinking to him. The idea of getting his hands on a young woman was about as far as he could reason it out. Oh well, he'd meet her and get his chances eventually, even if he didn't get to catch her himself.

"Wake up Jetty Jet! Jetty Jet, wake up!" a detached voice echoed. Suspended somewhere between dreamland and the waking world, Winnie drew the covers up tightly over her ears to drown out the offending sound, but the voice came again, this time louder and sharper, "Jetty Jet! . . . WINNIE, wake UP!"

"Oh please, make it stop," Winnie whined into her pillow, rolling over and wrapping herself up tight in the bedding like a burrito. Feeling a hand on her back she opened her eyes to Dallas, who was, for some unknown reason, beside her in the bed.

"Geez, Dallas," she said pushing her bangs off her forehead and rubbing the sleep from her eyes. She closed them again and reopened them. His hand was still on her back.

"What the fuck?" she said, sitting up in the small loft bed that she'd climbed up to only a few short hours before. Reaching out with his hand and placing it gently around the base of her neck, Dallas leaned in, softly kissing Winnie's lips. Winnie's first instinct was to pull away, but curiously, she was enjoying it; getting into it even. When the kissing stopped, and they drew apart they continued to make awkward eye contact for a second or two. She wasn't sure what to think or how to react, but Winnie averted her eyes first.

"I have to go pee," she said uncomfortably as she unwrapped herself from the bedding and slid off the bed. The loft was too small to stand fully up in, so Winnie crawled over to the edge and made her way down the steep stairs to the bathroom below. When she came out of the bathroom, Dallas was sitting outside on the steps smoking a cigarette.

"Hey," she said.

"Hey," he said back.

She sat down beside him. "Can I have a drag?" she asked.

"You don't smoke."

"I know, but I feel like smoking this morning," she said.

He handed her the cigarette and she took a puff and immediately coughed. "Like I said, you don't smoke," Dallas said taking the cigarette back from her.

They sat in silence for minute. "Sorry about what happened up there," he said finally.

"It's okay," she said.

He turned to look at her and they both started to laugh. Dallas stood up pulling Winnie up with him. "Let's go make you a new girl!"

Because they'd gotten in late at night after dark Winnie hadn't had a chance to form any first impressions of Hooker, Oklahoma, but as they made the drive into town from the ranch where they were staying, her appraisal was notably bleak. Where the desert held a certain craggy charm, the panhandle, it seemed, was a vast expanse of pure nothingness . . . well, and tumbleweeds, lots and lots of tumbleweeds. If Jimmy had thought LA was ugly and flat, he'd most certainly have an aversion for this austere terrain. Winnie knew little about the region, other than what she'd learned from watching a Ken Burns' documentary about the Dustbowl on PBS. In the 1930s, the Great Plains were devastated by drought and dust storms during the Depression, but in the 1940s, the oil and gas industry saved Hooker, clearly evidenced by the sprinkling of many refineries surrounding the town. As they got closer, Winnie pointed out a sign prominently displaying a "lady of the night" that read "Hooker Chamber of Commerce Welcomes You," followed by another that read "Home of the Hooker Horny Toads American Legion Baseball Team."

"Awesome," Winnie said, snickering as they drove past.

"Hey nothin' wrong with being proud of your town!" Dallas said laughing too. The downtown's main street featured a few thriving businesses mixed in with a fair amount of "For Lease" signs and boarded up storefronts. Like most towns across the country, a lot of the businesses had moved to strip malls out by the highway where there was more foot traffic and rents were cheaper.

A couple of blocks from the center of town, Dallas pulled the Tercel into the driveway of a ramshackle house on a rundown residential side street. The paint was peeling off the wood structure and weeds, which grew up between the cracks in the sidewalk, had also long replaced grass in the tiny front yard where an assortment of kids' toys—Big Wheels and other miscellaneous outdoor playthings were scattered about.

Dallas and Winnie walked up to the porch and Dallas rapped his knuckles against the wood that held together the tattered screen door. Someone inside opened the door about an inch and peered out at them.

"Snake?" Dallas inquired. "Is that you in there?"

"That you Dallas?" countered a scratchy voice with a distinct southern drawl from within.

"It is, my friend," Dallas said, opening up the screen just as the door was being opened.

"Hey you! Where you been, you skinny-ass bastard," Snake asked as he emerged from the house stepping onto the porch and seizing Dallas in a big, burly bear hug. A large and rather scary man with wild eyes and long curly hair that cascaded down his back, Winnie watched in awe as Snake lifted Dallas' thin frame into the air and spun him around in a tight squeeze before setting him down and clapping him several times on the back hard, nearly knocking him off the porch.

Like Alice in Wonderland, Winnie tried to make herself small behind one of the posts, hoping Snake might forget to notice her. No chance. He spotted her right away. Pushing Dallas off to the side, he came slinking toward her with a petrifying smile on his face.

"And who is this sweet girly girl?" he said lunging menacingly closer and closer to her. Cringing and preparing for God knew what, Winnie squeezed her eyes shut tight. When nothing seemed to be happening and she opened them up again, the big guy was kneeling down at her feet and grinning like a nut.

"M'lady," he said with all the flourish of an English knight as he reached out and procured her small hand into his large hairy one, daintily kissing it. Not used to the princess treatment, Winnie actually blushed. This was probably the strangest, albeit sweetest thing that had ever happened to her in her entire life!

Dallas came forward and pulled Winnie away from Snake's clutch. "She's ain't no malady, Snake. She's a girl who needs a new name," Dallas said.

"Ah, so this isn't a social visit," said Snake as he hauled himself up using the porch post for support. "Come on in and we'll get to it then."

Crazy, wild-eyed Snake, *aka* Bruce Burnell was all business as they sat down at the kitchen table to fill out the paperwork. Despite his appearance or maybe because of it, Snake had a lot of connections with a diversity of people—good and bad alike—from petty criminals to people in law enforcement, people who worked for the government and at the hospital—all places that could supply him with vital information for crafting fake IDs and documents. While Snake was busy rifling through various papers and forms Dallas felt compelled to explain things to Winnie.

"Snake here," Dallas said, waggling a finger at his friend. "He's one of the most upstanding citizens of the Hooker community." Snake looked up, nodded, grinned. "His wife Lucy," he continued, "Also upstanding. She's at work at the courthouse right now." Dallas wasn't finished yet. "Their kids go to the local school, and his son . . ." Dallas tapped Snake on the shoulder, "What's your kid's name again Snake?" he asked.

"Jem," Snake answered without looking up.

"Jem, that's right," Dallas said. "Well Jem plays softball as a junior Horney Toad."

"Wow," Winnie said, visibly impressed.

"And not only that, but Snake here, he's an actor in the local community theater company! Ain't that right, Snake?

"Yep," Snake said, nodding. "Sit down," Snake instructed Winnie, moving a pile of medieval props and costumes off the chair. "We're doing *Camelot* this year," he said. "And can you believe it, me? As Lancelot?" he said chuckling.

"So, Ms. girl-with-no-name, I'm assuming you're looking for a new one, am I right?" Snake asked.

"Uh, yes, Mr. Snake . . ."

"Call me Bruce," Snake interjected.

"Yes . . . uh Bruce, I guess I do need that," Winnie answered glancing at Dallas for guidance.

"She's on the run, Snake," Dallas volunteered. "She needs a sosh and an ID card and . . ."

"I want to be Jetty Jet," Winnie interrupted.

"Jetty Jet?" Snake asked, shaking his head. "I don't know, that sounds a little too out there. You might want to go with something a bit more vanilla," he said, throwing out a couple of examples, "Debra Smith, maybe Mary Olsen . . .?"

"I think she's pretty set on Jetty Jet," Dallas added.

"Yes, definitely Jetty Jet," Winnie repeated.

Snake sighed. "Well, here's the deal, for legal purposes, when you need to sign your name somewhere, it really needs to be something that doesn't raise a gazillion red flags, you get me?"

Winnie nodded understanding, but seeing her crestfallen look, Snake offered up an alternative, "Okay, here's a compromise," he said. "How about *Jenny* Jet? Your friends can call you Jetty, Jet, whatever, but legally, Jennifer Jet isn't going to stick out too much and as good as I am, you don't want anyone digging into your ID too deep."

"Okay," Winnie agreed, her face brightening.

"You'll need a common last name, though," Snake said. "Does Jones ring your bell?"

Winnie nodded. Jenny J. Jones would be just fine.

Bruce/Snake gathered up the necessary information and told Winnie to come back in two days to pick up the IDs, along with it offering some parting advice: "Stay under the radar, don't bring attention to yourself. Don't become prominent in any way," he cautioned. "And whatever you do, don't get arrested, don't get fingerprinted."

Two days later, they drove back to town and Snake had delivered; one day after that, Winnie and Dallas were employed at a dusty diner along the interstate near Guymon, about 10 miles southwest of Hooker. Except for the dust that blew in and settled on the tables whenever anyone entered or exited the place, this new dive was about the same caliber as The Bus Stop. Wiping down tables and chairs and booths was an unremitting routine for Winnie, not to mention having to go outside every couple of hours to clear away the seemingly never-ending assemblage of tumbleweeds that rolled up and blocked the entrance.

Mixed in with the dust though were grainy bits of sand that managed to lodge in her uniform and then creep down, seeping into her bra and panties, and making her feel itchy and uncomfortable all the damn time. She took full advantage of the Fluff & Fold's open 24-hour policy and dutifully did her load of clothes at night. Except for some minor details, the laundromat was just like any other in any city, like the one she used in New Mexico. Funny she thought, just like when I was a kid. New schools and laundromats are just places that weren't as strange as the people who came and went.

After chucking the wet load into the dryer, she dug more quarters out of her pocket and fed them into the machine. It would be another 30 to 45 minutes of drying before she could go back to the house and get some sleep. At least she didn't have to be at work until 11:00. Yay, more time for rumination, she thought. So far, there had been no more strange phone calls, and nobody seemed to be looking for her at the moment, but she still felt jumpy and on edge and maybe even a little paranoid.

Why did that man over in booth #3 keep looking over at her? What's that black car doing in the parking lot? Why does that woman at the counter keep glancing down at her watch? And what's in that paper sack she's carrying?

If that wasn't enough, complicating things further were the feelings she had been having about Dallas. Ever since that morning when he leaned over and kissed her, she'd felt sort of excited about the prospect of him maybe doing it again. You know. Kissing her. Like that.

Seven weeks ago, which seemed like an eternity now in retrospect, she had abruptly walked out of her life, leaving everything behind—her education, most of her possessions, her chance at a satisfying career, and most of all, the man she loved; the man she expected to marry someday. Maybe being on the run, hiding, trying to survive these past weeks had spared her from having to face the reality of her situation. But as she stood now, teetering on the precipice, poised to cross the threshold into some wild new, unpredictable, crazy life as a completely different person, she wasn't expecting to feel this despondent. Sure, she'd cried a lake of tears when she was alone and living in the motel in Albuquerque, but for some reason, tonight, and really ever since picking up her new IDs from Snake, her emotions suddenly felt achingly real and raw and wrenching and final.

She had imagined many times in her mind Jimmy coming home, finding the note, wondering what the hell was going on. It pained her to think that she couldn't contact him, explain herself, at least let him know that she was okay and that she hadn't meant to hurt him this way. She had nearly broke down a couple of times, one time actually dialing his cell number from the motel, but hanging up before it started to ring. The only thing that sort of comforted her and helped her feel less like a complete shit was the thought that maybe he had gotten that job in Portland, had moved there, and was carving out a new life for himself, too. Sitting alone in the empty laundromat, Winnie wept. She wept for Jimmy. She wept for her former life, and she wept for herself.

Nothing was predictable anymore. That part was over. She'd just have to get used to it and move on. And Jimmy was part of that old life that didn't exist anymore. She would have to extricate him from her brain somehow too because she wasn't going to be Winnie anymore. Winnie was weak. Winnie was scared. Winnie was gone. She was Jetty Jet now, well technically Jenny. "Je-tee Jett," she enunciated out loud to the empty room.

Just then, the dryer stopped. Winnie wiped the tears away with her hand, folded her clothes quickly, placing them in the basket with the laundry soap, softener, and dryer sheets, and loaded the basket into the trunk of the Tercel.

Dallas had walked the few blocks over to the sports pub to down a few beers and watch a basketball game on the big screen TV while she did the laundry. He was coming out of the door just as she drove up.

"Perfect timing!" he said cheerfully as he swung open the car door and hopped into the passenger seat. "How was laundry time?" he asked.

Winnie placed her hand on his knee. "It was good," she said smiling back. A look of startled curiosity crossed Dallas' face when she didn't immediately remove her hand.

"Something's different about you," he said.

"Really, you think so?" she asked.

Dallas smiled and leaned forward to look at her face while she drove. "I dunno, you tell me," he said.

She drove into the dark garage and put the car in park. Winnie cut the engine but made no move to get out. She looked over at Dallas who was looking at her. "What is it, Winnie?" he asked.

She leaned close to him and placed her index finger to his lips. "It's Jetty Jet," she whispered before kissing him softly on the lips and pressing onto him on the seat.

"Let's go inside," Dallas said.

"Okay," she replied.

It was dark, the porch light was off, and for the life of him, Dallas could not get the key into the dead-bolt lock fast enough. "Dammit," he cried as he fumbled with it. Visions of Jimmy danced briefly through Winnie's mind, but evaporated when Dallas pushed the door open, pulling her inside where they both tumbled awkwardly onto the futon.

Wild with unrestrained passion, Dallas began to kiss her arms, her elbows, that super ticklish part at the crook of her neck, her lips, her eyes, every exposed body part he could find. And then, with skilled hands, he unbuttoned each button on her blouse. He carefully removed her bra and fondled her exposed breasts, licking and nibbling and tickling her nipples with his tongue. Besides the obvious heightened sexual arousal, something else was happening inside Winnie. She was a snake, shedding her old skin, leaving it behind and emerging a new person; a wild, uninhibited, sexy, beautiful new creature—Jetty Jet. Making love with Dallas was the most exciting, magically erotic adventure she had ever experienced. And even though she knew she wasn't *in* love with Dallas, she loved what he had awakened in her.

Breathless, they collapsed backward on the futon and laughed. Laughing seemed like the only appropriate response for what they'd both just experienced. It *was that* much fun. Who knew that a skinny fry cook could be so good in bed? Jimmy tried hard, but his inexperience always got in the way. For him, foreplay meant five minutes of vigorous tongue kissing and a bit of rough nipple fondling. Come to think of it, she couldn't remember a time when he had ever brought her to orgasm. It was priority #1 with Dallas.

"Oh my God," Jetty Jet gasped. "That was something." Dallas turned his head in her direction and smiled a dreamy that-was-dayum-good grin. He looked sleepy and spent, and she expected him to roll over now and go to sleep. That's what Jimmy always did. Instead, he turned on his side and pressed up next to her. He traced a heart around her belly button with his finger.

"*You* are something, Jetty Jet," he said, as he began to trace an invisible line around her birthmark. Starting at her shoulder, he slowly ran his finger along the edges, up and around, and all the way back down her arm. Jetty lay quietly, completely exposed to him, for once, not scrambling to pull the sheets up to hide herself.

When he was finished, he leaned over and kissed her shoulder. "You are beautiful Jetty Jet," he whispered. Don't let anyone ever tell you you're not."

She looked at his face, so serious and earnest, before reaching out with her hand and touching the scar on Dallas' cheek. "How did you get this?" she asked. Dallas sighed as he folded back against the pillow, placing his hands behind his head. He paused as if he wasn't sure that he wanted to tell. "You don't have to tell me if you don't want to," Jetty said.

"No, it's okay," he said. "It's just . . . it happened a long time ago . . . when I was in jail."

"Really? You were in jail?" she asked, genuinely curious but not terribly surprised. "What for?"

"Oh, just stupid shit, dope," he said. "I got tangled up with some pretty gnarly meth people for a time."

Jetty sat up. "You mean like *Breaking Bad* type people?" she asked excitedly. "Wasn't that filmed in Albuquerque?"

"Yeah," was all Dallas said.

"So . . ." Jetty pressed him."

"I thought you said I didn't have to tell if I didn't want to."

"Okay well, I lied," she said with a smile.

Dallas couldn't help smiling either. "Okay, Miss nosypants, if you have to know, I was a mule. I drove a truck across the border."

Jetty was intrigued. "Wow, it was just like *Breaking Bad* then."

This was new, Dallas thought. Drug running stories had never impressed girls much before. It felt sort of good that Jetty thought it was cool. He told her the much less glamorous story about how he'd gotten busted and ended up serving a six-month sentence in jail.

"And that's when you got that scar?" Jetty asked again.

"Yeah," Dallas said. "The STGs put me on the Bad News List," he said.

"STGs?" Jetty asked.

"Security threat groups, gangs," Dallas said. "I was young and dumb and thought I could get away with not paying my drug debts. Turns out some of the guys I owed money to were in jail too."

"Oh," Jetty said. All joking aside, it must have been horrible. "I'm sorry," she said. "I don't mean to make light of it."

"Getting cut wasn't the worst part," Dallas continued. "They raped and beat up my girlfriend." Jetty gasped.

Dallas bit his lip and looked away. "I didn't even go see after her when I got out," he said. "Too scared. I just changed my name and disappeared." She wanted to say something, but she couldn't find the words. Life sucked. Her life sucked, but Dallas' life had really sucked.

They stayed that way, quiet, the silence hanging over them like a dark cloud, lying next to each other for a while before Dallas finally broke the silence. "What's your plan Winnie . . . er, Jetty?" he asked.

She turned over onto her side to face him. "My plan?"

"Yeah," he said, "your plan." She shrugged her shoulders, not sure what he meant or where he was going with this. "Listen," he said, sitting up now. "I've been glad to help you, but I'm involved now," he said. "So I need to know more. For one thing, I don't know anything about you, and if we're going to, you know, be together, I need to know what's going on, what we're dealing with."

She knew, of course, this day would come. How could she realistically expect Dallas to just keep on helping her? Who knew how much danger she was placing him in? She didn't know for sure herself. This was all new to her, too. She sat up, facing Dallas. "But are you sure you want to be involved? Because if you don't, I'll understand. I really will."

Dallas clutched her arm, "I'm in," he said.

"Okay," she said, taking a deep breath before beginning. I told you that my dad was in the witness protection program, right?" Dallas nodded.

"Well, I was six when he left," she explained. "We were living in Philadelphia at that time. I have a few memories, mostly good

ones, you know, the usual father/daughter shows of affection."
She told him about the night he had been arrested. "It was scary,"
she said. "We were eating dinner—spaghetti, I think—and
all these men in black suits burst into our house with guns. I
remember being frightened and knocking my plate on the floor
by accident. After they handcuffed him and took him away, all
my mom said afterward was, 'clean up that mess.'"

"I bet that was hard for you," Dallas said.

"It was. I didn't understand, but a few days later he came back
home, and we were all packing to leave." Jetty Jet paused before
speaking. "But then, at the last minute, he and my mother got
into this huge fight. They fought all the time, but this one was
different. They were yelling back and forth at each other, and
she'd tell me to pick up my suitcase, we're going, and then he'd
say, no put your suitcase down. The next thing I knew, he was
scooping me up and giving me a hug, saying he loved me and that
he was sorry, and then he was gone."

Dallas shook his head. "Wow."

It was evident that the memories cut deeply, and Dallas
didn't want to upset her more, but it was important that he
understand, so he pressed on. "So he went into the Witness
Protection Program without you two?" he asked.

"That's how I understood it, yes," Jetty answered.

"You didn't know?"

"I didn't know where or why he was going then. I was a little
kid," she said. "But over the years, I got bits and pieces from my
mom, usually when she was pissed off."

"Like what?" Dallas asked.

She seemed even more uncomfortable revisiting this
particular part of her past. "Well," she sighed, "when I'd ask her
questions about him, she would get really angry. She said he was

a no-good, rotten gangster; she was glad he was gone, we were better off without him."

Dallas snorted. He couldn't help himself. He was trying to be sympathetic, but her description just struck him as funny. "A no-good, rotten gangster?" he asked trying not to snicker.

"Oh my God, you are so mean," she said pummeling his shoulders with her fists, feigning anger, and trying not to laugh too.

With the tension broken, she was able to fill in the blanks about what she did and didn't know. What she did know: Dad had been involved with the mafia in Philly. He was arrested. He accepted a deal to turn state's evidence and entered into the Witness Protection Program.

What she didn't know: Why had he called her? Was she really in danger? Had someone in the mob found out where he had been relocated in the program? Why after so many years? Without access to the Internet, she hadn't been keeping up with the news. The same for newspaper and TV; she had been so focused on dealing with her own situation, that she hadn't been paying attention to anything else that was going on in the world.

Dallas leaned over and gave her a quick kiss on the forehead. "We can talk about this tomorrow," he said taking her in his arms and cradling her. With Dallas lying next to her, Jetty Jet couldn't help feeling content, and for the first time in weeks, safe.

The next morning, she woke up to Dallas scooting off the futon and pulling on his pants and shirt. "Where are you going?" she asked, sleepily.

"We need to go to the library," Dallas said.

"The library? Why?" she asked, rubbing the sleep from her eyes.

"We need to get on the Internet and Google some stuff."

The only name she knew to look for her dad was Jason Jensen. A lot of Jason Jensen's came up in the Google search, but a second search with "Jason Jensen" mafia Philadelphia yielded dozens of news articles about a mob boss by the name of Julian "Mad Man" Scibelli. The first newspaper article they read reported that Scibelli had been indicted on multiple charges ranging from petty crimes and fraud to murder, but also named in the story was a Jason "Jet" Spade, who also went by Jensen along with a variety of other aliases. Spade had made a deal to turn states evidence. Dallas looked over at Jetty Jet who was staring at the screen in disbelief.

"Jet," she said. "That's where it came from. I remember it now." She leaned back in her chair and began describing a memory to Dallas: A group of men were gathered at their house for a BBQ, drinking beer and smoking cigars, telling jokes, and slapping one another on the backs. She is about three or four and comes running at full speed across the yard. "Who is this one, Jet?" they ask her dad. "That's my little Jetty Jet!" he replies as he grabs her and scoops her up in his arms and they all laugh.

"I had forgotten," she said. "Hell, I never knew my real last name was Spade either. I knew Hooper was my mom's maiden name and that it was my 'legal' name, but I always thought I'd been born Winnie Jensen." With dismay, she realized that the Winnie identity that she'd just dropped had been almost as fake as her new one.

Dallas took her hand and kissed it and after a few minutes of letting that sink in, they got back to digging. Another story, dated a few weeks later, stated that after being let out on bail, Scibelli had fled the country. Typing in 'Scibelli' in the news search yielded a boatload of hits. Apparently, about two months ago, Scibelli had been recaptured in Greece and the old crime boss was facing extradition back to the states to face trial, a trial that could potentially lead to the arrests of many more high-profile members who had escaped prosecution with the disappearance of Scibelli.

"Oh no," she said.

"What?" Dallas asked anxiously.

A look of dawning comprehension crossed Jetty Jet's face. "Two months ago," she said. "That would have been right before I got the phone call from my dad."

She frowned. "I wonder if they found him. But why would they want me?"

"I doubt they found him," Dallas said. "The point of the witness program is to not be found, but they might think you know something or know where he is," he suggested. Dallas leaned back in his chair, slowly rubbing his fingers through the strands of hair on his chin, thinking. After a minute or two he said, "I know you don't want to think about it, but this is worse than I thought. The drug cartel is bad, but these people . . . these people aren't people you wanna fuck around with, Jetty. I think we need to think about getting the hell outta Dodge again."

The transitory feeling of safety she had felt last night began to dissipate as the fear came creeping back in again. She felt like crying. Was this how it was going to be? Running for the rest of her life? What would Jason "Jet" Spade do? she thought. He probably wouldn't be thinking about crying or giving up. And then, it struck her.

"Mom!" she blurted. "Of course, mom. She had to know something about where dad went." Maybe that's why she was constantly uprooting them. The reasons always seemed to stem from the boyfriends she chose, but maybe it was more than that.

"Yes!" Dallas said excitedly. "So where do we find Mom?"

His boss was not happy. "You haven't even been here a month and you want a week vacation?" Jimmy just nodded, he'd made it clear he wasn't asking for a paid leave, but he could see that no real response was going to help with the angry editor. "Hell, take your time, then come back in and we'll see if there is anything we need you for."

That sucked, but Jimmy had half expected to be summarily fired, maybe when he brought Winnie back they'd forgive him and remember why they hired him in the first place. If not, well the job wasn't what he'd expected anyway and neither was Portland—it was perpetually damp and the people were annoyingly quirky weird and worse, the women didn't at all seem impressed with a low-level newspaper guy just recently out of his first and only relationship.

It took forever to pack. It surely wasn't because he needed lots of clothes or cared which he took. He just wasn't sure about what he was doing. Yeah, he missed Winnie; sometimes it hurt more than he could bear. Other times, he was so angry it almost physically pained him as much as the loneliness. He desperately needed to know why she'd run out on him, but he was also afraid that if he knew, it might hurt even more. Finally, despite his dithering, he'd shoved a week's worth of the clothes into a duffel bag with his shaving kit, toothbrush, comb and other junk. Maybe, just maybe she'd come back with him, which would certainly make it worthwhile.

The old, untrustworthy Mazda coupe that he'd coaxed up I-5 probably wasn't any more ready for the trip to New Mexico than he was, but it was probably cheaper than the bus, especially if Winnie's return trip were factored in. Getting through Portland's

evening traffic required his attention—it really wasn't as bad
as southern California traffic, but he still felt very out of place
among the drivers here. It wasn't until he'd hit the highway
outside Gresham headed East toward the Gorge that he could
ponder what he was doing, and what he might expect.

Quickly he realized that thinking about Winnie wasn't
productive. She'd left him. She had his cell number. She was
alive. As hard as he tried to imagine scenarios where she wanted
him to follow her to New Mexico, he couldn't fool himself into
believing. He'd even come close to turning around a few times.
At best, he figured, she'd give him a reason for what she did
and maybe, if he forgave her, he could convince her to give the
relationship another chance.

Over the nearly two months since she'd left, he'd examined
seemingly every aspect of their relationship to see if there was
something he'd done. He'd found plenty. He knew he was a bit of
a whiner—he got out-of-context angry about such trivial things.
He knew that he'd taken her for granted. Back when she was
around, he'd believed that their sex life was outstanding. Winnie
let him have sex pretty much whenever he wanted. Since she left,
he'd come to realize that he'd been so content with that, that he'd
stopped bothering to make sure Winnie would enjoy it too.

They'd been each other's first, and only lovers. There had
certainly been no need to get each other revved up at first when
everything had been new. It had been naturally exciting. As he
drove painfully reliving every second of his failed relationship,
he'd come to realize that neither of them had even tried, nor even
thought about replacing that early excitement. Even until the
last time, only a few days before she'd left, there had been plenty
of physical response, well, at least he'd been horny. For nearly
the entire two months she'd been gone he'd been wondering if

she'd been dissatisfied and blaming himself for not even thinking about it until she was gone.

Annoyed with the semi-erection resulting from that train of thought, he forced himself to think of something else, settling on the odd FBI visitors. At the time he'd thought little except that finally, someone besides himself wanted to find Winnie, but something wasn't right. Why would the FBI be interested? Winnie was no criminal, and no one had reported her missing as far as he knew. Furthermore, the attitude of "agents" just didn't fit with the image he had. He was smart enough to know that television shows were not reality, but he also knew that they were mostly really good at capturing the outward appearance and mannerisms of real cops.

Finding radio stations that were usefully distracting wasn't worth the effort as he drove on through the mostly empty lands. Even meal and fuel stops were instantly forgotten as he chewed up the miles in the car. If it weren't for the squirrely highway handling of the well-worn Mazda, he'd have fallen asleep more than once. He'd traversed the entire catalogue of internal discussions multiple times . . . examine the sex life, get a boner, think about the FBI, remember himself rolling onto and off of Winnie, wonder who those guys really were, think of a new way to please Winnie . . . The ever-flattening landscape he found himself traveling through provided little distraction from his ruminating thoughts—becoming ever more desolate and filled with fucking tumbleweeds, it reminded him of what hell must be like. He rolled down the window but the hot dry air blasting in his face only elevated his dislike of the desert.

When he saw the sign indicating he was entering New Mexico, he jerked a bit with surprise, almost sending the skittish vehicle onto the shoulder. He'd been speeding slightly the entire way, and he knew (thanks Google maps) that the drive was about 21 hours, but because he'd basically been hypnotized by the road and his looping thoughts, the past few hours seemed like minutes. In a panic, he looked at the fuel gauge. Still a third of a tank! Well, the car was a handful to drive on the freeway and anything but powerful on the steeper passes, but it did get pretty decent mileage. One more gas stop and he should be in Albuquerque at about dinnertime. *I hope Winnie has the dinner shift* he thought to himself.

It was actually closer to 4 p.m. when he pulled in front of the Bus Stop cafe. It was hard to believe anyone would work there, not only was the place deserted, but there pretty much wasn't anyone on the streets either, outside of a couple homeless people sitting by junk-laden shopping carts near the bus station across the street.

Just as he was getting out of the car, a shiny red Porsche pulled into the space beside him. Jimmy gave it an admiring glance; he'd have been here a couple hours sooner if he had that ride. The big man that got out of the car looked exactly like the stereotypical slightly over-the-hill wannabe playboy. His silk shirt was unbuttoned halfway down to reveal a tangle of black chest hair and thick gold chains to complement the gold distributed over his wrists and fingers. Slicked back hair and wrap-around mirrored sunglasses completed the look. Jimmy was slightly amused, but quickly turned back to the cafe.

The inside was even less impressive than the exterior. Jimmy thought it had probably been rundown before he was born and had only gotten worse over the decades. He headed for the counter, only barely registering that "Porsche man" had followed him inside and was taking a seat at a table directly behind him.

An older, obviously tired waitress wearing a name tag that read Meg came down the counter carrying a coffee pot and a plastic-encased menu. "What can I get ya sugah?" she asked in a weary drawl. Jimmy had planned on asking straight away about Winnie, but with the man right behind him and the promise of coffee in front, he impulsively decided to wait until he'd settled in a bit.

"I'll have coffee and a cheeseburger with fries," he said, waving away the menu. He had skipped lunch, and come to think about it, breakfast had merely been a donut from a gas station in the very wee morning hours. He'd get some food into him, then he'd ask about Winnie, heck, maybe Winnie would arrive any minute for her shift—the waitress certainly looked tired enough to be at the end of hers.

The slick guy ordered a Rueben and a coke. As he watched the waitress post the orders on the old circular clip stand in the opening to the kitchen, he saw an older man shamble up, glance at the orders, and start moving items onto the grill. The man seemed even more exhausted than the waitress.

When the waitress, Meg, came back by to refresh his coffee, Jimmy found his voice. "I'm looking for Winnie, which shift does she work?" he asked. The woman frowned at the name, like it tasted bad.

"Ah, Winnie doesn't work here anymore sweetie. She ran off with our fry-cook last week."

"Ran off?"

"Yeah, her and Dallas hit it off right away. They were a great team in here, but if I'd known she was going to take the best fry-cook we've had, I'd never have hired the little thing."

"Do you know where they went?"

"Not really, Dallas said something about going home, I think he's from up in the panhandle—a little town in Oklahoma. They didn't give us any notice at all, just finished their shifts, asked for their pay, and took off." The bell rang and the waitress turned to grab his order then slid the plate onto the counter in front of him.

The burger was huge and sitting in a sea of hot greasy, delicious-looking fries. Jimmy grabbed a fry and tossed it into his mouth, then realized it was way too hot and reached for the glass of water. As he took a moment to savor both the taste of the now sodden fry and relief from the iced water, the order-up bell rang again. The waitress turned and grabbed the Reuben for Porsche man and walked out to deliver it.

At about the same time, the sweaty old fry cook came out from the back and mumbled to Jimmy, "the town be Hooker, that's where Dallas were from. I remember it cause it were funny." The old guy grinned, showing where a few teeth still remained, then shuffled back to the kitchen.

Jimmy wolfed down the burger and fries, which were surprisingly good. At the same time, he was Googling "Hooker, OK" and plotting a route. It looked like about a five-hour drive. He was beat, but figured he could make it to Santa Fe and get a room and be in Hooker before noon tomorrow. Leaving a pretty good tip, Jimmy nodded to the cook and the waitress as he walked back out to the car. He didn't notice the Porsche man leaving right behind him, more than half his Reuben untouched.

As soon as he hit the road, his mind seemed to explode with all the implications from what he'd learned in the cafe. Winnie seemed to have hooked up with some fry-cook named Dallas! Damn! Once again, he found himself vacillating between turning around and slinking back to Portland or carrying on to Hooker.

It seemed even less likely that Winnie wanted him to come
find her. The fantasy of a joyful reunion didn't seem promising,
but closure seemed even more important than ever, and he'd
come all this way. Jimmy imagined just how bad Winnie would
feel, knowing that he'd come all this way to find her. It felt like
revenge, and that helped take the edge off the exhaustion that
was creeping over him as the sun set and he came into Santa Fe.

The parking lot of the cheap motel on the outskirts of Santa
Fe was mostly full. Thankfully, he found a space among the
minivans and pickup trucks and discovered that there were still
a few rooms left. With sleep deprivation weighing him down, he
trudged back to the car, grabbed his bag and climbed the exterior
concrete stairs to his second-floor room. He didn't notice the
red Porsche parked in the corner of the lot or the big flashy guy
walking into the office.

As tired as he was, sleep didn't come easy. A couple in the
room next door was rhythmically pounding something against
the wall. For an instant, Jimmy didn't understand, then he heard
a woman's voice moaning out "oh my god!" over and over. A wave
of contradictory feelings washed over him. The first was guilt
and embarrassment for "intruding" on their privacy, which he
knew was silly, but he couldn't shake it. Worse, he found it a bit
of a turn-on, which stoked the guilt again, then frustration and
anger that they were disturbing him so.

Eventually they stopped, but not before the pounding and
the moaning had reached a crescendo that Jimmy was slightly
in awe of. They may have stopped, but Jimmy's mind was still
churning. Implausibly, he wondered if maybe that was Dallas
and Winnie, but no, they were surely hundreds of miles away,
and that woman didn't sound anything like Winnie.

In fact, Winnie was always quiet during sex, Jimmy recalled. He'd beaten himself up quite a bit during the long drive, but now it occurred to him that maybe it wasn't all his fault that their sex life hadn't evolved over the years. He may have taken Winnie for granted, but she had taken no responsibility either. In the beginning, she'd made herself eagerly available, and indeed, that felt very much like participation, but over time the eagerness had fled, and she had become merely available.

Damn! We were just sleepwalking through our sex life. Neither of us knew any better. As he drifted into a troubled sleep, he pictured Winnie with this new guy (Texas?, no, Dallas). They were in the room next door and Dallas was showing Winnie what she'd been missing, and Winnie was responding and actually participating and telling him what she wanted . . . the dream was so real he awoke with a start, and a painfully full erection. The couple had obviously recovered from their previous bout and the woman was vocally, and explicitly coaching her partner.

Still groggy from sleep and the need for more, he listened to the woman describe actions and body parts that needed attention while he stroked himself. A few minutes later, he finished and cleaned up before they'd come close to stopping. Despite that, he had no problems falling back into a thankfully deep sleep.

Light through the faded curtains awoke him. It was morning. A quick shower, two cups of the instant coffee provided, and he was ready to hit the road. As he exited onto the highway, he realized that he was feeling pretty good about things today. The weird night seemed to have let him come to peace with his own role in Winnie's abandonment. Now, he wasn't going to Hooker so much to make her feel bad for walking out, but to let her know that he was going to be okay. He still had a lot of questions, and some lingering anger over the manner of her leaving, but somehow, he felt as if he'd dropped the guilt he'd secretly been carrying.

Hooker wasn't even a real town as far as Jimmy could tell. There was a sign announcing it, some campy half-jokes about the name, but not much else. It was lunchtime, and he'd planned on eating in the first cafe he found in Hooker, half expecting Winnie and this Dallas dude to be working there. The problem was, there was only one restaurant in the town, and it appeared to have been closed for years, maybe decades from the dust on the windows.

He thought about looking on the backstreets, but of course, Hooker had none. Finally, after cruising through the main street three times, Jimmy pulled into one of the few businesses that seemed still extant, a mom-and-pop grocery with a couple gas pumps out front.

Grabbing a soda and a bag of chips, Jimmy went to the cashier and asked, "Where's the nearest greasy spoon?" and immediately felt like an idiot. Two days on the road didn't qualify him to talk like a long-haul trucker.

"Walll," the old man minding the till drawled, "that'd be Tillie's Cafe in Guyman, about 15 minutes down the Interstate."

As Jimmy headed back to the service road leading to the interstate, he noticed a flashy red car parked on the side of the road. He recognized it as the Porsche man from the diner sitting in the driver's seat. "Wow, what a coincidence," he thought dismissively as he turned toward the freeway. It wasn't entirely unusual to fall behind and catch up to other travelers on long road trips, especially when there wasn't much else to look at in terms of scenery.

Walter knew he'd been made but wasn't at all worried. The car was noticeable anywhere, but out here in this wasteland of dust and rolling weeds, it was a beacon. Rather than a liability, Mario considered it a sophisticated form of counter-camouflage—people would notice the details of the car sure, but probably only "see" a caricature of the driver. That he was personally outfitted to match the car's flamboyance didn't bother him either. If and when he needed to, he could ditch the car, the jewelry and fancy clothes—he'd done it before. Without them, he'd become just a guy. Hell, he could walk up to an eyewitness and ask for a description without raising any suspicion. All the flash hid every real detail.

The kid he was tailing didn't even seem to be that alert. As those idiots who'd called him to let him know that the guy was likely to go looking for the girl had suggested, this guy, Jimmy, was a bit of a loser, all love-sick and probably thinking about nothing but getting the girl back.

Hell, even if he were suspicious, Walter didn't care. With luck, when sad sack showed up, the girl would tell him to get lost and he'd turn around and haul his sorry ass back to Portland. Mario would hang around to get a positive ID on the chick, then scoop her up once it was clear.

A few hours later he'd drop her at the meeting house, call those scumbags to come out, get their money and do their jobs after he'd had a chance to build a solid alibi back home. It was a fairly simple job, low-risk and his part was clean. He'd done a couple risky "wet" jobs when he was getting started, but the stress and danger weren't worth it. Moving up enough in the organization to get away from that stuff had been a huge relief.

He didn't let himself think about what would happen to the girl once the goons got her—he was nothing but a guy getting paid a bundle to give her a ride to where she needed to be.

"So, where do we find mom?" Dallas said leaning back in the library's rickety wood computer desk chair.

"She lives in Costa Mesa." Jetty said.

"Where's that? California?" Dallas asked. "Is that where you're from?"

"Sort of," she answered.

"What do you mean sort of," he asked.

"It's where we landed," she said. "We moved around a lot." Jetty Jet briefly described her nomadic childhood to him; of her mother's parade of boyfriends and poor choices; how when she was in high school her grandmother had left her house to them after she died, and it was the first more or less permanent home she'd ever had.

When she paused, Dallas asked, "So this running away, you're used to it, then?"

A puzzled look crossed her face. "What are you saying?" she asked.

Measuring his words carefully, he answered, "Well, you spent most of your life running away, right?" She nodded. "So it just seems like you'd be more . . ." he paused before adding, ". . . I dunno, more hard-core, I guess."

She hadn't considered that. "Yeah, I guess so," she said. "But it's been a long time since I had to run away and besides, I was just a kid along for the ride." Without giving away too much background on Jimmy, she explained how she had just graduated from college, had hoped to start a career as a photojournalist.

Dallas chuckled. "That explains the camera."

"Why do you want to know all this stuff," Jetty Jet asked.

Suddenly becoming very serious he said, "Because I've never met anyone like you. I've been around a lotta crazy women; drunks and druggies and ditzes, but I always wondered what it would be like to have a pretty *and* smart girl," he said. "Now I know. I can die a happy dude."

Uncertain how to respond, Jetty Jet simply smiled and said, "Thank you."

"Oh shit, look at the time!" Dallas said pointing to the clock on the wall and jumping up out of the chair. "We're gonna be late for work."

"What about contacting my mom?" Jetty asked.

"We'll have to figure that out later," he said as they rushed out of the Hooker library into the bright morning sunshine.

Work was actually good therapy, thought Jetty. She and Dallas had both quickly absorbed the differences in menu, layout, and clientele and with no little pride, she noticed that the shift manager seemed impressed. Despite the physical demands, the hours flew by until just before their shift ended, Snake and a plump woman wearing old-style cat-eye glasses and a conservative business suit walked in.

Dallas burst from the kitchen as they approached Jetty. "Hey Snake!" he boomed, oblivious to the startled customers at the counter.

Jetty's "Hi Snake," was lost in Dallas' outburst, but she had already turned toward the woman, "You must be Lucy. Snake and Dallas have told me so much about you."

The woman smiled brightly and answered, "You must be Jetty. Bruce couldn't stop talking about you, and now I see why!"

Jetty noted the slight, but unmistakable emphasis on the word Bruce, and determined that when Lucy was around, she'd refrain from calling her husband Snake. Other than that slight verbal cue, the woman did seem happy to meet her, and something about Lucy made Jetty feel comfortable.

When Dallas tried to find out what they wanted him to cook up, Bruce waved him off. "Nah, we're not staying, we've got to get home to the kids. We just came to invite you two over for dinner tonight."

"And," interjected Lucy, "to take you out to see Bruce's play tonight—it is opening night, the hottest ticket in Hooker!" Delighted, Jetty looked over at Dallas to see if he was as excited as she was about attending a live performance. He was frowning! Just as Jetty started to open her mouth to beg him to accept, Dallas broke into a big grin.

"It's a date!" said Dallas, laughing at Jetty's childish yelp of glee. "When do you want us?"

"The sooner the better," replied Lucy, also laughing at the byplay. "Yeah," added Snake, "we're afraid to be alone with the kids without adult backup, so when your shift is over, do what you gotta do and come on over!"

Jetty nearly set a record in prepping her station for the dinner-shift waitress, then found herself tapping her foot impatiently when she wasn't aimlessly pacing behind the counter. How dare Brenda not be here for her shift already! Finally, she arrived, a good 10 minutes early, but in Jetty's mind, unforgivably late.

Dallas made a show of slowly removing his apron and hairnet until Jetty punched him in the arm. Then it was a quick trip back to their crash pad, a change of clothes and they were on their way. "Wait! We need to stop at the store and pick up a bottle of wine or something!," Jetty said when the house was in sight.

Without missing a beat, Dallas smoothly pulled a U-turn and drove to the nearest market. "I know Snake has a preference for Napa Valley Pinot Noir, well, if it is a 2003, '07, or possible the '09," said Dallas in a totally deadpan voice.

Taking the bait, Jetty looked dubiously at the small, slightly ramshackle grocery store. "Do you think they carry those here?" she asked earnestly, sending Dallas into almost hysterical laughter.

"Not a chance babe!" he managed as he gasped for air. "Let's just grab a six-pack of cold beer, any vintage will do!" he added as Jetty's fists playfully pummeled him some more.

When they arrived at the house, Lucy answered the door beaming, then looked down at the six-pack in Jetty's hand and frowned. "Domestic beer?" she sneered. Jetty felt her cheeks flame and she really did want to hit, and hurt, Dallas for bringing this humiliation on her, then both Dallas and Lucy started laughing. Relief and a new impulse to pummel both Dallas and Lucy fought in Jetty's mind, then she broke into laughter as well.

"How'd you do that?" she asked Lucy, when they were inside and seated. It had seemed like a rehearsed routine between her tormenters.

"Girl!" exclaimed Lucy, "you're just so earnest, it comes natural." Earnest? Jetty didn't think so. Bringing wine when you were invited for dinner was expected, wasn't it? True, when she was Winnie, she and Jimmy never did, but then, they only really went to their parents' houses, mostly his, for dinner. Still, she'd seen people do it almost without fail on TV and it seemed to be just standard etiquette. However, both Snake, er Bruce and Dallas nodded in agreement, so Jetty put her supposed earnestness aside to examine later.

At home, without the business suit, Lucy seemed much more an appropriate fit for her huge, rough-looking, mate. But then, Jetty noted, Snake certainly acted much more the part of "Bruce" than he had when she'd been here while Lucy was working.

After a beer or so, Bruce and Dallas went out the sliding glass door to the patio to get the briquettes fired up. Jetty followed Lucy toward the kitchen to watch as she pulled a large plate with thick steaks out of the refrigerator.

"You know, Dallas is a bit of a wild man, but he has a real good heart. He and I even dated, well sorta, back in 7th grade. He's the one who introduced Bruce to me and helped get Bruce to settle down here in Hooker. Of course, just after he did that, he took off again. Dallas doesn't seem to be able to stop anywhere for very long," Lucy said, watching Jetty's face for reaction.

Slightly taken aback, Jetty hesitated. She didn't really know Dallas very well, and she certainly hadn't even begun to come to grips with her feelings about him. How could she tell this woman anything when she didn't even know herself? "Well, um, you know, we really only just met a few weeks ago and uh, you know, uh . . ." Jetty was flailing on how to say that it had only been since yesterday that they'd gotten physical.

Lucy smiled, "Relax! I'm not his mother. I know he's the kind of guy that has to grow on you, and that takes time. Bruce tells me you have lots of other things on your mind too. I just wanted you to know that I think he's a good guy. If you just want to roll in the sack with him for a while before moving on, well, he seems to be enjoying that. Just don't think because he seems tough that you can't hurt him."

Jetty gulped, damn, this woman seemed to be able to read her like a large-print book. Then she realized, it wasn't her that Lucy was reading, but Dallas. Looking at the matronly woman, Jetty met her eyes and nodded, "Yeah, Dallas has helped me out when he didn't have to, I don't want to hurt him, ever." With that, the slight tension that had been building between them evaporated and as if on cue, the men came back in for replacement beers and to report on the progress of the coals. Jetty noticed that Dallas had a slightly guilty, slightly pleased look on his face and she guessed that he'd been outside talking to his buddy about her. Just as obvious, Snake/Bruce was searching both her and Lucy's faces for clues—obviously he knew what Lucy had probably said.

Once everyone had filed away their impressions, they all accompanied Lucy and the steaks outside toward the grill. Two small children swung noisily on an old swing set, arguing about who was going higher. A boy and a girl, they each appeared to Jetty's untrained eye to be about the same age, 7 or 8 maybe.

"Are those your children?" Jetty asked, unnecessarily.

"Yup, that's Scout and her brother Jem!" responded Bruce, obviously proud of the pair.

"Like in *To Kill a Mockingbird?*" asked Jetty, delighted by the unexpected literary allusion.

"Yup, and their Daddy is Boo Radley, the mysterious scary man!" quipped Lucy. "Scout's eight and Jem is, well, he insists he's 7-and-a-half . Truth is, they are barely 9 months apart, I didn't know just how potent that man was back then!"

As the steaks grilled, and the beer was consumed, Jetty got swept into the glorious domestic normality of the evening. Longtime friends, comfortable with each other in a way that only comes from shared time, children safe and playing, a backyard barbeque—it was what she'd always hoped she'd have one day.

Dinner was wonderful, Lucy made a mean potato salad, just the way Jetty liked it. Fresh corn on the cob dripping with real butter went perfectly with the juicy steak. A peach cobbler for dessert was almost too much, but Jetty gritted her teeth and managed to wolf down a generous helping.

After dinner coffee seemed a bit formal to her at first, then she remembered that Bruce was going to be in a play this evening—he probably didn't want to go on stage with even a little beer buzz.

The play was surprisingly enjoyable, even if most of the actors were almost comically bad and obviously hadn't studied their lines enough. As the lovelorn Lancelot pining after fair Guinevere, Bruce was the star of the show, and he didn't forget a single line. Even his acting wasn't bad, especially in comparison to the collection of farmers, ranchers, and overly nervous young folk that made up the novice community acting troupe.

Afterward, things became a blur for Jetty as she was swept along with a crowd of celebrating thespians and most of the audience as they overwhelmed the local bar. At some point, they made it back to Snake and Lucy's place where a whiskey bottle made it around the fire Snake had built in his backyard fire pit.

Dallas sat beside her, his arm draped around her shoulder as if to show the dozen or so people who'd made it from the bar that he had a real girlfriend. At first, it kinda bothered her, then she kind of liked the idea that he was so proud of her, then she had another swig of whiskey.

As she limped toward wakefulness, she remembered lots of boisterous talking and laughter and the fire slowly transitioning from mostly flame to mostly embers. She also vaguely remembered making out with Dallas at one point, and even having to stop him once when his hand slid into her blouse.

Well, she thought ruefully, *I did stop him eventually—God, I hope no one was watching!*

Then the transition to being awake took a nasty turn. She had to pee, her head was throbbing, and it tasted like the fire pit had been extinguished in her mouth. Worse, she was disoriented and didn't know where the bathroom was. Tentatively, trying not to move her head at all, she swung a leg down from her prone position on the couch and found Dallas.

Evidently, he'd been semi-awake already, because he grunted, "g'morning, I think." When asked, he pointed her toward the bathroom and struggled to sit up.

It wasn't until she came back that Jetty noticed the smell of fresh coffee. A note on the small dining room table said: "Help yourself to coffee, cups in the cupboard above. Cream in the fridge and sugar on the table. Didn't want to wake you. Make some noise and we'll come join you!"

Smiling, Jetty grabbed a pair of mugs and let them pound slightly onto the counter before filling one for Dallas and one with lots of cream and sugar for herself. Dallas had barely made it to the table and grasped his hot mug when Lucy and Bruce came out, wearing matching Popeye pajamas loosely covered by Batman robes. Lucy had absurd Hello Kitty slippers on, but Bruce's comical "hobbit-feet" slippers totally stole the show.

Somehow sensing it was safe to come out, Scout and Jem appeared, incredibly sporting Popeye pajamas of their own. Jetty felt herself emotionally yanked violently. She'd been prepared to laugh and joke about her host's silliness, but then, seeing the entire family together, she felt her eyes well up—that much cuteness wasn't fair to a hungover girl on the run! She lost it and it only got worse when she heard little Scout (or was it Jem) ask "Mommy, why is the lady crying?"

It was futile trying to refuse breakfast. It was evidently a big deal in this household. The kids set the table while Jetty escaped outside with Dallas as he smoked his morning cigarette. When Jem had come over to her and patted her hand and told her "don't cry, it's going be alright" she'd snorted as she'd tried to stop the tears and stifle a laugh at the same time. Both the kids were fascinated with her birthmark. And after staring shyly for a few minutes, Scout bravely asked, "Are you a witch?"

"Oh for heaven's sake Scout!" Lucy cried. "Where are your manners?" Scout slinked embarrassed behind the chair.

"Oh no, no," it's totally okay," Jetty interjected while motioning for Scout to come back over.

"I'm not a witch," Jetty said to Scout and Jem, who was peeking out from behind her mom. "It's something much better. It's my superpower!" Jetty said fast and loud while raising both arms in the air for drama and effect." Both of their eyes got bigger.
"What does it do?" Jem asked shyly. Hmmm, Jetty had to think fast.

"Well," she said, making it up as she went along, "it has the power to scare people away, but only bad people are scared."

"Really?" Scout asked, "how does it know who's bad?"

Jetty turned her eyes up, thinking, and then replied, "I'm not sure, but somehow, like magic, it knows."

Jem stepped out from behind his mom and piped up, "but I was scared of it and it didn't do nothin' to me!"

"So see, you weren't really scared, right? Or else you would have run away," Jetty said.

Jem and Scout weren't convinced and commenced arguing every fine point they could think of to debunk Jetty's superpower claims, until Bruce came in and shooed them off.

"Leave Jetty alone now you two," he boomed in his scary Snake persona voice. "If she says it's her superpower, it's her superpower, now scoot!"

Breakfast, lots of coffee, and double-doses of pain reliever helped settle her emotions, and lessen the worst of her hangover, but it didn't leave a lot of time before she and Dallas needed to get to work.

They scuttled into Tillie's just a couple minutes past 11:00, both tying their apron strings, pretending that they weren't hungover as Jetty hurried to the back to clock in and Dallas headed for the kitchen. "Yer late," barked Jesse, the shift manager. "Yeah, yeah," Dallas said as he expertly grabbed a couple of spatulas and quickly began scraping the excess grease off the grill from the morning rush. He turned and winked at Jetty Jet as she emerged from the back and whisked by him with pad and pen, ready to take orders and kick butt during the lunch hour blitz.

Jesse couldn't complain too much about their tardiness. The first time he'd seen Jetty Jet and Dallas work together in perfect synchronicity, he knew he'd hired a good team. Good cooks and waitresses that worked well together were hard to come by. He planned on holding on to these two.

Around 1:30, the lunch crowd had thinned out. Only a couple of patrons lingered at their tables chatting over frosty glasses of iced tea. Jetty strolled over and leaned against the counter. It wasn't quite time for her break yet, but the momentary incline allowed her to rest one foot and then the other. Dallas peered out through the window at her.

"We 'bout done?" he asked.

"Yep," she answered. Despite her aching feet, she felt good. Things were happening. Yesterday had been like a vacation of sorts. They'd decided to contact Missy after work the day before, but instead, they'd spent yesterday evening and this morning with Snake and his family. It had been marvelous, despite the hangover. For an entire day, she'd been able to become Jetty and hadn't even given Winnie's problem more than a few brief thoughts.

But that was yesterday. In a couple of hours, they'd be off work and they could maybe track down her mom. It felt good to have a plan. And it felt especially good to have someone by her side now; a friend, a lover, a companion. She glanced back over at Dallas who was busy cleaning the grill. She caught his eye and smiled at him. He smiled back.

Just then, a gush of hot air blew through the door as a customer walked in. Without looking up, Jetty Jet tossed the towel she was using to wipe the counter over her shoulder and started walking toward the door. But when she looked up her eyes widened in disbelief.

"Jimmy?" she gasped.

Jimmy regarded her, but the person addressing him by name didn't register at first.

Of course, it didn't, she thought. Her badge read "Jetty" and her short black hair . . . well, she certainly didn't look anything like Winnie anymore.

What are you doing here Jimmy?" she cried.

Stunned, Jimmy said, "Winnie?"

Before either could say a word more, another hot gust of wind blew in when the door banged open behind Jimmy and a tall, stocky man wearing a pair of flashy mirrored sunglasses burst into the room. From his vantage point at the window, Dallas, who had witnessed the exchange happening between Jetty Jet and this Jimmy guy, had out of concern instinctively moved out from the kitchen in case she might need help. What happened next was like a crime drama, a nightmare in slow-mo. He watched as the man effortlessly flipped back the panel of his sport coat, reaching inside for the concealed pistol in his shoulder holster. Without hesitation, Dallas tore across the room to where Jetty Jet and Jimmy stood. Even though Dallas wasn't, by any stretch of the imagination, a big person, coming at the larger man at full force, he managed to tackle him hard from the side, knocking him off balance and sending him tumbling headfirst into the hard metal corner of the counter.

"Run!" Dallas screamed at Jetty Jet as he rumbled to the floor.

Grabbing Jimmy's arm, she dragged him out the back door of the café. "What's going on?" Jimmy demanded, as he reluctantly followed her out the door.

"Where's your car?" she asked calmly, but firmly.

"What?" he responded sharply, a trace of anger starting to creep into his voice,

"Why?" he wanted to know. She ignored him, her eyes wild, despite her calm voice.

Seconds that seemed like hours ticked by. A sticky hot wind danced around her knees blowing her apron up. At once, the loud crack of a gunshot exploded from inside the cafe. A warren of startled jackrabbits skittered out from behind an outcropping of rocks and brush. "Noooooo," Jetty Jet howled. It was all she could do to keep from rushing back inside to Dallas' side. But a voice inside her head kept repeating, what would Jet Spade do? What would Jet Spade do?

She spun around and faced Jimmy. "Where's your fucking car!" she shrieked. Still looking befuddled, he pointed in the direction of the Mazda. "Give me the keys," she demanded, "Now!" This time, Jimmy did what he was told, anxiously fishing them out of his pocket and tossing them to her. She jumped behind the wheel in the driver's seat and Jimmy tentatively opened the door to the passenger side and got in. He'd barely gotten the door shut before they roared out of the dusty parking lot and onto the interstate. In the rearview mirror, Jetty Jet saw a man staggering away from the café toward a red Porsche. Tears streamed down her cheeks as she punched the gas pedal hard. She would have to mourn Dallas later.

Tillie's could have been part of the same downtrodden franchise as The Bus Stop in Albuquerque, if anyone would want to franchise restaurants that were semi-shabby the day they opened and only deteriorated from there. Well, at least Winnie picks consistent places to sling hash, thought Jimmy to himself. With a sardonic smile, he embraced the road slang—slingin' hash indeed!

The truth was, now that he was presumably close to finding Winnie, he realized that he wasn't really sure what he really expected or even what he wanted. The motivation for chasing her really had never been something he'd examined. He had told himself he needed closure, but he wasn't sure he wanted the "Winnie chapter" of his life to close. Maybe he'd just play it by ear, maybe . . . hell, he knew this wasn't going to make him feel better, at least not for a while. This was going to hurt like hell, he grimaced, but I've got to hear her say it's over so I can get over it he told himself.

The place was almost deserted, just a beat-up import car, a rusty old Ford pickup, and lots of dust and tumbleweeds. Why would anyone put a café' here, why would anyone stop here, and why in the world would Winnie leave me to work in a place like this? He pulled into the lot and forced himself to get out before he could think about the scene that was likely to follow.

The well-worn floor literally showed a path from the door through a handful of mismatched tables and a few Naugahyde-clad booths toward the dingy counter. A dark-haired waitress at the end of the counter turned at the sound of the bell attached to the door. He strode toward her, already becoming resigned to finding that Winnie wasn't here, when she looked up and her eyes widened in shock.

"Jimmy?!?", she exclaimed in Winnie's voice. Stunned, Jimmy felt his jaw drop. It was Winnie! His eyes were immediately drawn to her left arm, the arm with the port-wine stain birthmark clearly visible in her short-sleeved uniform, something Winnie would never wear. And she'd hacked her hair short, and it was black, but it was her and she was asking him something. He knew he should listen, but he felt unable to do anything but look at her in surprise. His heart was about to burst, the months of pain and loneliness forgotten in a flash, and he felt himself stepping toward her to embrace her without really thinking about it.

Before he could even take a step, the bell rang again and he turned to see that Porsche guy, from before, walking into the restaurant. What the fuck?! He turned back to Winnie looking for answers, but at that moment a wiry dude in a greasy apron and paper cook's hat came from nowhere and tackled the big guy while screaming something. They crashed into the counter and Jimmy winced as the big guy's head make a cracking sound against the hard metal.

They were still rolling on the floor with the cook guy screaming, "Run!" Winnie grabbed his hand and pulled him urgently toward the kitchen and out a back door.

"Where's your car?" Winnie screamed at him. The question was simple, but he felt as if he were in a thick fog. "Give me the fucking keys!" she screamed. A loud crack from inside broke his paralysis and he fumbled the keys out of his pocket and tossed them to Winnie.

Winnie looked back at the door, and he wondered if they were going back in, then they were running toward the front and his car. Winnie got it started and spun the tires in the dusty lot, both backing out, and then taking off. Jimmy looked back at the rapidly receding cafe and saw the big guy stagger out toward his Porsche.

"Shit!" he said. "That guy has been following me!" When he turned to see Winnie's reaction to that, he saw tears rolling down her cheeks.

They sped back toward Hooker. Winnie had the little engine of the Mazda maxed out and Jimmy was too scared, and still way too confused to even begin a conversation. He just held on and hoped Winnie wouldn't kill them both to death before they had a chance to even talk.

Damn! That couldn't have been more fucked up! He'd barely gotten into the restaurant when the skinny dude had come at him like a madman. Shit, Walter thought, he must have seen the gun when I reached toward my pocket for the crappy photo of the girl's mom he was going to use to convince her to come with him.

This was supposed to be the easy part, confirm that it was the right girl, wait for her to send the boyfriend packing, or if she didn't, then wait until the two of them were alone and disable the kid and take the girl. Who the fuck was that skinny guy in the cook's outfit? Her new boyfriend, some random hero? Well, whoever he was, he wasn't a problem anymore.

But he'd sure made a mess of things. Walter didn't like doing the contract hits, but really, he didn't mind killing when the situation required it. He didn't feel bad at all for plugging the cook, but he was sure pissed that now he didn't have time to do more than a quick search for the girl. Worse, now she was going to be even more careful.

When the cook had tackled him, he'd banged his head hard against one of the old tabletops. The guy had been wiry, and he was fighting like a fucking wolverine, but Walter had been in more than a few fights and had maybe 80 pounds on the guy. More importantly, the cook had made two fatal mistakes. He hadn't gone for the gun first thing, and he took a look at the girl when he yelled at her to run.

Even seeing double and afraid he might pass out, Walter was able to get the gun into his hand. The cook had tried to wrestle it away, but it only bought him maybe 30 seconds before he had it pointed right into his face. Funny, the cook never paused or stopped, even when he was looking down the barrel, only the bullet had finally made him stop.

Walter had heard someone in an office in the back but made a quick decision that it was better to get out of there and get after the girl. Whoever was back there probably couldn't get out in time to even see his car if he left quickly. It was less than a second since he'd killed the guy and made the decision not to hunt any potential witness.

He'd banged into the side of the restaurant door on his way out, giving him his first indication that he was more messed up by the fight than he'd thought. The still somewhat double eyesight was a bigger problem—he could just see a silver blur racing away down the road—was it a car, a truck, maybe a jeep? No, goddamm it he told himself, it had to be the boyfriend's stupid Mazda.

His Porsche was faster in second gear than that toy at its top speed. If he could get behind the wheel, he should be able to catch them. Fuck, you could see a tumbleweed coming for a hundred miles, it shouldn't be hard to find the fucking car. His arm and hand weren't moving right, but he eventually got his keys out of his pocket. A few seconds shouldn't make a big difference he told himself as the sports car roared to life and he spewed gravel as he took off.

Since spinning recklessly out of the Tillie's parking lot, Jetty Jet had not once taken her foot off the gas pedal. Her hands were tightly plastered to the steering wheel in a death grip and her focus remained solely on the road ahead of her. She didn't know if Dallas was dead. She didn't know if the guy in the Porsche was following her or not. All she could think about was getting away. Fast. It was amazing how motivating fear could be.

Clearly unequipped for driving at high speeds, the inadequate Mazda bounced precariously around the road, shaking at times like a teenager after a six-pack of Red Bull. It was all Jetty Jet could do to keep it in a straight trajectory. Exacerbating the situation, the wind had kicked up making it even more difficult to keep the small car on the road. Heading back in the direction of Hooker toward familiar landscape and where she sort of knew a few people seemed the logical plan, but she needed to somehow get off the main highway. Being in this wide-open, flat expanse, made them vulnerable to being seen by the guy in the Porsche. If he was able to catch up to them, which was entirely likely given the capabilities of sports car versus piece of shit car, he could very easily run them off the road, shoot them, and leave them in a ditch for dead. These days, Jetty always leaned toward worst-case scenarios.

Up ahead, she spotted a semi-truck offering her the opportunity she was looking for. Racing past him she then slowed down, tucking the Mazda neatly hidden from view in front of the truck. At the next exit, she veered off the highway, speeding down the off-ramp and hanging a quick left onto a frontage road that led under the freeway overpass. She found a concealed spot to pull over, but which gave them a vantage point to see if and when the red Porsche drove past them. She turned off the motor and immediately, the adrenaline high evaporated and Jetty Jet's body fell limp against the seat. Taking a deep breath, she unclenched her white knuckled fists from the steering wheel and glanced over at Jimmy, who was staring vacantly out the window, still pinned against the passenger seat, his own hands clenching the dashboard in front of him. In her panicked-induced state, she had completely forgotten that Jimmy was in the car with her.

They looked at each other, neither wanting to start a conversation about what had just happened yet. The high-pitched whine of a powerful engine revving at extreme rpms broke the silence between them as they observed the red Porsche roaring past on the highway above them at an incredible speed, disappearing quickly into the horizon.

"Oh my god," Jetty Jet said, putting her face in her hands and expending a protracted breath of relief. Jimmy removed his fingers off the dashboard and wiped the sweat from his brow with a corner of his cotton T-shirt, and when he looked back over at her, a wave of emotion overtook him.

"Winnie," he said, impulsively grasping her arm. He moved over next to her wrapping his arms tight around her. She resisted at first, unsure how she felt about seeing him again, but then, she flung her arms around him, burrowing her face into his neck.

" Oh Jimmy," she cried, tears streaming down her cheeks.

They stayed that way for a few minutes, neither wanting to let go, but knowing that sooner or later they would have to. Winnie was the first to extricate herself from his clutch. "Sorry for yelling at you back there," she said, wiping tears away from her eyes. After what they'd just been through, the fact that she was apologizing for yelling at him seemed entirely comical to him and as inappropriate a response as giggling at a funeral, Jimmy couldn't help snickering, which in turn, made Jetty Jet laugh, which turned into weeping again. As much as laughter broke the tension between she and Jimmy, it also reminded her of Dallas and the very real possibility that he might be dead.

This time Jimmy apologized, "I'm sorry for laughing," he acknowledged. "It just seemed silly that you were saying you were sorry for yelling," he said as he took her hand in his. "It was okay to yell at me," he reassured her. "I deserved to be yelled at. You don't need to cry." It suddenly occurred to her that Jimmy had totally misinterpreted her tears. So much had changed for her in the past seven weeks. Seven weeks ago, she apologized to Jimmy for everything; for forgetting to turn on the porch light; for existing. But that person was gone now, and there would be no going back to the way they used to be. Jetty Jet withdrew her hand from his, and said, "You're right, it is silly. I don't know why I said that I was sorry for yelling at you," she admitted. "I'm upset because I think my friend might be badly hurt or dead," she said, her eyes tearing up again.

"Who?" Jimmy asked, "that greasy looking cook that told us to run?"

Jetty Jet's eyes widened in anger and disbelief at the sheer callousness of Jimmy's comment. "He wasn't just some greasy looking cook," she said, her voice mounting in rage.

Jimmy could feel his anger building as well. Of course, he had missed Winnie, or Jetty Jet, or whoever the hell she said she was now, and yes, he was ecstatic to have finally found her, but seven weeks of worrying and wondering came swiftly simmering to the surface.

"You slept with him, that cook, right?" he said accusingly.

Jetty Jet looked him squarely in the eyes, something Winnie would never have done. "Yes," she said defiantly. "I did."

Jimmy was livid. "How could you?" he demanded. "I can't fucking believe it." Exasperated, he threw up his hands and reached for the door handle. "Did you run off with this guy, or is he just some dude you met on the road and decided to fuck?" Without a word, Jetty faced forward and calmly started up the car. "What are you doing?" Jimmy bellowed as he opened the car door and got out. "We're through, do you hear that Winnie . . . through!" He slammed the door and Jetty Jet pulled back onto the road, leaving Jimmy behind, for the second time.

About three quarters of a mile down the road, she pulled over and made a U-turn. Of course, she wouldn't leave Jimmy behind. But she was absolutely not going to deal with this right now. Not now when they could be in real danger. Jimmy was sitting on the ground leaning against the concrete wall of the overpass when she drove up and gestured for him to come over and get in. Reluctantly, he stood up, brushed the dirt off his butt, and walked slowly over to the car. He opened the passenger door and leaned in. "This is MY car you know," he said.

"I know it's your car, so get in," Jetty Jet replied.

They got back onto the highway and drove in silence until pulling into the garage at Jules place. "Where are we?" Jimmy asked. "We're at a friend's house," she answered without looking at him. Jimmy was tempted to ask if this was yet another "friend" she was fucking, but decided not to; not now anyway. Jetty Jet retrieved the common key that she and Dallas had left under the big moss-covered rock when they'd left for work this morning. For Jetty Jet, the pain of bringing Jimmy here was twofold; Jimmy would know that this was where she and Dallas had been staying together, along with having to remember their time here and the probable realization that she would never get the chance to even tell Dallas goodbye.

She led Jimmy into the tiny house. It was the way they'd left it this morning, basically, a mess because they had expected plenty of opportunity to clean in the future. Breakfast dishes littered the small coffee table, and she hadn't had a chance to put away the folded laundry. The basket of clothes still sat on the floor in the middle of the room.

Jimmy scanned the room imagining Winnie shacking up with some guy in this dump before plopping down on the futon. "Now what?" he asked, looking up at Jetty, who was making herself busy clearing away the dishes and the overflowing ashtray. It occurred to her that these were the last cigarettes Dallas had probably smoked as she dumped them into the garbage receptacle. She sighed resignedly.

"We wait, I guess," she said shrugging her shoulders as she walked into the kitchen area.

"Wait for what?" Jimmy snapped. "Wait for some crazy ass murdering dick in a red Porsche to just show up and kill us?"

She spun around and faced him. "Goddamnit Jimmy," she wailed. "Do you have any idea how serious this is? We have just been through a horrifyingly traumatic experience. My friend was probably murdered back there." She paused, taking a breath to try to calm down. "All I'm asking is that you please, please give me just a few minutes to get it together," she implored. "And stop calling me Winnie!"

But Jimmy couldn't let it go. He'd waited too long. How could she expect him to hold it in any longer? "You owe me an explanation Winnie," he said on purpose. He clenched his fists tightly. His face was turning red and his body shook with anger that had been building to this crescendo for a long time. "I came all this way to find you . . ."

"And I didn't ask you to, did I," she tossed back at him furiously. "I don't even know why you're here."

Jimmy leapt to his feet, as if being at the same physical level as Winnie would help him win this argument.

"I'm here," he said, trying to pull back, to control his pent-up feelings, "because I thought you loved me, that we had something," his voice cracking a bit. "You left me a note for crissakes! No explanation, nothing. Did you think I would just shrug my shoulders and say, 'Oh well, she's gone' just walk away, and go on like nothing had happened? How would you feel if I'd left you like that?"

Jetty hung her head. Of course, he deserved an explanation, she thought. He was right. She hadn't handled it well at all. "I'm really sorry," she said and meant it.

Jimmy backed down a notch from his rage and hesitated before gently asking, "So, can you tell me now?"

She really wanted to focus on more pressing issues, like who that guy was in the red Porsche and why he was following Jimmy, but she knew that the circumstances of her leaving abruptly had to be addressed first. It was the only way to get Jimmy on board. She walked over to the futon and sat down, and Jimmy sat down beside her; looking at her, waiting.

Jetty took a deep breath. "You had left that morning for Portland," she began. "I came home that evening after work and was fixing some mac and cheese when my cell phone rang. I thought it might be you calling to say that you were there, but I didn't recognize the number. Normally, I don't answer those calls," she continued, "but for some reason this time I did," She paused, "now I wish I hadn't," she said, turning away and staring at the wall.

"So who was it?" Jimmy asked.

"When I said hello, a man said, 'Winnie, this is Jason Jensen.'"

"Who the hell is Jason Jensen," Jimmy asked.

"My dad," Jetty answered.

"Your dad?" Jimmy was confused. "I thought you said you never met your dad, or that your mom never told you who he was, or something."

"Jetty sighed. "I knew him," she said, "but I didn't want to tell you that I did."

"Why not?" Jimmy inquired. "Was he a crook or in the witness protection program, or something crazy like that?" Jimmy said jokingly. When he saw her face, he knew that his dumb joke was closer to the truth than he'd anticipated and he wished he could take it back. Dammit, why did he always have to be so flippant about everything? No wonder she left him! "Winnie, I'm sorry. Is that true?"

She hated when he said things like that, but the fact that he'd apologized helped and she continued her story. "Yes, that's exactly true," she said. "From what I understand, he went into the witness protection program because he was going to testify against a mob boss named Julian Scibelli. We, my mom and I, were going to go with him, but they got into a fight, and he left without us."

Jimmy was stunned. "Wow," he said. "I had no idea. Why didn't you tell me?"

"I don't know," she said, looking away, "I guess I was embarrassed. I didn't want you to think I was like my parents or that I was a bad person, too."

Jimmy took her hand. "I would never think you were a bad person," he said, and he meant it. Jetty smiled at him. Jimmy could be really sweet sometimes.

"So what did your dad say to you?" Jimmy asked.

Jetty continued. "Well, I was in shock. I mean, I never expected to hear from him again, but before I could respond, he sort of yelled into the phone, 'they're coming, run!' and then I heard some shuffling noises like someone was trying to take the phone away from him, and then click, he hung up. I didn't know what to think, so I called my mom."

"And what did she say?" Jimmy asked.

"She said I should run."

Jetty did her best to explain why the note she had left him was so brief and vague. She didn't want to give away any information in the event that whoever was coming came. "I was really scared," she said. And she hadn't wanted to involve him, especially when he was right on the verge of starting his career. "It didn't seem fair to tangle you up in my messy life."

"Thank you," Jimmy said when she had finished speaking.

"For what?" Jetty asked.

"For telling me what I needed to know," he said. He was still angry for a lot of reasons, the fact that she'd apparently slept with this Dallas dude for one, but he figured they could hash that out later. "I want to be tangled up with you, Winnie," he said reassuringly, "no matter how messy it gets."

Jetty and Jimmy felt better after their talk. She was glad now that he had insisted that she explain her actions. There were issues, sure, tons of them, but at the same time, she was glad Jimmy was here with her now. Everything in her life over the last eight hours had been turned upside down, again; and after Dallas, she no longer wanted to face what lie ahead alone.

Still, decisions needed to be made right now and Jetty wasted no time bringing up the subject of what should be done and where they should go from here.

Without mentioning the fact that Dallas was part of the original plan, she said, "Before you showed up, I was going to try to get in touch with my mom."

"Your mom is gone," Jimmy said.

"Gone, gone where?"

"When you disappeared, that was the first place I went to look for you," he said. "Nobody was there. There were newspapers piling up on the porch."

Jetty leaned back in her chair contemplating this news. "Hmmm," she said. "I wonder if she got a call too, maybe after I spoke to her? Maybe she just figured if I was in danger, so was she?"

"Where do you think she may have gone?" Jimmy asked.

"Well, the only place I can think of is the cabin in Montana," Jetty said.

"Your mom owns a cabin in Montana?"

"It's not exactly something she owns," Jetty explained. "It's more like what you would call an abandoned hunting structure."

Jimmy raised his eyebrows indicating amazement. "There are so many things I don't know about you Winnie, er, I mean Jetty," he said remembering that she'd asked him not to call her Winnie anymore.

"You know I never talked much about my mom," Jetty reminded him. "We aren't close and that's just the way it is," she said, getting up and clearing away the lunch dishes from the small table.

Jimmy nodded in agreement. It was true, she didn't talk much about her mom. Come to think of it he knew very little about her childhood at all. Winnie had always been sort of closed off, a bit of an enigma, but he had always figured she'd tell him when she felt like she needed to. He felt bad now that it hadn't occurred to him to ask her. Maybe knowing about the dad's past might have helped him understand her better.

"We have to go to Montana," Jetty announced as she returned to the living area from the kitchen.

Jimmy looked up incredulously from the *Rolling Stone* magazine he was flipping through and said, "What? Why?"

"Because mom is the key to finding my Dad."

"Why would we want to find him?" he asked.

Jetty told him about "the plan," which really wasn't much of a fleshed out one, just an idea mostly to talk to mom and see if she had any sort of inkling about his whereabouts, and if she did, to try to locate him and hope the local FBI might help.

Over their years together she had gotten pretty good at reading Jimmy's reaction to things, and she could tell by his face that he didn't think much of the plan, but when she was finished, he didn't say anything about it. Instead, he asked, "Why don't you just call her?"

Jetty Jet answered, "I don't have a cell phone anymore. I dumped it. I was afraid someone could trace me through it."

Jimmy rolled his eyes. "That's what disposable phones are for Winnie," he said. "Didn't you learn anything from watching *Breaking Bad?* He was right and she suddenly felt dumb. She thought she'd gained back some self-confidence over the past seven weeks, but all it took was a few condescending remarks from Jimmy to totally deflate her.

"You need to stop calling me Winnie?" she blurted. "Right now. You need to just stop!"

Jimmy looked confused. One minute they had been talking about disposable cell phones and out of the blue she was getting angry about something completely different. "Why?" he asked.

"Because it's not my name anymore," she said.

"You changed your name?" Jimmy asked.

Jetty Jet walked over to the futon, opened up her satchel and grabbed a small black wallet from inside, flipped it open, showing him her driver's license and social security card with the name Jenny J. Jones.

"See," she said, pointing at them.

It didn't have the impact she hoped for. Jimmy looked at them and said, "So you went to all this trouble to disguise yourself and get a fake ID, yet you didn't think to get a throwaway cell phone. You could have used it to call me."

"Oh jesus christ, Jimmy," she said, tossing the wallet back into her purse and walking away. "I guess I wasn't thinking clearly," she said sarcastically. "It's not like something like this just happens to people every day, you know."

Jimmy didn't understand why she was so angry. He was simply trying to point out the obvious. Sometimes, she could be so sensitive, he thought.

But he managed to convince her that the pressing issue at hand was figuring out how to get a hold of a burner cell phone. Jetty was hesitant to take the car out, fearful that the guy in the Porsche or any number of other bad people could be watching and waiting for them to come out of hiding. She was pretty sure there was no store that carried them in Hooker. The closest place would be Guymon, about 15 miles southwest of them and she thought there might be a big warehouse store there, but going anywhere was a gamble. But she had an idea.

Jimmy had decided it was best not to speak. He'd let her figure it out if she really wanted to. "I think I know how we can get a phone," she finally said, breaking the palpable silence hanging frozen in the air between them.

"What are you thinking," Jimmy asked.

Jetty Jet sat down next to him on the futon. "I have a sort of friend here in town," she began. "Well, more like an acquaintance really, but I think maybe he could help us out.

"Him?" Jimmy asked trying not to sound too suspicious, but after the Dallas fling, he was feeling more than a little sensitive himself, and still angry, although he would try to restrain his urge to lash out. Jetty knew she needed to tread softly with Jimmy. She wasn't the only one with flayed and raw emotions.

"Okay, he was the guy that helped get me new IDs," she said. "He lives in Hooker and I was thinking maybe if we could somehow contact Snake, he could drive to Guymon and get us a phone."

"Snake?" Jimmy asked. "Seriously?" Ironically, Jimmy had sometimes teased Winnie about tattooed bikers named "Snake" that would whisk her away into the night if she wasn't careful.

Realizing that Jimmy would make the Snake connection, Jetty quickly interjected, "His real name is Bruce . . . something, I forget. He's married, has kids. He's like an involved citizen."

Jimmy slapped his hands against his knees and stood up. "Sounds great to me," he said. "How do we contact Snake?"

Deciding that the safest bet was to wait until after dark, Jimmy and Jetty passed the time during the rest of the afternoon and early evening reading magazines, watching TV, napping, cleaning up, but otherwise avoiding discussing topics of any gravity. Instead of being the happy reunion Jimmy had hoped for, the distance between them was an even wider chasm filled with conflicting emotions of anger, love, distrust, and need.

At any given moment, he wanted to tell her to fuck off and walk away; the next he longed to touch her; to grab her and feel himself inside her again. It was the elephant in the room that each tiptoed around as they waited for it to get dark.

At around 8:30, Jimmy slowly backed the car out of the garage and they headed toward Hooker. Jimmy chuckled when they passed the Welcome to Hooker sign emblazoned with the not-so-subtle image of the "ladies of the night," as most people did the first time they saw it. For Jetty, it was a bittersweet memory of coming into town that first night with Dallas. He'd said that people in Hooker were proud of their name and they'd both laughed. Instead of laughing with Jimmy, she turned away and looked out the window at the passing prairie.

Jetty directed Jimmy to Bruce's house. She was surprised she remembered where it was, but even in the dark it was easily recognizable because of the abundance of kids' toys littering the front yard. Jimmy pulled up to the curb and cut the lights and engine. He started to get out, but Jetty stopped him. "No," she said, touching his arm to stop him. "I think only I should go," she said. "He's a little skittish around people he doesn't know."

Jimmy nodded agreement and sat back against the seat. "Okay, sure, no problem," he said. Jetty grabbed the door handle. "I'll be right back," she said before jumping out and closing the door. He watched her scamper up to the porch.

Jetty Jet knocked lightly on the outside screen door. She felt bad showing up unannounced, and it was nearly nine on a school night. She barely knew Snake; he'd been a terrific host that one night, and helpful with the ID, but really, he'd done all that for Dallas, not her.

All kinds of scenarios played out in her head. Would he be angry that she showed up on his doorstep? He was sort of a big, scary guy. How would she tell them about Dallas, did they already know? Would Lucy blame her? Would Snake? She could be potentially putting them as well as little Scout and Jem at risk by coming here. She knocked again, a little harder. The porch light flicked on and the door opened.

Lucy cracked the door and said, "Come in, quickly," opening the screen door for Jetty to enter. She had barely sat down on the couch when Snake entered the room. He barreled over in his usual big, lumbering way and gave her a big hug.

"Jetty," he said. "I'm so glad you're here."

Jetty was perplexed. "You are?" she asked and began to apologize. "I'm sorry to show up so late, but I need your help," she said.

"I know all about it," Snake said before he began peppering her with questions. "How did you get here? Did you walk? Are you alone? Where is the car you were driving?"

"The car is out front, and . . ." Before she could finish her sentence, Snake leapt from the chair and rushed over to the window to peer outside through the curtain. "Oh Jesus," he said. "We have to get that car out of sight, right now!" She started to tell him that Jimmy was with her, but he was already out the front door. Jimmy froze when he saw a very large man with crazy wild hair rushing toward the car. It truly was the Snake he'd warned Winnie about. Snake grabbed the handle on the passenger side and opened it. "Who are you?" he demanded.

"Jimmy, uh Jim . . .," Jimmy stammered.

"Well get the hell outta the car Jimmy or Jim," Snake bellowed.

Jimmy wasn't sure what was going on, but he wasn't about to disobey the orders of a lunatic the size of a mountain. He got out of the car and Snake hopped in, started the engine, put the car in reverse backing down the street in breakneck speed. He quickly pulled back into the driveway and Jimmy watched as the electric door of the garage slowly opened up and a slight woman with a long braid began to come into view. Without waiting for it to fully open, Snake drove inside the garage and the door came back down, entombing it inside.

Wondering what had just happened, Jimmy stood on the curb, unsure about what to do next. Was this Snake guy pissed? It was hard to tell. Should he go up and knock on the door or just wait outside for Winnie to return? As these thoughts rushed through his head, the front door opened and Snake yelled out, "Get in here Jimmy or Jim!" Jimmy didn't hesitate. He bounced up to the porch and Snake ushered him inside.

Even though he was a journalist, trained to notice details and never make assumptions, the house was not at all how Jimmy pictured a badass biker's house to look. It was normal. Pictures of kids and award plaques, semi-new furniture, a large 70-inch

TV screen mounted to the wall and hooked up to a video game console; and a variety of games scattered around on the floor.

Winnie was sitting on the couch with the pocket-sized women he'd seen in the garage. "Bruce Burnell," the large man said reaching out to shake Jimmy's hand.

"Jim Carson," Jimmy countered.

"For some reason, people want to call me Snake," Bruce said with a hint of a smile. "That's my wife Lucy," he said pointing to her on the couch.

Lucy nodded. "Hello," she said.

Jimmy looked back at Snake. "So, what's going on Bruce, um Snake? It is alright if I call you Snake or do you prefer Bruce or Mr. Burnell?"

"Snake'll do," Snake replied. "Sit down," he told Jimmy. "I have something to show you two."

He picked the remote up off the coffee table and switched the TV on. He scrolled through the DVR until he came to a saved entry. The reporter, a woman Jetty recognized, from a local news channel and the red and blue flashing lights of a police car filled the screen.

"We're reporting live from Tillie's restaurant on highway 84 outside Guymon where a shooting occurred inside around 2:30 pm this afternoon," she said. *"Witnesses say a lone assailant entered the restaurant and pulled out a concealed pistol. An employee, Daniel Lindsay, tackled the gunman, apparently injuring him, but in the process, was shot and died at the scene."*

Jetty's jaw dropped. "Dallas," she whispered. Snake nodded sadly.

The report continued. *"Witnesses also report seeing two people, an unidentified man and a woman, fleeing the scene in a late model economy car with the alledged gunman, driving a red Porsche, in pursuit. The owner of Tillie's tells us the woman may be Jenny Jones, a waitress employed at the restaurant."*

Jetty's name and driver's license photo splashed across the screen. Jetty's hand instinctively went to her mouth as she audibly gasped. *"The Guymon police department is asking the public to notify them if they have any information or see either of these vehicles . . ."* Snake paused the DVR, and then walked over to Jetty, placing his hand gently on her shoulder. Lucy reached out and grasped her hand.

Tears rolled down Jetty's cheeks. She couldn't stop them even if she'd wanted to. She had held on to some hope that Dallas may have survived; that he was only injured and lying in a hospital bed right now watching bad reality shows and cracking jokes with the nurses.

Jimmy hung back to the side. He understood that Winnie was sad, but it was difficult to watch her weeping over a man that she'd cheated on him with.

Sensing the tension between them, Snake walked over to Jimmy. "How 'bout a beer?"

"Sure," Jimmy said, following Snake into the kitchen and leaving Winnie on the couch with the box of tissues.

Snake grabbed a couple of cold brews from the fridge, popped the tops off, and handed one over to Jimmy.

"Thanks," Jimmy said, raising it in a mock cheer.

Snake took a swig of his own and said, "Look, Jimmy, I don't know you from Adam, but I suspect you had some sort of relationship with Jetty here . . . from before." He paused before saying, "She leave you? You come lookin' for her?" he asked.

"Something like that, Jimmy answered sardonically.

"Okay, well, you're gonna have to set your relationship issues aside for a bit," Snake advised. "You get what I'm sayin'?"

Jimmy heard. It was crystal clear that after that newscast, whoever was looking for Winnie knew right where to find her and him, too.

Snake looked directly into Jimmy's eyes. "You're in this now," he said. "There's no going back to wherever you came from. You know that, right?"

He knew. And part of him deeply regretted it, but another part of him also loved that girl—Winnie or Jetty—to pieces and would probably drive off a cliff for her, if he was being honest.

The conversation turned to small talk as Snake and Jimmy lingered in the kitchen finishing off their beers, giving Jetty time to compose herself.

"So, Jimmy, whatcha do for a living?" Snake inquired.

"Journalist," Jimmy said. "You?"

"Businessman myself," he said.

Only in Hooker, Oklahoma could there exist a businessman that looked like Snake, Jimmy thought.

Jimmy and Snake retreated to the living room to wait for Jetty to come out of the bathroom. When she emerged, although she had scrubbed her face, her eyes were puffy and bloodshot from crying. He felt bad for her. Losing anyone had to be hard, even though he hadn't experienced it, he tried to be empathetic—something he was really trying to work on, especially when it came to Winnie.

Jetty sat down on the couch and Snake told them what they needed to do.

"Okay, you two," he began. "Here's the deal. I have good news and bad news. It just so happens I have spare cell phones." Jetty's face brightened knowing that they wouldn't have to risk driving all the way to Guymon to get one.

"The bad news," he continued, "is that you can't stay here. You have to go, and you have to go tonight."

"But how are we going to do that," Jetty asked. "They're looking for the car; they're looking for us."

"You won't be in your car," Snake said. "I'm gonna keep the car right here in the garage until I can dismantle it and part it out."

"So are you going to drop us off somewhere, or what?" Jimmy asked. "How do we get out of here?"

Snake stood up and grabbed a flashlight from a drawer in the buffet. "Follow me," he said. Jimmy and Jetty followed Snake out through the back door of the house, around the back, and then down a path that led out to a rundown lawn shed. They walked around the back of it and Snake shined his light on an old Winnebago that looked like it had been parked there since the last century.

"You're kidding, right?" Jimmy asked. "Does it even run?"

"It runs," Snake assured them. "After I saw what happened on the news, I came out here and started it up in case you two showed up."

Jimmy shrugged his shoulders. "Well, I guess it's as good as anything."

They went back into the house and Snake gave Jetty the cell phone and Jetty immediately dialed her mother's number. Missy picked up on the first ring. Jetty left the room to talk to her and returned a few minutes later.

"Just like I thought, mom is at the cabin," Jetty told Jimmy. "She said we should come right away. We'll be safe and she'll explain everything when we get there."

"All right then," Snake said. "Come on Jimmy, let's go fire up the beast."

Snake opened up the side gate as Jimmy drove the sputtering Mini Winnie out through the backyard. Jetty frowned now that she could see it better under the light from the streetlight. It was a hideous piece of junk. Truly. It had a dozen or so dents along the body. The vibrant yellow color it had probably once been had faded to a hue evocative of piss. The inside wasn't nearly as horrible as the outside, although it had also seen better days.

The fabric in the curtains was thin and fraying, the upholstery fading too. Fortunately, the stove and refrigerator seemed to be in working order. The lights worked and the bed was reasonably comfortable, although it emitted a bit of a permanent bad smell.

"Keep your heads down," Snake said as Jimmy and Jetty pulled away from the house. Lucy waved and Jetty waved back.

"So, Montana?" Jimmy said to Jetty.

"We have to go to Jules first," she said, "to pick up my clothes and my camera."

Jimmy shook his head no. "I'm sorry Winnie, we can't go back there. Snake said that's probably one of the first places the cops will go."

Jetty was adamant. "I don't care about my goddamn clothes," she wailed, "but I *have* to get my camera. I have to!" She was glad that she'd decided to wear the jeans jacket and beret today that she had bought in New Mexico. She could get by without the other clothes. But leaving her camera behind? No way, not an option. There were pictures she'd snapped of Dallas.

He was torn. He knew how much her camera meant to her but wasn't sure it was worth the risk. At least until he looked over at her and saw how stricken she was. Despite everything, he would try to do this one thing for her.

They drove through the silent streets of Hooker, past the signs on the way out and down the dark back roads back to Jules place on the outskirts of town. A little way up from Jules place, Jimmy veered off onto a dirt road and parked the RV in a stand of skinny trees to try to conceal it.

"What are we doing?" Jetty asked.

"Stay here," Jimmy told her. "If I don't come back in 20 minutes, you leave."

"What? Why? I want to come with you."

"No!" he insisted as he jumped out of the RV and disappeared into the darkness.

It was more than dark. Out in the country with no streetlights and no moon, he could scarcely see two feet in front of him, but Jimmy kept walking straight until he reached the stone driveway leading up to the garage and the small house. He fumbled around in the dark trying to find the rock that he'd seen Winnie tuck the key under. Finally finding it, he unlocked the front door and went inside, leaving the lights off. Where would she put that camera? he thought just as he stumbled over the laundry basket hitting the floor and banging his knee up against the table. "Damn it!" he cried out, grabbing his knee in pain.

Just then, car lights reflected off the glass window. A dog barked. Staying down on the floor Jimmy crawled over to peer out the window. Cop cars, two of them, their lights flashing, were heading down the road. In a panic, but still determined to find that goddamn camera, Jimmy jumped up and began blindly feeling his way around the room. She had taken photos today. He knew that. It had to be somewhere in here and the room wasn't that large. The lights were getting closer. Where was it?

He was about to give up, but quickly did one more pass around the room, feeling his way in the dark when his fingers made contact with something hard. He grabbed it. It was the end of the camera's lens. "Oh sweet jesus, mother of god," he whispered under his breath, thanking someone, although he wasn't particularly religious, as he made his way out the door and raced far and away from the house in the opposite direction mere seconds before the police cars rolled into Jules driveway.

Hoping to backtrack around to where the RV was hidden, Jimmy made a wide arc through the desert. He felt like he was a character inside of a cartoon. Everything was so flat out here, it was difficult to hide, so as he rushed through the night, he found himself taking refuge behind every bush or tree that he could find. Running a few yards, stopping to hide, running again. Along the way, he ran into several tumbleweeds, the sharp dried out parts of the dead diaspore cutting into his bare arms. Twice, he tripped on large rocks that he didn't see in the darkness until it was too late, falling and gashing both of his knees. Finally, he decided to jump back on the road. Trying to maneuver through this harsh landscape was proving futile. He was limping, but he made a run for it. As he dashed down the road, a memory of high school track popped into his head; of losing against Donald Winters, the fastest runner in school, in the 100-meter race. He was devastated at coming in second, but now it didn't seem all that important. This race tonight was the one he couldn't afford to lose, and it propelled him faster in the direction of the RV and Winnie . . . no, Jetty Jet.

Twenty minutes had passed, and Jetty was scared. She'd seen the two cop cars roar past on the road, heading straight for Jules's house no doubt. Jimmy said she should go, but she didn't think she could bring herself to leave him behind, not again. Her mind raced. Two more minutes, she thought. I'll wait two more minutes. I don't need the stupid camera. I need you. I don't want to be alone. She waited. He didn't come. She reached out to start the engine and then suddenly the passenger door flew open. It was Jimmy. Jetty gasped. Traces of blood trickled down both arms. His pants were ripped, and blood showed at his knees, too, but her camera dangled from its strap around his neck.

"Oh my god, Jimmy?" What happened?" Jetty asked, trying hard not to panic.

"Scoot over," he said. She jumped back into the passenger side, and he dived in, turning the key in the ignition. The RV's engine sputtered at the first try but roared up on the second. Jimmy put it into reverse and slowly backed down the dirt road, lights off, careful not to make any noise. Neither dared speak as they made their way back down Jules' road, and finally turned onto the highway on their way to the interstate, and Montana.

Despite its appearance, age, and general shabbiness, Jimmy found the RV actually drove significantly better on the freeway than his abandoned Mazda had. True, it was a massive boat, but the big Ford V-8 purred. It wasn't nimble, and even 300+ horses couldn't accelerate the thing quickly, but it didn't seem to have any trouble at all maintaining a steady 70 MPH, just a tad below the rest of the light traffic.

Winnie was slumped in the passenger seat, and he could see that she was mentally exhausted. She'd fiddled with her camera for a few minutes, swapping lens, then switching back to the telephoto lens. Fortunately, she'd left the small gear bag snapped onto the camera's strap so that when he'd rescued the camera, he'd also brought along the extra lens, the charger, and a few extra memory cards and a battery. Even though he'd been furious at her for the risk she'd forced him to take, he was glad that he had done it. Sometimes he had no idea how to make her happy, and after everything, he discovered that making her happy was still very important to him.

It was only a few minutes longer when he heard gentle snoring next to him. His first instinct was to reach over and shake her awake—there was so much they needed to talk about. Ultimately, he didn't. Only partly because she looked so peaceful, and he knew she needed it. Mostly, he grudgingly admitted to himself, he let her sleep because he himself was too mentally exhausted to have any of those conversations.

Jimmy couldn't even guess how long he'd been driving, and with a jolt, he realized that he'd been on the edge of sleep himself for some unknown time. The freeway was still mostly empty, it was still dark, and they were still in their lane, but an amber light was flashing next to the fuel gauge. Weird, Jimmy thought to himself, I was basically asleep but probably doing everything on autopilot and he wondered if somehow that flashing light had been what had brought him back from the brink.

Fortunately, there were signs signaling a truck stop with gas and food at the next exit. The fuel needle wasn't below the E, but it wasn't above it either. He'd grab some coffee and get the beast filled up.

"Wha! Why are we stopping?" the mixture of sleep-slurred confusion and panic made Jimmy smile to himself a bit. Looking over at her, the deep crease on her cheek where her face had rested again a seam in the upholstery and the delicate thread of sleep-drool hanging from her chin only made him smile a bit more.

"It's OK, we're just getting gas babe," he murmured reassuringly. In fact, they'd just pulled into a small truck stop. There were maybe a dozen trucks parked in the back, where the diesel pumps were located. A pair of older gas pumps were in front of a combination restaurant and convenience store. He guided the RV into the garish blue-white flicker of the harshly lit island.

Without thinking about it, he hopped out, pulled his wallet out and slid his debit card through the pumps reader as he grabbed and removed the nozzle. Momentarily he panicked as the pump activated and he realized he had no idea where the fuel tank was located. Somehow though, he'd pulled up almost perfectly aligned to the small door housing the cap. Realizing that his tension was simply silly—no one was watching, and even if they were, no one would care that perhaps he'd "forgotten" where the gas tank on his RV was. Setting the nozzle to autofill slowly, he went up to the passenger door and asked Winnie if she needed anything from inside the store.

"Um, I'm starving, I'll eat anything," she said, then frowned in concentration before asking "did you use your card for the gas?"

Jimmy didn't understand the question at first. "Uh yeah?" he mumbled just before it dawned on him that they were on the run. He recovered with typical Jimmy-like quickness. "They obviously know I'm in the area, and even if they are somehow watching my account, we'll be days away from here before it even shows up at the bank."

Jetty nodded dubiously. She'd been on the run for less than two months and had made some dumb mistakes that had ultimately led Jimmy and the Porsche man to her, but she wasn't really sure Jimmy was wrong. Besides, she only had about $15 in tip money on her and she doubted Jimmy was carrying much if any cash. Anyway, it was too late to do anything about it now, she thought, just as the nozzle clicked off.

Jimmy went back to finish off the fueling, and Winnie decided she might as well go inside with him, although she took the precautionary measure of pulling the hood of her sweatshirt up over her head before climbing out of the RV. The inside of the place was somehow both dingy and even more fluorescently bright and flickering than the island had been. The store and the café were barely partitioned from each other by a large table with a row of yellow-tinged heat lamps keeping various foil-wrapped parcels somewhat hot. A hand-scrawled erasable board proclaimed that the parcels were "delicious cheeseburgers" 3 for $10 and "giant corndogs" 4 for $10.

Feeling like an alien in some foreign place, Winnie scooped up an armful of what she presumed where some of each and managed to liberate a large bag of Funyons that had been hanging from a metal strip next to the table. She trudged up to the counter and dropped her prizes and immediately turned and walked back to the beverage section.

Jimmy had a package of cookies and two oversized Styrofoam cups filled with coffee and a handful of creamers and napkins. Winnie shook her head slightly—cookies and coffee were pretty much Jimmy's choice for any road trip. She found the dairy section, grabbed a large carton of chocolate milk, then on impulse, she grabbed a dozen eggs. "Eggs in a convenience store?" she thought to herself, but there they were, and she'd claimed them. A loaf of over-priced balloon-style white bread joined her collection.

The bored clerk rang it all up and even found a couple plastic bags for them when they asked. Before they even got to the RV, Winnie had an idea. "Hey, Jimmy, you should get some cash from the ATM so we won't be so easy to track." Dutifully, Jimmy nodded and dropped his share of the parcels inside the step-in door and turned to go back inside.

Winnie had barely gotten the stuff put away, or in easy reach of the driving seats when Jimmy came back. "Damn, I knew I was cutting it close, but it is worse than I thought. This is all I could get," he exclaimed, holding up a single $20 bill.

"Oh well, at least we've got a full tank of gas and some food," she replied cheerfully, though she felt a new knot of worry tying itself up in her guts. "Let's get back on the road and have a picnic!"

It turned out that Jimmy hadn't driven that far in a trance, they hadn't yet reached Texas. By the time they did, the sky was beginning to lighten, and Jimmy's coffee was beginning to lose the battle with his exhaustion. At the next truck stop, they pulled in and parked back by the big rigs.

For the past couple hours, he and Winnie had simply drove (and sat) while munching on snacks and downing their coffee and chocolate milk. There was still so much to talk about, but somehow, they both needed the quiet and consistency of the road and the hum of the RV. Feeling how stiffly his muscles had knotted over the night, Jimmy stumbled back to the RV's bedroom, dropped his trousers and took off his shirt, barely getting it done before he plopped onto the semi-comfortable queen-sized bed.

Somewhat bemused at his robotic and silent trek to bed, Winnie sat for a few moments in the passenger seat. Her first thought was that she should climb into the bed above the cab, or maybe drop the kitchen table and turn it into a bed. Those were the options she gave herself, yet when she finally got out of the seat and scrambled back, she found that she'd decided to join Jimmy in the back.

Her jeans hit the floor, and then she pulled her arms inside her shirt and removed her bra. It felt great to be free of the demonic device. Even though Jimmy was turned away and seemingly already asleep, she'd learned long ago that merely exposing her breasts in the same room somehow could awaken him. Without any further conscious thought, she plopped into the bed and snuggled closely into Jimmy's backside.

It was hot in the RV when she awoke. Jimmy was exactly as he'd been, but she noted he was covered in a light sheen of perspiration and had at some point one of them had shrugged off the light blanket. More from waking grogginess and long familiarity than any semblance of a decision, she threw an arm over him and pulled him closer as her hand gently caressed his chest.

As he stirred slightly her hand accidently swept lower and she brushed against the head of his "morning" erection. "mmphmmmhp," or something like that was all Jimmy could say, but he smoothly rolled toward her. Any words they exchanged from there were less comprehensible and more guttural. Sometime later, they found themselves both covered in much more than a sheen of perspiration surrounded by a virtual whirlwind of sheets, blankets, and discarded clothing.

Both of them lay on their backs staring at the ceiling as their respective heart rates and breathing slowly returned to normal. Jetty's mind was awhirl. Why had she done that? She certainly hadn't planned it. Hell, she'd slept with Dallas less than a day ago. But, somehow, she didn't regret it in the least. It had happened naturally and been authentic. As mixed as her emotions were, she realized that at least her feelings for Jimmy were still there. But she still hadn't decided if that was a good thing or not. Being Winnie was easy, but she wasn't sure she didn't want to be Jetty Jet too. Would Jimmy ever forgive Winnie, would he even like Jetty? Man, the sex had been easy and uncomplicated, but nothing else was.

Jimmy casually caressed one of her breasts as he tried to make sense of what had just happened. Half-awake in the beginning, he'd almost convinced himself everything from the last two months had been a bad dream. Then, even as Winnie writhed above him, he'd thought of her sleeping with that fry cook. But then, well, it had been a long time . . . and she seemed different somehow, less inhibited, more confident. Normally, she went to great lengths to cover up her birthmark, but now she hadn't even bothered. It was as though all the insecurities about it had been lifted and he wasn't sure where that came from. With the immediate urgency spent, he wasn't sure exactly if he was angry more at her for dumping him and hooking up with some dude, or because she had so easily caused his anger to be pushed aside, at least temporarily. Damn, he wasn't even sure if he was mad at Winnie, or her alter-ego Jetty Jet.

"Let's go inside and splurge on a shower," Winnie finally suggested. By the time they'd gathered their clothes, Winnie had reconsidered. She was a mess, and the excursion could easily be incredibly embarrassing, not to mention maybe a bit elicit— they'd bought no gas, supplies or food here and had little money even if they'd needed those things. However, it had been her idea, and the truth was, she really wanted, no needed, that shower.

Fortunately, it turned out that mid-afternoon wasn't prime time for truck-stop showers. They'd only had to pass one grizzled-looking driver sitting by a phone bank on the way in. When he saw her, he mumbled something in the direction of Jimmy. She felt Jimmy tense, and his hand on her back pushed a bit, helping them rush past the man and into the door marked

"Showers-Men". There was no door marked "Showers – Women". If not for Jimmy obviously rushing her away from the man, she would've have aborted the plan, stickiness be damned.

Her stomach knotted a bit more when she looked around the place. There were three shower "stalls" against one wall, and three beat-up wooden dressing stalls on another. The third wall was lined with sinks, mirrors, and metal shelves for toiletries. The place seemed clean enough, but Winnie couldn't get past the realization that the showers were not truly enclosed, only separated by short tiled half-walls, maybe 3, 3-½ foot high.

As if reading her mind, Jimmy said, "Let's just do this as quick as possible and get the heck out of here!" Winnie bit her lip and nodded as they ducked into one of the changing booths. Although she stripped down, Winnie brought most of her clothes out with her, this was probably as close to a laundromat as they'd see for a while. Although Jimmy had his suitcase from his car, she only had the clothes she'd been wearing.

The hot water was delicious! The steam even helped give her just a smidge of relief, if she didn't look, she could pretend that the steam was so thick that no one could see her if they came in. Nonetheless, she washed herself in turbo mode using the harsh green liquid soap from the dispensers, while simultaneously trying to wash her undergarments and blouse. After a moment's debate, she decided she simply had to wash her hair, despite the time it would require, not to mention the green soap.

"Hey asshole, get outta here!" Jimmy yelled while she was still massaging the green glop into her short hair. Without thinking, Winnie spun around to see who Jimmy was shouting at. Even as she did, she realized that whoever it was would get an eyeful. With suds dripping off her head, she flailed her arms to cover herself as best as possible and through soap-stinging blurry eyes, she could see the old guy from the phone bank.

Incredibly, he had his penis out and was masturbating and grinning at her. "Ew," Winnie said with utter disdain. Jimmy, despite being naked and himself lathered up, took an angry step toward the guy. Winnie grabbed his arm and said, "No Jimmy! As long as he just stands there, let's just rinse off and get out of here." She knew better than to mention that as old as the guy was, he outweighed Jimmy by maybe 100 pounds and was fully clothed and shod in boots.

It seemed every second took forever, but it was probably less than a minute before she'd put the wet underwear, bra and blouse on while the steamy water finished rinsing the last of the goo from her hair. Finally, she turned back around, fully aware that even semi-dressed she was far from modestly attired.

When she glared at him, the creep said, "nice tits!" grinned at her, and hustled out the door. Jimmy, despite having to go to the dressing booth to retrieve his clothes had dressed faster than Winnie could believe. He seemed ready to explode and Winnie realized that he planned to go fight the perv now that he was dressed. "Jimmy! We shouldn't even be in here and beating that guy up is just going to get the cops out here."

He nodded but didn't look too happy about it. Winnie wasn't sure his agreement would hold if the man was out there and certainly if he were still grinning. Fortunately, he wasn't, and they hurried back to the RV. They sat in an uncomfortable silence as they maneuvered back onto the freeway. After about five miles or so, Jimmy turned to her and said, "I guess it is fitting that it took a dirty old man to get us clean so fast." Winnie snorted; the joke hadn't been that funny, but all the tension was released, and the absurdity of their odd shower kept her laughing and giggling a bit for at least the next five miles.

Over the course of the next few hours, they each seemed at different times almost willing to broach one of the many topics they absolutely had to discuss, but each time, instead opted to talk about the route ahead, the rare, interesting landscape feature that Winnie was taking photos of out the window, until darkness shifted the discussion to the occasional car or truck that passed them. But shortly before midnight, Jimmy said, "we're coming up on Denver soon, maybe an hour or so. We've got a problem though; we're burning through the gas and we won't get much past Denver. What do you want to do?"

Damn, Winnie knew it would be close at best, but this wasn't even close, Denver was only about halfway way to the cabin in Montana. They had Jimmy's $20 and her cash, so a total of about $35. Even with the relatively low gas prices right now, that wasn't enough to fill the tank, and she really had hoped to be able to buy some more food.

"Well, let's stop for the night just outside Denver and maybe we'll come up with some ideas. Look for someplace we can park for free, we're pretty broke."

"I don't think that'll work," Jimmy replied. "We're going to need to hook up to power tonight. It's awful cold out there." Indeed, Winnie hadn't really noticed because the road was dry and clear, but alongside it, she could see that snow now covered more of the ground than not.

"Maybe the heater in this thing runs on propane?" she said, looking back at the control panel that Snake had given them a brief introduction to.

"I'm sure it does, and there is certainly at least some propane in the tanks or Snake couldn't have shown us how to light the stove. But the furnace needs the fan to blow the warm air, without electricity, the furnace probably won't come on at all."

"Yeah, that's sounds right," she acknowledged. "Maybe we can find someplace real cheap."

For a change, luck was with them as the freeway sign showing services available at the next exit included the little campsite icon. The place was tiny, and really little more than a glorified parking lot. Jimmy wondered who would choose to "camp" in such a place, then ruefully acknowledged that he and Winnie were exactly the types who'd need a place like this.

Despite the early morning hour, a neon sign in front of a large, older travel trailer was on, flickering wildly, but promising both vacancies available and that they were "open 24-hours". When Jimmy rang the service bell under the awning, a middle-aged woman in a faded terry-cloth bathrobe answered the door and immediately held out a registration form and said, "$15 a night, noon checkout, fill out your license plate and sign it." Jimmy quickly scribbled in the info and handled over the crumpled bills Winnie had given him. "Spot 34 B, turn left and it'll be about halfway down the loop on your right." Even as the last word of her directions left her lips, the woman grabbed the clipboard and closed the door.

It took two tries for Jimmy to get into the spot correctly, he'd guessed wrong on which side the electrical hook-up would be and had to back into the space to get them aligned. Then it took him a good 10 bone-chilling minutes to find the right key to unlock the little plastic door enclosing the coiled-up power cord and another five to find the right power plug adapter to actually connect to the park's 20-amp outlet. Finally, he got it connected, but then had to fiddle around to find the reset switch that the directions on the power-pole sign instructed him to turn on.

The lights inside the RV suddenly grew significantly more intense as the electric lights augmented the yellow-tinged battery-fed lights. By the time Jimmy got back into the RV, he was shivering. Winnie had already figured out how to activate the furnace and he could hear the gentle whoosh of the propane burners, but the fan hadn't yet kicked in. "The gauge says we have a little better than half a tank of propane, but I have no idea how long that lasts," Winnie said, as she moved back toward the bedroom to make the bed that was still in disarray from their earlier adventures.

"I have no idea either, but hopefully it'll get us through the night," Jimmy replied, through shivering teeth. He'd packed for a quick trip to New Mexico and hadn't even included a jacket. Basically, he had his shaving kit, a toothbrush, half a travel-size tube of toothpaste, a comb, deodorant, a couple light shirts, a couple changes of underwear and socks, and that was it. Winnie had even less.

The RV seemed to have also been outfitted for warm-weather trips. There were plenty of sheets, once they plundered the over-cab bed and the storage under the convertible kitchen table-bed, however, there was only one threadbare light blanket and a couple of bedspreads that weren't much heavier than the sheets. Fortunately, the RV was still retaining some heat from the regular engine-based heating system.

Even cuddling together under all the sheets they could find, it would be a miserable night if the furnace didn't engage the blower. When the slight whistle of the fans did start up, both Jimmy and Winnie/Jet visibly relaxed.

Grabbing the bag holding their leftover hamburgers and corn dogs, Jimmy did his best to warm them up a bit over a gas burner, with less than stellar results. Truth was, it didn't matter much, they were both hungry enough to have finished off the sad meal even if it had been frozen. Much more successful was Winnie's attempts to coax drinkable coffee from the boil percolator she'd found in one of the cupboards and a half-empty can of Folgers in another.

As Winnie placed the mismatched, chipped mugs of coffee down on the table alongside the scorched, yet cold food, she said, "So, I guess we need to talk." This elicited a grim smile from Jimmy, along with a nod indicating that he agreed it was time.

"So, what are we doing, really, Winnie? What has really been going on?" Jimmy began. For a second, Winnie almost corrected him—she truly had become Jetty Jet in some ways, but looking into his open and earnest face, she realized that in maybe even more ways, she would always be Winnie too.

"Well," she began, "you know a lot, but let me start at the very beginning. It probably won't make sense, but after I've told you everything, you can ask questions and maybe you'll have better ideas about what to do than I've come up with so far. Does that sound right?" When Jimmy nodded, she closed her eyes and began telling what seemed to be her life story.

"I remember Jason--dad. He would be gone, it seemed like forever to me each time, but was probably weeks at a time. It was always fun, but scary when he came home. He'd take me to the park, the zoo, out for ice cream and buy me an Orange Crush while we drove around. It was like he was trying to do everything in those few days that we couldn't do together when he was gone. Of course, I didn't think of it that way then, I just knew that when Daddy came home it was playtime.

"But for me, even though the park and the zoo and the ice cream were fun, it was spending time with my father that meant the most," she said. You know, I remember how he used to kiss my hand with the birthmark and tell me that I was special and beautiful and that I should never let anyone ever tell me otherwise. I could tell that he loved me. I felt it."

Winnie hesitated, gazing past Jimmy wistfully, as if trying to catch and hold on to this one good memory before continuing her story. "The scary part was whenever Mom and Dad were together. They yelled all the time, and mom was 'sick' even more than the other times. I don't think I really understood at the time, but Missy drank a lot and "sick" pretty much meant drunk, hungover, or badly in need of a drink."

"Wow, that must have sucked, how old were you?" Jimmy asked. He'd suspected the part about her mother, in fact, he couldn't really envision her mom as anything but an alcoholic.

"Little, I think this was before I went to school, so maybe 5 or 6," Winnie replied before continuing. "One day, the police came to the house and took Dad away. I remember Mom trying to scratch the policeman who was holding Dad's arm. She was really drunk and instead of getting the policeman, she fell down and started to cry."

Dad came home the next day and he and Mom were screaming a lot for a long time in their bedroom. I was scared, and then I heard a big crash, and the door slammed. I was supposed to stay in my room when they were fighting, but I couldn't. I went to their bedroom and called out for Dad, but no one answered, so I was going to go downstairs, but Mom was lying on the stairs about halfway down."

I guess she'd fallen; she was, of course, drunk. I asked her if she was okay, she just moaned at told me to leave her alone. I went back upstairs and went into their bedroom to find Dad. He was on the floor and his head was bleeding. I think Mom probably threw something at him, there were broken things everywhere."

I thought he was asleep, but when I called out, he shook his head and got up. He gave me a big hug but didn't say anything. Instead, he started putting more clothes in the suitcase that was on the bed. When I told him that mom was on the stairs, he just nodded. Finally, he finished packing and closed the suitcase. Then he grabbed me and sat me next to him on the bed."

"He was sad, I never saw him that sad, even when he and Mom would fight. He goes, 'Well, little Jet, I don't think Mommy wants to go with us. Let's go pack your suitcase.' Jimmy's eyes widened at her mention of the name Jet. It made sense now.

Winnie continued the story. "So while we packed, Dad told me that Mom would be alright and when we could, we'd come back and see her."

Dad helped Mom up and took her to the couch in the living room, but she didn't say anything for a long time. Then he went back upstairs and got our suitcases. As soon as mom saw my suitcase she started screaming again. I didn't really understand, but she kept telling him that he might be able to hide, but she'd always find me, which, in retrospect, doesn't make a lot of sense because she didn't behave like she liked me. Anyway, I guess he believed her because he hugged me for a really long time, before standing up and letting go of my suitcase.

'Winnie, be good for your mom, and try and take care of her. Missy, you've got to get it together—Winnie needs you.' Missy just yelled some bad words at him, and he left."

Winnie paused again before going on, "She didn't come out and say it until I was older, but the truth was, she was embarrassed of me because of the birthmark. So, you can see why I was confused why she wouldn't let dad just take me."

Jimmy was aghast, both at the story and how Winnie, despite appearing and speaking calmly, had tears streaming down her face. This new piece of information explained plenty. Jimmy knew that as a child Winnie had been teased about her birthmark, but he could only imagine how traumatic it must have been for her knowing her own mother was embarrassed of her. Missy was more of a monster than Jimmy had thought. It made him very angry. In fact, he could feel his hands clenching, and he wished Missy were here right now so he could give her a piece of his mind. How could anyone do that to a little girl?

Winnie could see Jimmy's jaw tensing up and knew he was getting angry, but now that she'd started with this story, she was on a roll; she needed to keep going. "Well, Missy went crazy for a while, throwing and breaking lots of things before drinking more whiskey and falling to sleep on the couch. In the morning, she made me pack some things, then she loaded all the suitcases in the car, and we left.

"At first, we stayed in hotels and drove a lot. Then, one day, probably a few weeks after Dad left, she was really mad and told me he had taken all our money. I didn't understand at the time, I thought he must have come when I was asleep or something, but it was probably just the banks freezing their accounts.

"I remember sleeping in the car often, but we went to lots of people's houses too. Sometimes for maybe a week or two. I figured out pretty quickly that mom almost always parked us by a bar. I also learned even more quickly not to talk to the men who'd come out to the car with her, even if we were following them to their house. I never unpacked my suitcase. Even when the men tried to be nice, I didn't like to talk to them because I knew mom would say it was my fault when they kicked us out.

"That went on a long time. We were always driving, or Missy would be trying to get money for gas and food so we could drive more. She didn't talk to me a lot, but we were in that car an awful lot. I found out that Dad was a dirty, no-good mafia scumbag stoolie, she told me that sometimes, but more often I'd overhear her telling one of the men about Dad.

"Then one day the car was broken. It was really cold, and we didn't have anything to eat. Mom got a job at a strip club. She said it was my fault her boobs were too saggy, and she couldn't make the 'big bucks' dancing, so she had to serve drinks. She'd leave me in the dressing room where the ladies, some of them were dudes dressed up like ladies, would put on their costumes and stuff while she worked. It was warmer than the broken car, and the car had been towed away anyhow. The ladies were mostly nice to me, but I was really glad when we got an apartment, and I could stay at home when she worked.

"Even better than the crappy apartment was school. I was a year older than the other kids in 1st grade, but I loved it! Before 2nd grade, they decided I could go right to 3rd grade. My favorite part was the library because I could bring home books to read and when I had a book, I could pretend I didn't even know that mom had brought home some guy, and more important, I could pretend that they couldn't tell I was there either."

She wasn't sure when it had happened, but Jimmy was holding her hands on the table, and he too had some tears in his eyes.

"Anyway, over the years, Missy would just pick up and move us to another town, get a job in another dive, and drop me into another school. Once, I made the mistake of mentioning Dad, I think I may have asked her if he'd know where we were if he decided to come back for us. She slapped me and told me 'your

Dad is a fucking stoolie who'd just get us all killed.' I didn't know what that meant, but I learned not to talk about Dad.

"Mom finally found a boyfriend, Roy, that stayed around more than a couple weeks. He smelled bad, but he had a job working in a mine or doing something with oil wells, at least he talked a lot about drilling. Even though Roy moved in with us, Missy would still bring other guys around sometimes when he was out at work.

"Well, one day I came home from school, I was probably in 6th grade or so and Mom had a black eye, and her arm was broken. Evidently, Roy had come home unexpectedly and found her messing around with another guy. There'd been a big fight, Missy said that she'd gotten hurt because she hadn't gotten out of the way fast enough, but that Roy was surely coming back, and we couldn't be there when he did.

"So we hopped in the car and drove. We ended up in Montana and found the cabin where we're heading now. It wasn't much, but with a fire, it was warm. Missy got another job waiting tables in another bar. She wouldn't let me go to school in the little town down the road. She was afraid Roy or the mob (the great bogey man she used to scare me) would find us if I registered.

"Fortunately, we weren't there long. My grandmother, who'd moved to California, died and Missy inherited her house. We picked up and moved into your neighborhood. You pretty much know the rest," Winnie finished.

"Man, that's messed up Winnie, no wonder you don't like talking about your childhood. I don't know how you turned out so "normal" after all that!" Jimmy said sincerely.

"Ha, normal! I've spent most of my life hiding right in front of everyone, making sure no one notices me. I've done almost nothing ever that wasn't designed to keep me from being noticed or to avoid any hint of a scene. I've lived in the shadows my entire life just waiting for "Daddy" to come shine some light and make things safe."

"Yeah," soothed Jimmy, "but you found me in the shadows, and you found a way to survive and get a college degree. You're not a shadow person to me."

Winnie could see that he was sincere, but it didn't help that much. She wanted to tell him how often she'd swallowed her own anger at him and tried to ignore any of his shortcomings over the years. It had always been her first instinct to simply absorb any and every potential source of friction and dampen it deep inside herself.

She knew her list of grievances with Jimmy were not only trivial, but really not even his fault. Yes, he nagged about silly things like the porch light, and she'd accepted blame even on the not too infrequent times when he'd actually been the last to leave the apartment, but it was really her fault for not addressing the issue. She couldn't really blame him for all the tiny unresolved arguments that she had worked so hard to avoid, hell, she'd done everything she could to make sure he never even knew the squelched arguments existed. Now wasn't the time to get into that though.

"Well, that's just a long story that just sets up what happened when you went to Portland," she said. "As I told you before, Dad called, somehow, I knew it was him even before he told me. He was in a hurry, like he expected someone to come back and stop him from talking at any minute. He told me to run and hide, "they" were coming to get me. Then he hung up before I could say a thing."

"OK, that explains why you left," said Jimmy, "but it's been, what, 15 years, why would "They" come after you now? And it doesn't really explain why you didn't tell me."

"The long-time part is easy, my dad's old boss was finally captured in Greece and extradited back to the states. Dad didn't tell me that, I, well . . . we found it on the web at the library back in Hooker when we were doing research. It was actually pretty big news back east." Taking a deep breath, Winnie decided to avoid the second question and change the subject, especially because she'd just uncomfortably referenced Dallas. "It was easy to figure out that they haven't been able to get to my dad to stop him from testifying, so they must have figured if they could get me, then Dad wouldn't dare."

"That makes sense, but doesn't answer the question," Jimmy said. Winnie realized that she should have known better, Jimmy was great at getting interview answers, even from people that didn't want to answer.

With her eyes down, Winnie reiterated what she'd briefly told him before back at Jules place, "I didn't want you to get involved. You were on a job interview for christsakes, your life was just getting started and I didn't want to ruin your life too." Winnie looked up to see Jimmy studying her intently with a crease of concentration marring his forehead.

"I get that Winnie, I really do, especially after hearing about your childhood on the run. But I'm not your mom. You were willing to run away from me because it didn't seem worth it to explain it to me, or because you thought I couldn't or wouldn't help?" There was a touch of anger and betrayal in his voice and Winnie thought to deny it, but Jimmy continued, "so you figured you'd leave me a note and it would be all over, but you chickened out on that too!"

Now Winnie was surprised and confused, "No, I didn't! I left you a note! You even told me you found it!"

"Yeah, yeah," now there was anger in his voice. "You left me a note, but you couldn't bring yourself to even give me a reason, even a lie . . . anything that might let me start healing. You cauterized your own wound, but you just left me bleeding with a million questions!"

"Oh my God Jimmy! You're right. It never crossed my mind that I had "closure". I knew I couldn't tell you the truth or you'd follow me, ruining your life, but I should have lied, said something to end it for you. I'm so sorry!"

Immediately, Jimmy felt something dissolve deep within him. It felt for all the world as if a massive weight had just been lifted from his back. The hurt was still there, a bit, she had chosen to leave him, but the anger was gone. Finally telling someone about her troubled childhood, especially Jimmy, was huge, and cathartic for Winnie as well.

"Okay, I guess I'm mostly up to speed now, but we've got to talk about what we're going to do now," Jimmy finally said after a few moments of digesting everything.

"I think we need some sleep, then when we wake up, we can talk about what to do next," suggested Winnie. Jimmy looked over at her and realized that telling her story had been at least as traumatic for her as it had been for him to hear it. He was also surprised to realize just how tired he was. The heat from the furnace had quickly warmed the RV and combined with the food in his belly and the long day driving had pretty much overwhelmed any energy the coffee had lent him.

As they lay down on the bed, Winnie snuggled up to him and said, "There's one more thing. I need to tell you about Dallas," she said. "I was all alone in New Mexico, scared and lonely .

. . ." Jimmy listened and tried to understand. Despite himself, as Winnie continued her story, he became almost glad she'd managed to find someone to help her out. Even when she got to the part where she tried to explain that yes, they'd slept together, and yes, it was more than just sex, but it wasn't love, and that she'd known it wasn't long term.

At one point, despite himself, he asked for more details about the sex. Winnie gave him a quizzical look, as if trying to judge whether Jimmie really wanted to know, then continued in the same calm manner. "We'd been together pretty much constantly since we'd met in New Mexico. I think we both knew we were attracted to each other, but nothing had come close to happening. Then, I'm not sure which of us made the move, it just happened. We were on the couch, we kissed, then it happened."

"What happened?" whispered Jimmy, now needing to hear more, even though he wasn't sure he wanted to.

"Jimmy, I'll tell you anything you want to know, but you've got to understand, I was Jetty Jet." She continued, "Yeah, I was me, Winnie too—I'm not crazy—Jetty is part of me that has always been there I think, but I always kept her pushed down."

When Jimmy nodded with understanding, she continued. "OK, here goes. Tell me if you want me to stop," her eyes closed, and she began describing the scene. It had been pretty steamy when it had happened, and Winnie would provide Jimmy every detail, reluctantly if that was what he needed. Surprisingly, she was finding it very cathartic herself. It felt as if by sharing her innermost secret thoughts on the experience was somehow releasing the guilt she'd harbored since Jimmy had reappeared. No matter how Jimmy ended up taking it, she realized that now, she needed to tell him about every sensation, every wet contact, gasp, and convulsion.

Jimmy's mind was spinning. As Winnie had begun, he'd felt the keen edge of jealously tearing into him, but as she opened even further, he felt drawn in. It was strange. The voyeuristic aspect was quickly pushed into the background as he realized that Winnie, by sharing everything, was destroying the barrier. Sharing at this level was more intimate than anything they'd physically done, and more intimate by far than what she'd shared with Dallas.

There were still problems to resolve between Winnie and him, but what had happened with Dallas wasn't among them, anymore.

Jimmy sat up and looked at Winnie. "Just one more question?" he said. "Why do you call your mom Missy?"

Winnie laughed sardonically. "Well, funny story," she said with little amusement. "When she was with Roy they'd sit around drinking the day away, and one day when they were both blitzed, Roy said something to me like, "hey kid, you know what? I'm gonna start callin' your mama Missy." I was watching TV and turned around and asked him why? Roy burped and said, "Cuz she never misses a chance for a drink! So . . . Missy!' They both fell over in a fit of drunken laughter like it was the funniest thing anyone in the world had ever said. From then on, she was Missy. Even though biologically she was my mom, I never felt like we ever had a mother-daughter bond anyway. It always seemed like she was a crazy aunt or maybe a big sister gone wild. It actually took a lot of pressure off of me not having to acknowledge she was my mother even though technically she was."

"So what was her real name?" Jimmy asked.

"Ruth," Winnie answered. "From The Bible."

A perfect pinhole-sized stratum of sunlight drew a straight line from a hole in the RV's threadbare curtains directly onto Winnie's forehead. When she opened her eyes, the bright light was disconcerting. Something like "eeeeoww," came burbling up from her half-asleep throat as she rolled over tugging the blanket up over her face to shield her eyes from the blinding light. Wrapped inside the blanket Winnie stretched her legs out, yawned, and arched her back. It felt good to stretch. The bed was serviceable, but after a couple of nights sleeping on it, she could feel the lumpy parts of the old mattress boring deep into her back.

What time was it anyway? Morning, she surmised. Winnie threw back the blanket and sat up. It wasn't necessarily warm in the RV, but it wasn't freezing like it was last night. Thank goodness Jimmy had his clothes—she'd left hers behind at Jules house. He'd loaned her one of his warmer shirts to wear, but he hadn't packed for cold weather either. Where was he anyway? She stood up and headed toward the tiny bathroom to pee. "Jimmy," she called out. No answer. That was a little odd. Normally, well normal in their old life, even on weekends she was up at the crack of dawn, leaving Jimmy in bed to snooze and snore for a couple more hours. She liked taking her camera and going out for walks before the day got started, when it was still and quiet. In her opinion, listening to the echoing sounds of birds calling out to each other in the trees was the best way to start a day.

After peeing, she glanced at her face in the clouded over mirror. Her hair was spiky and pretty much going in every direction. She wasn't sure if she even had a comb. She was without makeup too—it was in her backpack—at Jules. She did have an eyeliner pencil though. It accentuated her smallish eyes, but also gave her that outlaw Jetty Jet look that she was beginning to love. Speaking of which, it made her uncomfortable the way Jimmy had just so easily slipped right back into calling her Winnie. Understandably, it was the only name he knew her by; He hadn't been around for the Jetty Jet transformation. Yet, what it showed her was that he didn't really get how much she'd changed during their months apart. She wasn't quite ready to let Jetty Jet go and return to being Winnie—or at least the version of Winnie she was before. And she wasn't sure she could just pick up where they left off either. In her mind, it was complicated. She was relieved that Jimmy seemed not to hold her little indiscretion with Dallas against her, but at the same time, it was like he didn't want to acknowledge that she was different, not just in her appearance, but inside as well. If she chose to shove it under the rug, the way the old Winnie would, it could potentially be a problem. She'd have to find a way to gently bring it up.

As she was putting on a pair of socks that Jimmy had lent her, the creaky door of the RV opened, and Jimmy stepped inside. "Oh, you're awake," he said.

In his hand he held a bouquet of roses in assorted colors— some red, some yellow, some pink. "Where did you get those?" Winnie asked. "Picked 'em," Jimmy quipped. "You picked them? Where did you pick them?" she asked, suspicious. Jimmy smiled slyly and said, "From a yard down the street."

Winnie rolled her eyes. "Oh jeez, I hope they didn't see you do that."

"Nobody saw. I was exceedingly stealth," Jimmy assured her.

"For you," he said grinning like a big dope and handing them over to her. Instinctively she pressed her nose into the fragrant petals. "They smell nice," she said. Rummaging around in the cupboards she found a plastic container to put the flowers in. They both stood back to admire the arrangement sitting on the RV's small table.

For some reason, he had awoken early this morning, rare for him, but a particular lump in the mattress had been burrowing into his side all night. After lying awake staring up at the peeling faux wood on the old RV's ceiling for too long, he finally accepted the fact that he probably wouldn't be falling back asleep anytime soon, so decided to just get up. Winnie was sleeping hard. She didn't move a bit when he climbed out of bed. He layered up with two shirts before going outside. He'd read about Denver weather—one day it could be 70 degrees and then it might snow. But although it was chilly out this morning, it didn't feel like it was near freezing. The skies were clear, and the sun was just coming up. It felt good to get out of the cramped RV anyway. All that driving had been exhausting. He needed to stretch his legs and a brisk walk was just what he needed. He was both physically and mentally exhausted.

So much had happened over the last few days—they'd been shot at and chased by a maniac in a Porsche, they'd found each other, broke up, got back together; they'd barely escaped the cops getting Winnie's camera; driven across the country in a wreck of an RV, shared a shower with a pervert at a truck stop, ran out of money. Everything was uncertain, their lives, their relationship. It was great that they had talked. It was probably the most they had shared with each other, well . . . ever, but at the same time, it was overwhelming. And he was hungry, really hungry, which reminded him of their most pressing issue—they were down to their last few dollars.

All was quiet as Jimmy strolled between the rows of late-model trailers, beat up RVs, and rusty campers in the little rundown park. Some of the occupants looked like they might be regulars—their spaces were outfitted with clothes lines and lawn chairs and other miscellaneous items—one even had a pair of plastic pink flamingoes planted in the grass out front. Others, like Jimmy and Winnie, were only there for a night or two, before packing up and moving on.

As he navigated through the maze of vehicles, Jimmy tried to think of ways they could get hold of some quick cash. They couldn't get jobs, at least real jobs that didn't pay under the table; Winnie's Jenny Jones ID was useless now that she was a "wanted" person. Jimmy could do some sort of odd job, but that would require staying for a while and that wasn't really a good option either, considering the urgency of getting to Montana. They could donate plasma, or they could do any number of illegal things—steal someone's wallet, for instance, have sex for money. Jimmy mulled that last one over in his head for a minute wondering if Winnie might consider doing such a thing. Nah, probably not, he thought, but then again, maybe she would. She had this whole new Jetty Jet persona, maybe it was something Winnie wouldn't do, but Jetty Jet might. He wondered if it would be wise to even broach the topic. It had the likely potential of not going over well.

Lost in thought as he wandered the grounds, he finally found himself way on the other side of the park near the entrance. At the rear of the small building where they'd paid the lady in the bathrobe to stay overnight, stood a vending machine and it was bulging with bags of chips and snacks and candy bars—all the goodies that make a famished person salivate. Jimmy dug deep into his pocket and fished out some change. He knew he shouldn't do it, but that overpriced Snickers bar was beckoning to him like a Greek siren. He put the quarters in the machine and watched the mechanical wire spiral thingy starting to slowly turn. This was always the moment, wasn't it? Watching, waiting, hoping, praying that the snack you'd just spent $1.35 on would not get hung up in the wire. It was decidedly a first-world problem, but today, Jimmy didn't care; he was desperate for chocolate. It looked like it was going to go, but then, nope, it stopped, the candy bar was hanging precariously just out of reach, like a carrot on a stick.

"Oh goddamn it all to hell!" Jimmy said out loud. Impulsively, he kicked the machine, and immediately regretted it. He cringed as seething pain shot up through his foot. The good news was his little temper tantrum had caused the candy bar to dislodge and it was now awaiting him in the slot at the bottom. Jimmy pulled it out and eagerly unwrapped it, biting greedily into its gooey chocolatey goodness. Sweet victory! He closed his eyes and chewed, savoring the first bit of food he'd had since yesterday afternoon, but then, he stopped mid-chew. What about Winnie? She was probably hungry, too, he thought. He really should save half of it for her. As he was thinking about this, he absent-mindedly took another bite, which left only about a quarter of the candy, too late now to split it in half. Screw it, he thought as he popped the rest into his mouth and finished it off. She didn't really like Snickers anyway, he reasoned. Still, he felt sort of guilty. He'd have to find some way to assuage his guilt. He threw the wrapper in the garbage can and started walking again—this time out the gate toward the road. I spot of color caught his eye and from where he stood, it looked like flowers, a lot of them. Hmmm, Winnie likes flowers, he supposed.

Even though this was primarily an industrial section of town on the outskirts of Denver, a few small homes were tucked in here and there in between warehouses. As Jimmy neared the house with the flowers, he was more than a little amazed at the sheer volume of rosebushes there actually were in this one tiny yard. Row after row of bushes, bloomed in all colors. Winnie would love this. She liked taking close-up photos of flowers.

Jimmy glanced around. It was still early. There were no cars on the road, but he didn't want to take the chance of anyone seeing what he was about to do. He pulled from his pocket the trusty Swiss knife he always carried and slipped furtively into the yard. Working quickly, he lopped off a red, a pink, and a yellow rose and then hurried out of the yard and away from the house, no one the wiser.

The roses were nice even if he had pilfered them from someone's yard. "Thanks," Winnie said as she leaned over and gave him a peck on the cheek. Jimmy smiled. Mission accomplished.

But as she was heading back toward the bedroom to get dressed, Winnie stopped and looked back over her shoulder at Jimmy. "Oh, by the way," she said, "you have a little chocolate there on your teeth."

Oops. Jimmy ran his tongue along his top teeth. Busted. But she was smiling. That was a good sign. It meant she wasn't pissed off that he hadn't shared.

Winnie finished getting dressed and came back up to the front of the RV where Jimmy was waiting.

"So what's the plan?" she asked.

Jimmy scratched his chin. Normally, he was clean-shaven, but over the course of the last week, he hadn't bothered to shave, and Winnie noticed he was getting some stubble and she didn't *not* like it. It was kind of sexy even. Gave him a sort of an outlaw look. And technically, they were outlaws.

"Well," Jimmy started. "I have about $2 in my pocket."

"Sans the candy bar you bought this morning?" Winnie asked. Jimmy hung his head dramatically. "Yeah."

Winnie couldn't help giggling. "I'm teasing, silly," she said, punching his arm playfully.

Jimmy smiled back. "Yeah, I'm sorry," he said. "I was just really hungry. I shouldn't have bought it. And I was gonna share," he added.

"Well, since you were 'gonna' share," she said as she sat down across from him in the cramped RV booth.

"Speaking of sharing," Jimmy began. "I didn't bring you flowers primarily to assuage my guilt for not bringing you back half of the candy bar."

"Oh yeah?" Winnie said. "Why then?"

Talking about feelings had never been Jimmy's strong suit, but after last night, he could entirely appreciate the value in baring one's soul. If it had been cathartic for Winnie, it had been a major breakthrough for Jimmy and his idea about the kind of relationship he wanted to have with her. And he didn't want the old one—the one where they both simply went through the motions—eating together, drinking together, having rote sex, renting a movie, having superficial conversations about TV shows, their workday, or mutual friends. He realized now that it wasn't enough to share a home or sleep in the same bed with another human; you needed to fully engage with that person daily, share intimate details with them, and hold them close to you.

Because so much of life is made up of the mundane—of sleeping and eating, working, paying bills, doing chores—it was essential that at least a portion of it be devoted to love and adventure, silliness and fun, honesty and intimacy. Maybe her sleeping with Dallas was what it took to jar his senses; to make him see how much he had taken her for granted—going all the way back to high school when he had been certain that he was "settling" for her as his girlfriend.

"I want you to know how much I love you Winnie," he blurted.

Winnie was more than a little stunned by his words. Although she knew that Jimmy was fond of her, she could not recall him ever actually vocalizing it. Love. It was one of those words that they seemed to always dance around, but never say out loud to one another. And it was so unexpected. She wasn't quite sure how to respond. So she didn't, instead, she avoided it completely and started digging into her jean's pockets, pulling out a $5 bill, two ones, and 38 cents in change.

"I may have a dollar or two in my wallet," she said, "but that's it, roughly $10 to our names."

"Wow," was all Jimmy could manage to say both in response to their current situation and the state of their relationship. "We really are screwed," he said. "I knew it was bad, but not this bad."

He ran his fingers through his hair and stood up. "Well, we have to find a way to come up with some quick cash today. We're paid up through tonight, but we can't afford to stay here another night, and we need money for gas, not to mention food."

"Right," Winnie said.

Considering her nonresponse to his declaration of love, Jimmy contemplated bringing up the idea he'd thought of earlier—sex for money. It seemed like she didn't really give a shit about him anyway.

"Well, we could donate plasma," he suggested, "or, one of us could trade some quickie sex for some quickie cash."

He chuckled making it sound like it was just a joke, but Winnie recognized the derision behind it. He was angry because she hadn't acknowledged his love, and this was his passive-aggressive way of getting back at her. It pissed her off. It was insulting for him to even suggest such a thing, yet at the same time, she felt bad. When he told her that he loved her, she could have smiled, or at the very least said something, anything other than simply ignoring it.

This was how they interacted with each other though, despite the breakthroughs of last night. It was just too easy to slip back into familiar patterns. Well, they didn't have the luxury of delving into it at the moment, Winnie thought. They needed to do something and giving plasma seemed like the best idea.

"Plasma it is," she said. "Let's go visit those vampires at the blood bank."

Jimmy offered a weak smile as he pushed open the door of the RV and they headed out in search of the nearest clinic.

Three and half hours later, the wearied pair trudged slowly back into the RV park. Donating plasma proved to be a much more complicated undertaking than they thought. They found the clinic okay, but after filling out the paperwork, using aliases, of course, and sitting for a half hour in the packed waiting room with other "plassers" (other regulars and first timers also strapped for cash) they were finally called back, not for the procedure, but for an oral examination—did they smoke, did they have tattoos, did they have HIV, followed then by a full medical checkup. All this took up another hour, culminating with being sent back to the waiting room for more waiting. After finally receiving the green light, they were ushered into the plasma donation room where 40 or so couches equipped with a blood pressure cuff and a centrifuge were set up. A phlebotomist who drew their blood explained how during the 45-minute procedure the plasma would be extracted and separated from the whole blood and the protein-depleted blood flowed back into their arms to rebuild their nutrient supply. When they were finished, the receptionist handed them each a calendar and a debit card. "What's this?" Jimmy asked. "It's your payment for today's donation," she said sweetly. "And if you come back twice next week, you'll get a $10 bonus."

Winnie looked at Jimmy, her face a question mark. "I thought we were supposed to get cash?"

The receptionist had returned to her work when Jimmy said, "Excuse me, Miss, but I . . . we . . . thought you paid in cash."

She shook her head, "No, we haven't done that in years. Just take your card to any ATM." They found an ATM a couple of blocks down. They were able to use the cards but dismayed to find that each one held only $15, barely enough to fill the tank with fuel with virtually nothing left over for food. The crestfallen pair trudged back to the RV park.

Once inside the RV, they both headed for the back and plopped down on the lumpy bed. "That was a huge waste of time," Jimmy lamented for about the sixth time. Although they had given them cookies and juice at the clinic, they were both hungry and exhausted.

"What are we going to do Jimmy?" Winnie asked.

"I don't know, babe," Jimmy said, closing his eyes wearily, his voice fading away with a heavy sigh. Fatigue had set in and he was already nodding off. Within a few minutes, he was snoring. No such luck for Winnie. Sleep eluded her. She was a worrier. Ever since she was a little girl, Missy had called her a worrywart, among other things. "Stop worrying so much. You're such a worrywart. Stop it," she'd say. But Winnie couldn't stop it, and *somebody* had to worry about things because Missy certainly didn't spend more than a minute ruminating on anything. It was a lot of pressure on a little girl. It was a lot of pressure now. What could they do to get some money? The question rattled around and around inside her head like a gumball in a machine. The offhand comment Jimmy had made earlier about her having sex for money came to mind. It wasn't a terrible idea, she thought. No, no, she dismissed it, horrible idea, horrible, but . . . first off, it was dangerous; she could get arrested, and yet, what other option did they have?

Winnie got up and checked her purse. Tucked inside the pocket with the zipper she found another five-dollar bill. She sometimes tucked her tip money in there and forgot about it. She shouldn't spend it, but it was enough for one drink. On their way back from the clinic they had passed a bar just a few blocks down from the RV park. She would walk over there, hang out, mull things over a bit; see what transpired. As she was putting on her shoes, she caught a glimpse of herself in the mirror. She looked a bit disheveled. Fumbling around in the bath area she found Jimmy's comb and ran it through her short hair. She frowned. The black dye part was starting to grow out revealing the blonde roots underneath giving her, what she thought, was a cheap look, like she couldn't afford hair dye. She couldn't, but that was beside the point. She patted some water on her face and decided to apply a little mascara that she had found buried at the bottom of her purse.

Still not satisfied, she decided to rummage around some more through the drawers for other things she could use to accessorize. Most of the drawers were empty, but some contained odds and ends like dishtowels and kitchen gadgets and a tablecloth, remnants of inhabitants past. She opened up one in the bedroom and discovered that it was filled with an assortment of women's garments. At the back, she pulled out a purple paisley scarf. Perfect! She looped it around her neck, placed the beret on her head to hide the roots, and stood back and admired herself in the mirror. "Not bad," she said as she tilted her head and turned from one side to the other with hands on hips. In another one of the bathroom drawers she found an old lipstick, bright red. Normally, Winnie only wore lip balm, but she'd make an exception tonight. Taking a final glance in the mirror, Winnie, now Jetty Jet was satisfied. She put on her jacket, grabbed her purse, slowly opened up the creaky RV door so as not to wake Jimmy, and quietly disappeared into the night.

The tavern was your representative dive. Dimly lit, bar with a glass mirror behind it, jukebox, pool tables in the back. Winnie walked over and hopped up on a barstool. A couple of regulars eyed her—an old guy in a ball cap and ratty jacket nursing a beer and a bleached blonde mess of a women with an eye patch drinking something from a small, brown tumbler. She hoped neither one got any ideas about talking to her. Fortunately, both seemed to be focused on drinking and nothing else. The bartender, a middle-aged biker chick, her arms covered in tats, strolled over to her.

"What can I getcha?" she asked.

Winnie couldn't tell if the woman's raspy, sort of irritated tone was needling or if she was just being badass. It didn't matter. She was used to being around these people. The key to fitting in was to simply act like you did. She had long ago shed any fear of scary people. Most of them were mostly show; and the really truly scary ones were the normal looking ones that didn't act scary at all.

Winnie ordered a Dos Equis with a lime. She laid the five-dollar bill on the counter and the bartender brought the beer over, placing it in front of Winnie on a cardboard coaster.

"Anything else?" she asked.

Winnie shook her head no. "Thanks," she said, "I'm good." Now that her eyes were starting to adjust to the dimness, Winnie glanced around the room to see who else was hanging about. A pair of scruffy looking guys played pool at one table while a skinny girl sitting nearby on a couch looked on. It appeared the owners were in the process of trying to make the place a bit more funky and homey by adding a couple of loungy sofas, end tables with modern lamps and a coffee table to the space. Over the lamps they'd placed red kerchiefs for ambience and scattered a few random magazines on the table. Yet, despite the avant-garde trappings, against the juxtaposition of the rundown bar, they just couldn't quite pull it off.

Three quarters of the way through her beer and as yet nobody interesting had come in. She couldn't afford another. When it was gone, she would have no choice but to leave. Just as she was bringing the bottle to her lips for another swig, the door swung open and two men wearing trucker style hats, cowboy boots, and plaid shirts sauntered into the bar. Old scruffy guy and eye-patch lady didn't even bother to look up. The pool players glanced up but turned back to their game. Maybe these were regulars too. They both had a swagger like they owned the place. The first guy sidled up to the bar next to Jetty. His breath reeked of cigarettes and beer.

"Hey fancy lady," he said slurring his words. Fancy sounded more like fee-ancy. "Whatcha drinkin'?" his head bobbling over her beer as he tried to focus. "Get this fancy lady a beer. She needs a beer. Maggie!" he barked. "Maggie!" he shouted louder this time. Maggie, the bartender, walked over from the other side, a look of concern crossing her face.

"Now Les," she said, "leave this poor girl alone, will ya?" Les grinned stupid drunkenly. Maggie turned to Jetty and said, "Is he bothering you?"

Winnie smiled nonchalantly, "nah," she said, waving her off.

"Okay," Maggie said, "you're on your own." She plopped another Dos Equis on the table in front of her leaving her to deal with the fire-breathing Les. His buddy had wandered over to one of the lounges and seemingly passed out, his head slumped over the armrests to one side.

Les cozied up next to her on the barstool. "So, what's your name darlin'?"

Winnie winced at his bad breath—a mix of whiskey and stale cigarettes. Normally, she would have shied away from any contact with a person as drunk and disgusting as Les, but she was here for a reason and Les seemed the most likely prospect.

"Amber," Winnie lied. "My name's Amber." She thrust her hand out and shook Les' hand. "Mmmmm Amber," Les crooned into her ear, "I like that name a lot."

Winnie smiled weakly. She hoped she could keep up the charade. She hoped she could go through with it. She could get up and walk out, right now, but they needed money. "I can do this," she told herself bravely. She turned and faced Les, looked him straight in his bloodshot eyes, and as sweetly as she could muster said, "If you have money, I have time." She knew it sounded stupid the minute she said it. If Les were a cop she'd be busted for solicitation for sure. She'd never done this sort of thing before, but she was betting that Les was too drunk to be a cop.

Les' eyes widened and he looked like he'd lined up a row of 7s on the slot machine. "You got it, Miz Amber," he said, snatching her hand and pulling her unceremoniously off the barstool. Winnie looked at Maggie, who shook her head with disgust. They left the bar together and Les led Winnie out to the parking lot where his semi-truck was parked. He stepped up on the running board and unlocked a door that led to the sleeper in back of the truck's cab. "Hop in little lady," he said as he gave Winnie a hand up. Rather than merely a sleeping compartment, the sleeper was more like a small apartment, complete with a bed, TV, small refrigerator, a microwave. Winnie was impressed. She'd never been inside a truck before. Now she understood how women could be persuaded to join their trucker husbands on the road.

While Winnie was admiring the set-up, behind her Les was doing a striptease and when she turned around, he was completely naked and ogling her in a creepy come hither way. "Come on darlin'," he said. "Let's get it on!" Winnie barely had time to react before Les grabbed her and started pawing and groping her with his grimy hands. In the confines of the small space, he seemed much bigger and stronger than he had when they were inside the bar. She tried to back away, frightened now that she was locked inside a space that she wasn't sure she could easily maneuver her way out of.

"Come on now Amber," Les crooned. "Don't play coy." It was clear that he wasn't messing around anymore. She had offered services and he was taking them. He reached out, cupping her breast roughly. And then suddenly, he violently wrapped one leg around hers tripping her and causing her to fall backwards onto the bed. Winnie was scared now. Really scared. "No, stop it" she managed to say meekly as she tried to shove him away with her hands, but Les was strong. Holding her down with one elbow pinned across her chest, he used his other hand to try to pull her jeans down. The more she resisted, the angrier he became; his face was contorting into a grizzly mean snarl. Furious that she was fighting, he hauled off and sucker punched her in the cheek. The impact knocked her back and from somewhere that seemed floating outside of her own head she could hear herself crying out in pain. This was serious. "No, no, no . . ." she screamed, but Les had managed to get her pants off. He spread her legs apart and was preparing to penetrate her. The world was spinning out of control. He was going to rape her. Winnie squeezed her eyes shut and whimpered and it was her fault.

The next thing she heard was a loud thwack, and when she opened her eyes, Les had crumpled to the floor out cold, and his buddy, the other trucker, was standing over her. He picked her pants up off the floor and handed them to her. "Sorry about that. Les can be a real asshole sometimes," he said as Winnie scurried to put her jeans back on. She stood up, embarrassed, and started to open the door to leave when the trucker grabbed her arm. Winnie was terrified again, certain that he wouldn't let her go, until he said, "I know you're not a hooker, Jetty." Jetty? How did he know her name? "I know you're on the run, saw your picture on the news," he said, "and I know you're out of money." He let go of her arm then and pulled a $50 bill from his wallet. "This'll help a little," he said handing it to her. Winnie hesitated but took the money. "Thank you," she mumbled and quickly exited the sleeper.

She stepped down from the running board. It was starting to snow. And even though her legs felt wobbly, Winnie ran. She ran away from the parking lot as fast as she could go, and once she was on the road she continued to run until the lights of the tavern had completely disappeared from view. When she was certain she was far enough away, she stopped next to an empty field where there were no streetlights. Bending over to catch her breath, she immediately threw up. Her legs felt rubbery, and she was lightheaded. She dropped to her knees. She felt so weird all of a sudden; so fatigued. She hadn't drunk that much; maybe it was the fear catching up to her, but then it dawned on her—the plasma. That had to be it. They had both been given instructions about possible aftereffects following donation, but Winnie and Jimmy had brushed it aside, not bothering to read the paper the receptionist had given them. She felt like she'd been hit by a truck, but she knew she couldn't stay here. Somehow, she must make her legs move.

Using her arms to steady herself, Winnie rolled over and pushed herself up. She began to slowly walk. "Legs don't betray me," she said as she put one foot in front of the other. It was late when she finally arrived back at the RV, but on the way, she'd had time to think about things. The whole Les thing was just stupid. She didn't know why she even thought she could pull it off. She wasn't Missy. She'd never be like her mom. Not ever. And she wasn't Jetty Jet either, not really. Jetty Jet wasn't a different person like Winnie wanted her to be, but she was a part of Winnie. She had so wanted Jetty Jet to be her savior, to be this strong, independent, tough alter ego that could replace little Miss too nice, too introverted, too accepting Winnie. But Jimmy had shown her with his simple gift of flowers that she didn't need to be anyone but herself, because he loved her. Little ol' her. He had come right out and said so.

Too exhausted to think anymore, Winnie trudged back to the bedroom. Jimmy must have been dealing with the same fatigue as she was—he was sprawled out on the bed sound asleep. Winnie decided not to disturb him and instead, crawled up into the bunk up front. She was asleep as soon as her head hit the pillow.

Winnie woke up early. She felt better, but her legs still felt wobbly. She climbed down from the bunk and walked unsteadily over to the tiny bathroom area to pee. Jimmy was still asleep. She could hear him snoring. She rubbed her eyes, but when she opened them and caught a glimpse of her face in the mirror, she gasped. A huge bruise had formed on her cheek where Les had struck her the night before. Oh my god, how would she ever explain this to Jimmy? she wondered. She had an idea. She quickly dressed, grabbed her camera, and left the RV.

An hour later when she returned Jimmy was up and waiting for her. "Where have you be . . .?" he stopped midsentence when he saw the angry bruise on her cheek. "Oh my god, Winnie, what happened to your face?" he asked. Concerned, he touched her cheek and she winced. "It's okay," Winnie said. "Okay?" Jimmy asked incredulously. "What do you mean okay? What happened to you?"

Just then, Jimmy's legs began to wobble, and he started to lose his balance. Winnie reached out and grabbed his arm. "Steady," she said as she guided him over to the booth to sit down.

"Whoa," Jimmy said. "I don't know what just happened. I feel so lightheaded and, I don't know, weird."

"It's from donating plasma," Winnie told him. "The same thing happened to me this morning," she coolly lied. "I went out for a walk and on the way back I started feeling wobbly and dizzy like that. I fell and hit my cheek against a rock on the ground."

"Oh wow," Jimmy said. "I'm sorry Winnie. This really sucks. Are you sure it's from giving plasma?"

She pulled the piece of paper the receptionist had given them from her coat pocket. "Yeah," she said. "Says right here, 'over the next few days you may experience aftereffects such as dizziness, nausea or fatigue.'"

"Great," he said. He rubbed his hand across the top of his head and sighed. "All this for nothing. We still don't have enough money. Can it possibly get any fucking worse?"

Winnie sat down across the table from him. He watched as she dug around in her purse and pulled out a wad of cash and placed it on the table. Jimmy's eyes widened with surprise. He picked up the money and started to count. "20, 40, 60, 80… there's 250 bucks here. Where did you get it?"

Winnie smiled perfunctorily. "I pawned my camera," she confessed. She'd really only gotten $200 for the camera, but this way she didn't need to explain the $50 from the trucker.

"What? Winnie. No," Jimmy said, placing the bills back down on the table. "You didn't?"

"I did," she said. "We needed the money." Jimmy was still shaking his head. He knew how much the camera meant to her. It was like selling a kidney for Winnie.

She reached across the table, careful not to knock over the bouquet of roses, and took his hand. "I can get another camera," she said. "Really, it's okay, and I kept the memory cards with all the photos I've taken."

"Are you sure?" Jimmy asked. He felt so bad for her. "You," he said, "are confusing, but I love you."

Winnie smiled and said, "I know. I love you too."

The last few days had been a roller coaster ride, but right now Jimmy was on top of the world. They had some cash, but more important, he and Winnie were clicking again, well, if he was honest, they were clicking like they never had before.

The pile of cash sat on the table between them. A bit more than $200, maybe just a drop in the ocean for most people, but a huge wave of relief for them. Things were looking up! "Let's get something to eat, get gas, and get out of this dump!" Jimmy practically shouted.

It only took a few minutes and they had everything disconnected and quickly stowed away. The gas station down the road a bit had a café next door, between two massive breakfast orders that they wolfed down and the gas required to top off the RV, they still had $140, plenty to buy gas enough to get all the way to the cabin and keep themselves fed along the way.

Even with the heavy biscuits, gravy, pancakes, and eggs sitting in their bellies, they both felt buoyant. Things were finally going their way. As they were at the register, paying their tab with the gum-smacking cliché of a bored waitress, she did a quick, shocked double take as Jetty Jet's face appeared on the old television hanging in the corner by the door.

Instinctually, Jimmy turned to see what the waitress was looking at and saw the full-screen image of Winnie with the caption "murder witness spotted in Denver area" along with a phone number for the local FBI office. Heart pounding, Jimmy finished the transaction, accepting their change. Awkwardly, he was sure, he mumbled to Winnie, loud enough for the waitress to hear "Wow, that woman looks a lot like you! Isn't that weird honey?" Winnie, shocked, only nodded, and repeated, "yeah, weird."

Back in the motorhome, Jimmy kept an eye on the restaurant door, but he couldn't see if the waitress was looking out at them, but somehow, he knew she was. "We've got to get out of here and we've got to change the way you look," he said, looking into Winnie's still shocked face.

Shaking her head, seeming to clear the fog, Winnie nodded. "Um, let's find a thrift shop, I can probably find a wig and some clothes that at least aren't on the television." Jimmy nodded, but he hadn't even realized that the blouse Winnie was currently wearing was the same as the one she'd been wearing in the police photo; Pretty unlikely that the waitress would overlook that coincidence.

On this, still the somewhat seedy outskirts of the city, it didn't take long to find a thrift shop. It was next door to a sprawling Walmart. Jimmy pulled the RV into the Walmart lot near a few other RVs. "Hopefully, no one will notice one more old broken down beater RV," he explained.

"Good idea, and we can get some stuff in the Walmart too. I don't think we should go to any more restaurants, we can just cook in here," Winnie agreed.

The thrift store was rattier than most and the distinct used stuff odor that permeated all second-hand stores was much more pronounced in this one, but Winnie wasn't looking for high fashion, or even a wig that might pass as real. She decided that being over-the-top would be her best option. People would probably notice her, but certainly not associate her with the edgy, but dark, police image. She found a red wig that actually looked pretty good, if not exactly natural. A bright yellow sundress finished her selection.

Once they'd paid, Winnie went back into the changing room to put the dress on. As she dressed, she thought to herself that they'd pop into Walmart, buy enough groceries for a couple days, then hopefully they could put Denver behind them. Winnie found that her once vaguely hopeful plan of getting to Montana and her mother had become a fierce need. She knew it didn't make a lot of sense, Missy probably wouldn't be much help, but it was the only plan she had, and she was clinging to it.

Of course, the food section was clear on the other side of the humongous store. It was either coincidence, or possibly a slow news day, but as Jimmy and Winnie trudged toward the food, they passed the electronics department with roughly half the giant televisions once again flashing a picture of Jetty Jet. Despite himself, Jimmy stopped in front of one set with its sound on low, but clear enough to listen to the newscaster.

"Reports that person-of-interest Jenny Jones, wanted for questioning in the café murder in Oklahoma last week, may be in the Denver area in the company of a man and traveling in a 70s-era Winnebago. Conflicting reports have come in that she may have been working as a prostitute in the Greenwood Village area and may have been involved in an assault in the parking lot of the Alibi Inn, a local tavern."

Winnie felt her heart drop and her mouth go dry. Jimmy glanced at her, then back to the screen a few times, his jaw muscles rippling as he tried to make sense of the news report. "Christ Winnie! What are they talking about? I thought you pawned your camera?"

"I . . . I did. Man, I should have told you everything. I'll explain when we get back in the RV," Winnie said, clearly on the verge of tears. "Let's get some food and get out of here."

Though obviously confused, Jimmy nodded, and they quickly walked over to the grocery section and grabbed supplies for making sandwiches, coffee, and a bunch of snacks. No one in the store, not even the elderly lady at the register, gave them a second glance, despite the conspicuous wig and bright outfit Winnie was wearing—it was Walmart after all.

Emerging from the massive store they immediately spotted the police cars with flashing lights at the other end of the parking lot, right where they'd parked the RV. "Crap!" they both said in unison.

"OK, don't panic!" Jimmy said, panic infusing his voice. "Act normal and let's just walk this way and find a place to think about what we do next," he said with slightly less quiver in his voice as he guided Winnie onto the sidewalk leading in the opposite direction of the RV.

A couple blocks down, they spotted a Starbucks and darted inside. They could have been back in S. California, maybe Portland, well, almost anywhere in the US, somehow the corporate sameness put them both at ease, or at least relatively so. Placing their familiar orders also calmed them down a bit, even though Winnie almost told the barista her name was Jetty before remembering that now, Winnie was more "underground" than Jetty.

The place was almost empty, except for a group of four women sitting at a table and a couple of student-types sitting with laptops at two other tables. Choosing a small table near the women that gave both of them a clear view of the door, Jimmy and Winnie sat and collected their thoughts for a few moments as they pretended to be engrossed in tasting their drinks.

"What are we going to do? We're screwed!" announced Winnie after the silence had gone on just a bit too long. Jimmy wasn't sure, but he thought at least a couple of the women had overheard and it made him uncomfortable, but he didn't want to tell Winnie to lower her voice. He'd learned early on that Winnie didn't react well to being "shushed".

"Yeah. Maybe we can hitchhike?" Jimmy said tentatively, knowing that it was a pretty awful idea. Being visible enough to attract a ride was exactly the wrong thing to do, especially now that the police knew they'd lost their transportation. Winnie gave him a look of dismissal, letting him know that she knew as well that it wasn't a good option.

"We can lay low for a few days, then try it, I suppose," she countered. "Then again, maybe we could 'borrow' a car and get to Montana before we get caught."

Jimmy pondered that for a moment. "Yeah, I suppose that is a possibility, but I think it is risky. Maybe we just need to trust the police, turn ourselves in. We haven't done anything wrong after all, well, I don't think we have . . ." Jimmy let the implication sit there.

Winnie immediately felt her anger rise, but then realized that from Jimmy's viewpoint, he was absolutely right to have questions. "OK, I lied about falling. I was trying to make money and it was your goddamn suggestion! I couldn't go through with it though and the guy got mad, then his buddy saved me. That's all there was to it. I didn't want to tell you, because, well, I didn't want you know how close I'd came to doing that."

Jimmy nodded, accepting that for now, but telling himself he'd want more details later. Winnie, seeing that, shifted back to other question. "Yeah, I suppose if we have to. But once the police have us, whoever is chasing me and killed Dallas will know exactly where we are. I don't think we'll be able to convince the police that we'd be in danger in their custody, but I don't doubt that whoever these guys are, they aren't going to have problems getting around the local police or jailers."

Now it was obvious to Jimmy, the women were eavesdropping, despite Winnie having dropped her volume. He couldn't be sure, but he also had a strong feeling that they were discussing him and Winnie. He took a closer look at the group, trying to be as casual as possible, aware that they were doing the same to him. There was something just slightly off about the group. They were all of a similar age, perhaps early to mid-30s. Each of them individually may have been totally inconspicuous, but something seemed out of place.

Then it snapped in his mind—they weren't dressed identically, that would be too easy. However, they were dressed very similarly, with the same off-brand jogging shoes and something about them made him think "sisters", even though they didn't really have a family resemblance to each other. Then, he caught the eye of the blonde one and she gave a little nod to the rest of her group and cleared her throat.

"I think we can help," it was a matter-of-fact statement, as if she were responding to a question. "If you and Jetty can trust us, we can help you out," she ventured. Both Jimmy and Winnie visibly jerked with surprise—the woman had plainly called Winnie by her alias. Slowly, Winnie turned to look at the blonde spokesperson who was giving her best, "trust me" smile.

"And who are you, and why do you think my name is Jetty?" Winnie managed to challenge, without too much hostility.

"We're friends. We're always looking to make new friends. Come with us and we'll explain more, but we think it is best that you two get out of this area as soon as possible." The woman was confident and open, with a bit more authority and a lot more warmth than he'd ever expect from a stranger. He decided that not only could he trust her, but that he had little choice. Looking at Winnie, he could see that she was considering their options as well. It was obvious that Winnie hadn't decided to trust the woman, at least not to the extent that Jimmy already had, but when he nodded, Winnie exhaled loudly.

"OK, we certainly need help, so let's go!" she said.

The women were all traveling together in a nondescript Chrysler minivan. Oddly, Jimmy felt himself guided into the front passenger seat, even though he'd planned on sitting in the back, next to Winnie if at all possible. The blond woman, somehow not surprisingly, was the driver.

As they wound through the surface streets toward the freeway, introductions were made. "I'm Kim. In the back row are Becky and Sue. Marla is sitting next to Jetty." The blonde spoke directly to the front windshield, but occasionally glanced into the mirror to make eye contact with Winnie. Jimmy half turned in his seat to try and put faces to the names and began to reply with their names, including Winnie's "correct" name when he saw Winnie's eyes flare and she preempted him.

"Great! Kim, Becky, Sue, and Marla," she repeated, "I'm Jetty and this is Jimmy. We're pleased to meet you and really grateful for any help you can give us." All the while, she looked straight at Jimmy, trying to convey that he should let her guide what they told these women. Jimmy gave an almost imperceptible nod to let her know that he was onboard. "Can you tell us where we're going?"

"Nice to meet you too. We're going back to *the* Community." The slightest of pauses before the final word made it clear that it wasn't just a community, but *THE* Community.

"Well, we really need to get to Montana," Jetty said, establishing that she and Jimmy had goals that may or may not line up with the help this somewhat mysterious group of soccer moms was prepared to provide.

"When we get back to *The* Community, only about 45 minutes more, we'll meet with the others and discuss what we can do for the two of you," Kim said. The two women in the back were sharing a whispered conversation and taking quick glances at her "purple" hand, and when Winnie tried to engage them in light conversation, she quickly discovered that Marla would reply to any query only with a variation of "when we get back . . ." She decided just to wait it out.

After the adrenaline rush of finding the police at their RV and mostly nonstop action of the past few days, Winnie was almost lulled to sleep by the hum of the freeway and the indecipherable whispering interspersed with quickly stifled giggles coming from the back. There was something odd about these women and their Community, but at this point, Winnie had no decisions to make so she let herself drift off. In the front seat, Jimmy was already out, despite the double-shot latte from Starbucks.

A jolt from a pothole brought them both wide awake. They were on a graded gravel road. Looking back out of the window, Winnie could see nothing but mountains on the horizon and a haze of dust kicked up by their tires. No telling how long they'd been off the freeway. Kim, looking at her through the mirror announced, "About another mile and we'll be home." Jimmy glanced back at Winnie. There didn't seem to be anything ahead of them but a few copses of trees, gently rolling prairie land, and the occasional prairie dog.

Indeed, it was behind one of the larger screens of trees that they turned in. At first glance, it looked pretty much like any semi-rundown working ranch or large farm. There was an immense barn, a pretty large multistory farmhouse that may have been built anywhere from 150 to 15 years ago, and a mad scattering of cars, pickups, tractors, and other equipment parked at seemingly random disarray. Peeking out from behind the barn, Jimmy could see the corner of a late-model mobile home, the kind popular in Over 55 trailer parks.

Kim drove them past the house and down a well-packed dirt road to the front of the barn. "We're here! This is our Community. Ladies, why don't you escort Jetty and Jimmy into the meeting hall? I'll run up to the house to let everyone know we're back with guests." With that, she was already quickly striding back up the dirt road.

Getting out of the minivan, Jimmy stretched and shook his head, trying to become fully awake. The cool, verging on cold, mountain air helped a lot, and he could see Winnie gulping in big breaths as she too tried to shake off the aftereffects of the short, but deep nap. Still not fully verbal, the three remaining Community women let their guests stretch for a few more moments, and then simply began walking toward the immense barn doors.

The whispering women grabbed onto one of the sliding doors and pulling the doors apart revealing not a hay-filled interior, but rather, a partitioned space with a stage and stadium seating. Staring at the space, Winnie estimated there was seating enough for maybe 50 people. The seating was in a semi-circle, looking over the stage and toward the recently opened doors. The stage, no, Winnie corrected her impression, it wasn't a stage, but more properly a lectern, or pulpit was mainly bare but for a large wooden desk oriented to face the audience and a few other chairs also facing the audience.

Winnie was pretty sure they'd stumbled into some sort of religious group. The peculiar way they called it the Community, the odd way the women all seemed somehow linked, the remote setting. The barn was still a bit surprising, but not shocking, she could see that Jimmy had pretty much made the same guesses. They didn't have long to just stand around and gawk. Marla hurried through a door, presumably into other rooms within the converted barn and the other two led Winnie and Jimmy up onto the stage.

Before they even got to the chairs, a bell hanging in the rafters began ringing and almost immediately people began streaming into the amphitheater. As the two women arranged things on stage so that the desk faced the chairs perpendicularly to the stands, Winnie studied the people taking their seats. Already the stream seemed to have ended, people were quickly finding their seats.

They seemed for the most part to be fairly young, with many probably in their 20s, most in their 30s, and Winnie guessed a few might be in their early 40s. Although they'd come through the doors seemingly at random, they'd all paired up with the result that the seating was perfectly arranged man-woman-man-woman. They pretty much filled the first three rows, about 40 total Winnie estimated. There had been a heavy buzz of conversation as they arrived and even once they were seated, but suddenly it cut off.

Kim, a man, and a middle-aged woman, scurried into three seats that had been left open in the front row. Right behind them, entering through the barn doors and bounding up the stairs was a large, shockingly handsome, deeply tanned man with a flowing mane of silver hair. He moved directly to the front of the stage, surveyed the audience, spread his arms wide, and announced, "Hey Everyone, isn't this a wonderful day!" Winnie imagined she felt his deeply booming voice vibrating her very bones and immediately she suspected he must be wearing a microphone.

When he'd taken a moment to survey the smiling, nodding faces in the crowd, he finally turned around and looked at her and Jimmy. Looking directly at him, Winnie could feel a blast of charisma that threatened to overtake even his bright toothy smile. His eyes, crinkled slightly from the grin were tropical beach blue. He was wearing a simple patterned button-down shirt and khaki slacks, but he wore them with more authority than most men she'd met could muster in a formal suit.

In two bouncy steps, he was directly in front of them. She didn't remember standing and could not have told you if she'd stood up when he first came on stage or just a split second ago. He held out a large, manicured hand and Winnie felt her hand fully engulfed in his. His gaze lingered a bit longer on Winnie's discolored hand before he pulled away gently and gave her a brief hug. He repeated the handshake, and the hug with Jimmy, then stepped back half a step to take them both in, all the while, the dazzling kind smile and dancing eyes never faltered.

"Welcome Jimmy and Jetty! I'm Archibald Golden and *this* is our community." As he finished on the word community, his arms gestured to encompass the audience. "I know it probably seems a bit overwhelming, but we're a tight-knit community and we've found it best if everyone gets to meet our visitors as soon as possible. It also makes it easier on the visitors too—you only have to answer each question once!"

Winnie could see that Jimmy seemed totally charmed and at ease, he was smiling back at Golden. Although she knew intellectually that charisma existed, she'd never encountered anyone with this level. She could feel herself relax and knew she was smiling back at the man, even though a part of her was still aware that he'd done nothing, really, to earn her trust.

That small part seemed to fall far into the back as Golden seamlessly shifted into a conversational mode. Winnie realized only after she'd answered a number of questions about her life, right up until her flight, that rather than a conversation, Golden had interviewed, in fact, had almost interrogated both her and Jimmy. She'd almost forgotten that there was an audience; it felt like talking to an old friend and catching them up on recent events.

It was only the trauma of being on the run, and probably Jimmy's confusion and mixed feelings about those events that stopped them both from blithely spilling everything. When neither she nor Jimmy readily extended their stories into the recent past, Golden chided Winnie gently. "So, you started calling yourself Jetty Jet and moved to Oklahoma, right?"

Winnie realized that this wasn't a group that ignored the outside world. Kim had known who she was right away—they had to know about Dallas being murdered, and almost certainly the accusations from that slimeball trucker. She found that she wanted to trust these people, she wanted to trust the earnest, smiling man asking her so many questions.

"Well, first I moved to New Mexico. My dad, who went into the witness protection program when I was just a kid, called me and told me to run. So, I grabbed a few things and ran. Jimmy was on a job interview in Portland, so I left him a note saying goodbye."

Golden cocked an eyebrow at that and looked over at Jimmy. "So, when you got the note saying she'd left for New Mexico, you followed her?"

"Well, not exactly. The note didn't say anything but goodbye. I had no idea where Winnie had gone, or why. I went to her mom's house, but she was gone too. After a few weeks, I took the job in Portland and moved up there. I figured she'd dumped me, and I'd better move on with my life. Then a couple cops, well, guys who said they were cops, they came to my office and said Winnie was in New Mexico. I went there, but she'd left already.

I asked at the place she'd been working, and they told me they'd probably gone to Hooker, Oklahoma, so I went there."

"They?" asked Golden, frowning in concentration as he tried to follow the story.

Winnie answered quickly, not wanting Jimmy to have to explain about Dallas. "Yeah, I met Dallas in the café where I was working in New Mexico, he helped me out. I wasn't real sure about how to be underground, I'd used my real name and social security card to get the job—that's how Jimmy, or those fake cops at least, found me."

"In Hooker, Dallas knew a guy that got me a fake ID, then we got a job at another café. We hadn't been there long when Jimmy found me. But some guy in a red Porsche had been following Jimmy and when he came in the door, I was talking to Jimmy and Dallas saw that the guy had a gun and he tackled him and told me to run. We didn't really see what happened, just heard the gunshot. Then we saw the guy stumble out of the front of the restaurant. We were able to lose him, we saw him driving like a maniac down the freeway.

"From there, we went back to see Dallas' friend. We traded Jimmy's car for the RV and decided to drive up to meet my mom in Montana."

"I assume you ran out of money for gas, right? So what is the story with the truck driver?"

Winnie blushed a bit, but Jimmy jumped in. "She was going to. We didn't seem to have any choices, but then she changed her mind, she couldn't do it. The trucker was drunk and hit her, but fortunately his friend came and knocked him out. Then, Winnie hocked her camera. We'd just filled the RV up and went to get some food at Walmart, but when we came out there were police all around the RV. We walked down to the Starbucks and that's where we met Kim and the others."

"Well, that's a pretty incredible story," said Golden as he sat back and looked out at the audience who had been stone silent through the entire process. He seemed to study the crowd for a minute then turned back to Winnie. "I have some questions. Why has your dad been in witness protection so long and only now called you? That seems odd, and it seems odd that you'd just run away with nothing but a call saying 'run'. Why didn't you go to the police in Oklahoma?"

Winnie filled in the information about her dad, how he was supposed to testify against his mafia boss, but before the trial, the boss had fled the country, leaving poor old Dad in limbo. She also explained that she really didn't know his situation, so had no idea why he'd never called her before, nor did she know how he'd gotten her number or even knew she was in danger, but that as Winnie, she'd been pretty easy to find online. She even volunteered that dad probably still had at least a few friends in "the family" that might tip him off that his daughter was in danger. She also told him how her and Jimmy had discovered that the mob boss had recently been captured and was being extradited back to the US.

Again, Jimmy picked up the next question. "There were a couple reasons we didn't think it was safe to go to the police. The first was that we weren't sure we could trust the police. It seemed that they had set me up to find Winnie so they could follow her. But, more importantly, we knew if we did turn ourselves in, there would be lots of media and the mob would know exactly where we were. The police are all about catching bad guys and holding them in cells, they aren't really concerned with protecting the people in those cells." Winnie noted by the near simultaneous nodding of agreement that the cynical portrayal of the police seemed to be easily accepted by Golden and the audience. Any community outside the mainstream probably had a well-deserved mistrust of the authorities.

Golden nodded as he visibly considered their answers. After a few seconds, the crowd began whispering among themselves. Golden calmly surveyed the crowd again. Winnie knew that he couldn't possibly hear any particular conversation, but she figured he could probably sense the mood of the crowd. This went on for a few minutes, as Winnie and Jimmy traded worried glances.

Golden stood up again and turned to face the crowd. "These people have asked for our help and our shelter. I'm convinced that they are deserving of this community's assistance." He paused again briefly, before announcing unexpectedly, "And one of them is quite special." He turned his head slightly and glanced in Winnie's direction. The crowd grew hushed, waiting in anticipation of Golden's next revelation. Winnie wasn't sure what to expect. Golden beckoned to Kim, who dutifully came forward. He whispered something in her ear and stood back waiting while she walked over to Winnie and delivered the message: "Archibald would like for you to remove your shirt please," Winnie stiffened.

"What? Why" she whispered back to Kim, but Kim just shrugged her shoulders. She looked over at Jimmy, who like her had no clue about what was going on and hadn't heard what Kim had said anyway. She shifted nervously from one foot to the other and when she turned to look at Golden, he bestowed upon her a smile that could melt butter. The crowd began shifting around in their seats and murmuring softly, waiting for something to happen. Winnie hesitated, anxious because everyone was staring at her, yet feeling oddly buoyed by Golden's pronouncement that she was somehow special.

Finally, grabbing the bottom of her sweatshirt, Winnie slowly pulled the fabric up and over her head. Standing alone in her sports bra, she surveyed the crowd. You could hear a pin drop. After a moment, Golden stood up and joined Winnie center stage. He raised his arms again, "Behold the firemark!" he roared. The crowd gasped. "Is it not beautiful?" he asked the crowd. "She has been touched by the hand of God himself and he has delivered her to us, here at *the* community!"

At once, the crowd was on their feet, clapping and basically going wild. Winnie had never witnessed anything like it. Did they think her birthmark was some sort of religious sign? What had he called it? A firemark? It all seemed so crazy and surreal, but she could also feel herself getting caught up in the moment; of being the focus of so much attention. All of this . . . for her! Crazy. Jimmy was stunned as well. It was all very weird and bizarre, but he could see, and feel, how religious people got so caught up in the energy of groupthink.

The clapping went on until Golden pressed his hands down to indicate that they should sit down. "Of course, I am but one person in this community," he said. His voice grew stronger, louder and more forceful as his arms spread wide and with much flair and drama, he said, "The community is bigger and more powerful, and vastly more important than any one person! I see. I feel. I know the community is here, right now. It is strong! Let the Community decide!"

As Golden had made his speech, continually ramping up the level of anticipation and rhetorical flourishes, the worried glances between Jimmy and Winnie quickly shifted to fear and confusion. When, after the final booming word was still reverberating, the entire barn seemed to erupt again as everyone in the audience jumped to their feet and shouted in a single voice, "The Community Welcomes Them!"

Turning back to Jimmy and Winnie, Golden said in a stage whisper "that does it then, you are provisionally part of our community." He winked at them before turning back to the excited throng. "We'll have a potluck tonight so everyone can meet our new arrivals. Set aside whatever can be set aside until the day after tomorrow. Go now and prepare. Tomorrow, we'll have a proper celebration to strengthen the bonds of our community!"

Almost immediately, the people began streaming out. Unsure about what to do next, Jimmy walked over to Winnie, who reached down and plucked her sweatshirt from the stage and quickly put it back on. Kim, the man, and the woman who'd entered with her, worked their way onto the stage. "Winnie, Jimmy, I'd like to introduce you to my wife, Veronica," then with a small smile, he added "yes, I'm afraid we are Archie and Veronica. There are indeed a few Betties in the Community, but they're each happily married." The little joke was obviously one he probably told every time he introduced his wife, yet she smiled dutifully. Winnie didn't get the reference right away, but when Jimmy gave a polite chuckle and asked if there was a "Jughead" in the community as well, it snapped into place.

Golden gave Jimmy a brief smile, then turned to introduce the man with Kim. "You've already met Kim. This is her husband, Darby. Kim and Darby are basically the ones that keep everything going around here. I guess you could call them the general managers. They've been the core of the community from the very beginning. But, you've had an incredible day already and I bet you're overloaded with questions and probably plenty of concerns. Let's go up to the house, have a little lunch and I'll tell you what the Community is all about and then you can ask all the questions you want. After that, Kim and Darby will show each of you around and you can ask more questions if you'd like." They were already halfway up the path to the house when Golden finished. It struck Winnie that when this man made a suggestion, it was already being implemented.

The inside of the house wasn't at all what Winnie had expected. In the books and on TV, cult leaders always seemed to live in high style while their acolytes were kept in either abject poverty or sterile dormitories. She hadn't seen how everyone else lived, but Golden's house appeared to be exactly what it looked like from the outside, a simple country farmhouse.

Well worn, but sturdy furniture in the living room was arranged around a fireplace with a modest flat screen TV above the mantle. Small pillows and throw rugs were scattered throughout the room. The room was slightly crowded with couches, loveseats, and overstuffed chairs, but otherwise nothing special. The wood floor was clean and polished and accented with old-fashioned oval hooked rugs. Veronica led them into a large dining room. The roughly hewn table was large, with benches rather than chairs except for the chairs at each end. As she indicated that they should take a seat on a bench at the table, she asked what they'd like to drink, "We have coffee, tea, milk, and lemonade, oh, and I think we have some ginger ale Barbara left here last time they were over?" Once everyone settled on coffee, she scurried off to the kitchen.

Not surprisingly, Golden had taken the seat at the head of the table; Kim and Darby were on a bench on the other side facing Jimmy and Winnie. "So, you've got to be wondering just what kind of crazy cult you've fallen in with, right?" Golden opened with a self-deprecating grin. Seeing them a little shocked, but also nodding, he continued. "Well, of course we don't see ourselves as a cult in the way the media likes to portray any group outside the mainstream, but it is just a label anyway, so it doesn't offend us if you call us a cult. But, to be clear, we are not a religious group, at least not the way most people think of religions, although I was quite excited to see Jetty's powerful talisman." He looked over and flashed her his winning smile.

After a brief pause to judge if they understood, or had questions, he forged ahead. "We don't brainwash anyone, no one is being held captive physically, or mentally. We're simply a community that has discovered a way of living together that works. Society at large is no longer functioning in a way that works for the individual; well, actually, society hasn't worked for humanity maybe for thousands of years. However, as the world has gotten more crowded, the problems have gotten worse. Society is set up to sustain itself, but increasingly that comes at too high a cost to the individuals.

"The bonds of community have unraveled, and no one feels safe or at peace in public anymore. In the modern world out there, individuals and families are increasingly turning inward. They can no longer trust the bonds of community. It isn't safe to let your children play in the neighborhood or go to public school. It isn't even safe to interact with your neighbors. Everyone is closing their blinds, drawing the shutters."

It was a familiar, if depressing idea, but Winnie and Jimmy had discussed this very concept between themselves, albeit in less grand terms. However, they'd always talked about it as a southern California thing, or even just their neighborhood. The idea that it might be like that everywhere was depressing but considering the rise in mass shootings on the news, not a terribly surprising concept.

Winnie and Jimmy could see that Golden was warming to the topic, one that he felt very strongly about. "The problem is that we humans are highly social, we need a larger cohort than just ourselves, or just us and a mate to thrive. But at our core, we have a conflict. In particular, the males of our species are extremely territorial when it comes to reproduction.

Basically, we need community; we can't be happy and thrive without it. At the same time, it is a biological imperative for us to secure our personal reproductive bonds, which have always been in conflict with building strong communities."

"There was no apparent resolution possible to this fundamental conflict so as a species, we've negotiated and constructed compromises over the eons. Throughout history, civilizations have instinctually tried various ways to organize to deal with the conflicts—some worked fairly well, many, if not most, failed. However, there has always been a key false assumption that we never examined. For tens, hundreds of thousands of years, maybe even millions, our species naturally made no distinction between sex and reproduction, because for all practical purposes, there was none."

Winnie couldn't tell where this was leading, and from Jimmy's expression, he was as lost as she was. She could also tell that he was becoming slightly uncomfortable with the implications and discussion of a sexual nature. Winnie was well past slightly uncomfortable, it seemed clear that the Community was just another "free-love" cult. But before Golden could continue, Veronica interrupted by bringing in a large platter of sandwiches and a big urn of coffee with a handful of mugs.

"Ah, thank you Ronnie," Golden said when he saw the food, "I'm sure Jimmy and Winnie are famished, and no one should have to listen to me on an empty stomach!" Despite her increasing misgivings, Winnie found the big man's gentle self-deprecating humor and warm smile more comforting and reassuring than she'd ever admit. He was right too—she was starving, even if she hadn't noticed until the food arrived.

The sandwiches were simple, but divine. Thick slices of soft homemade bread were separated by generous slices of meats and cheeses and freshly sliced tomatoes. She grabbed a turkey sandwich, while Jimmy chose a sandwich that must have had nearly a pound of roughly carved ham. For the next few minutes, everything became subordinate to the enjoyment of the fresh food and hot strong coffee. When prompted, Winnie surprised herself by accepting a second sandwich—she normally would have struggled to finish one sandwich in a sitting.

As she continued eating, Golden, who'd finished off his roast beef sandwich, resumed his spiel. "I'm sure you've jumped ahead a little bit and are thinking, 'but Archie, there have been lots of free-love experiments and they all failed, most very quickly.' That's true. Famously, the Oneida commune in the 1800s was based on open sexuality, and all that remains of that is a silverware brand. More recently, the hippies started hundreds of small communes with similar ideals, but they eventually broke up and ended up working in offices and living in the suburbs just like their parents."

"What they all failed to recognize is just how strong and intractable the instinct is for our species to pair up. Procreation is essentially and unavoidably a two-person job and deep in our genes we have the instinct to close the doors to all others. In a real biological sense, jealousy is linked inexorably with the sex drive. Each of those experiments failed because they had too. They had all recognized the power of sex to unite and build an incredibly close-knit community, but they fooled themselves into believing that jealousy was just a learned behavior that they could dismiss."

"Throughout our entire history, procreation and sex have been linked. It is so ingrained, that we don't even examine it. Jealousy, however, is only a biological imperative tied to procreation. Even though we've come up with all manner of methods to separate sex from procreation from every form of 'safe sex' to highly effective contraceptives, we've never really separated the emotional aspects."

Winnie was confused now. Everything he'd said seemed to make sense in a way. She'd never really thought about the power of sex to form bonds, but when he mentioned it, it was obvious. However, she'd also seen how easily sex could destroy bonds.

It wasn't any revelation that sex was a powerful force and having someone explain that society had never been able to tame that force was not much different than someone telling her water was wet. "But no one really thinks about babies when they hear that their husband or wife has had an affair. They feel betrayed and jealous. Being told 'oh, I wore a condom, or I'm on the pill, doesn't fix it."

"Exactly!" said Golden, beaming at Winnie like a professor toward an especially bright student. Winnie couldn't help herself—she felt a wash of pleasure surge through her as she basked in his approval. "We don't separate sex from procreation and anyone who tells their spouse, 'I slept with the neighbor, but don't worry, we used protection' is likely to need a divorce lawyer because of that."

"However, there are exceptions. Can I assume that the two of you have a 'normal' monogamous relationship?" Immediately Winnie felt her face flush from embarrassment and a bit of shame, and she couldn't help but notice a flicker of anger and humiliation flash across Jimmy's face as he surely thought about Dallas. Quickly and intuitively sensing that he'd hit upon a still raw nerve, Golden immediately jumped to the correct conclusion.

"You slept with Dallas, right?" he asked Winnie, but it wasn't really a question as much as a statement and there was no hint of accusation. When Winnie nodded slightly, he continued, "Jimmy was upset about that and you feel guilty and angry at the same time, right?" Again, Winnie nodded. "That is a normal monogamous relationship then."

"So, either of you'd be jealous if the other had sex with someone else, right?" Winnie nodded immediately, but Jimmy hesitated.

Frowning a bit, he struggled to put forth his thoughts, "Well, when we were stuck in the trailer park, I actually suggested that Winnie might make some money turning tricks, then she almost did, but I wasn't jealous, I was just worried about her."

"Good, that is one of the exceptions I mentioned. Here's another: you're both young, healthy adults and like almost everyone else you both occasionally masturbate. You both know with almost certainly that the other one sometimes has sex without you, but it doesn't really bother you and you don't feel like you've cheated, right? Oh, we all feel a bit of puritanical shame, but it isn't anything like having an affair, right?"

When they both grudgingly nodded, he continued, "Now we're getting to what we have discovered and what is the core of our Community. The only problem with masturbation is that it can't build any bonds. It is by definition, solitary, even if you do it in a group or in front of each other, it doesn't have the power of mutual sex. But, what if, rather than using your hands on yourself, you reciprocate with another?"

Golden paused a second to look at each of them, "Of course, we're back to the jealousy thing. But that is only because we've all been conditioned to see sex as a monolithic 'thing'. We don't always agree on what 'having sex' with another person actually means—remember our former President quibbling over the term?—but really, we set the boundaries and there are many levels of sex. Clinton may not have thought receiving oral sex was 'having sex' or really cheating on Hilary, but almost everyone disagreed. But what if the President had instead gotten a back rub, or even a simple touch?" As he said this, Golden's hand reached out and came to rest on Kim's arm, caressed it gently, then withdrew.

"But, that isn't sex!" objected Jimmy, just before Winnie could say the same thing.

"Why, because there was no orgasm, or because no genitals were directly involved? Or is it simply because certain boundaries were crossed? Could it be as simple as expectations were not set and the bonds between a couple were threatened? That is the correct answer."

Before either Jimmy or Winnie could even form an answer to the questions, Golden seemed to shift from a man conversing mostly dispassionately about the nature of human sexuality into something more passionate. It was as if he were no longer talking to them, but rather delivering a sermon.

"Couples must have a 'sacred' and exclusive bond that they hold in mutual trust. Violating that is adultery and unleashes discord and destroys both partners and their ability to join in the broader community. However, that bond should only extend to that which it must, the sacredness of intercourse." At this, Winnie noticed that Kim, Darby, and Veronica all nodded deeply, as if hearing a prayer.

"With the bonds of marriage thus confirmed and limited, they become even stronger and more sacred while enabling us to use the power of our sexual natures to forge and sustain a true community with bonds stronger than any ever known on earth. This is how we, as humans were meant to live. We can, and must, celebrate our separate social and sexual natures if we are to survive as a species."

The fervor of his last few sentences was almost palpable. Winnie wasn't sure she totally understood, much less believed in what he'd just said, but she had no doubt that he firmly believed in it, as did his wife, Kim, and Darby. She met Jimmy's eyes briefly and could tell he was also in a kind of shock and just as awed by Golden's powerful delivery as she was.

"Whew! Discussing the foundation of our community always gets me going!" said Golden, returning to his standard easy-going conversational tone. It was as if a spell were broken, or thought Winnie, as if a preacher had said, Amen. "Maybe it would be best if you had a chance to actually look around and meet the people of our community. We can talk later and I'm sure you'll have many more questions after you've seen what we are about. Kim, why don't you take Winnie around a bit while Darby takes Jimmy. Ronny and I will see to getting them a place to set up. Why don't we all meet back here in an hour, then you can take them to their room."

Jimmy and Darby set off in one direction, toward the front of the barn, where they'd arrived, while Kim guided Winnie toward the back, where they'd seen a bit of a mobile home. It became obvious almost immediately that Kim was less interested in giving a real tour than she was probing Winnie's reaction to the long meeting they'd just left. "So, what do you think?" she prodded.

"Well," Winnie said, "I couldn't disagree with much he said, the world does seem messed up, always has been and is only getting worse. I don't know about the practical side, I mean, what it all means in practice." Winnie could tell that Kim was pleased with the answer and was anxious to begin telling about the "practical" side of the Community's philosophy.

"The big thing is that we are totally, rock-solid monogamous! There is without a doubt less cheating in the Community than anywhere else." This was obviously a huge point for Kim, as well as a great source of pride. "The key is what we call the sharing of the seeds of community. The more we share, the stronger the Community bonds become."

"So, what exactly is this sharing of the seeds?" Winnie had suspicions, it sounded like a euphemism, but she wasn't sure for what.

Kim didn't so much hesitate as suddenly become very careful, stopping so she could watch Winnie's reaction as she answered "Well, we women, we gather the seeds, you know, semen."

"What!? How is that not cheating?" asked Winnie, not totally surprised, but still taken a bit aback by Kim's matter-of-fact admission, so closely after expressing her pride at the Community's fidelity.

Kim laughed, as if she'd expected that reaction. "Blowjobs aren't sex! Making love is only for married couples and doing that with anyone other than your husband is cheating. Just like vegetable seeds, most are food, but some are for planting. It is a different kind of cheating if you don't share the seeds outside your marriage—that is cheating the Community!"

"So, you're married, and you only sleep with your husband, but you have a boyfriend that you have oral sex with?" Winnie couldn't believe she was having this conversation with someone she'd just met. Hell, this would be a surreal conversation with someone she knew extremely well.

"Boyfriend?" For a second, Kim seemed confused by the question, then her smile returned, and she gave a small chuckle. "No, it isn't about romance at all. Having an exclusive 'boyfriend' that you shared with would just make things complicated and you'd be back with all that jealousy stuff. Community is a web of connections. It is stronger when all the connections are strong."

"You mean, you perform oral sex on all the guys?" Just thinking about that made Winnie's jaw hurt.

Evidently, Kim was prepared for this, unlike the boyfriend question. "Certainly, but not all at once silly! There are 24 couples in the Community, well, 25 if you and Jimmy decide this is right for you. Some of the younger guys do share their seeds almost every day, but there are a couple dozen of us women that can help with the sharing. Most of the men only want to share every couple days, some even less."

"Oh," Winnie felt embarrassed and silly, of course there were equal numbers of men and women. "Then, can I ask how often you share?"

"Well, it's not something we encourage each other to keep track of. It isn't a contest, but I can tell you, I enjoy sharing and do it most days. Some girls need to be encouraged to share more often, but that isn't really a problem. I'd say the average is about every other day."

"But, it seems so one-sided," Winnie protested. Kim also seemed quite prepared for this too.

"I suppose it seems so, we do focus on the seeds of community, but it isn't as one-sided as you think. As long as we don't make love, we can receive pleasure from men other than our husbands. It's just that for most of us, it's not something we need or want that often. If a guy wants to 'share' in that way, he can usually find someone and if a woman wants that, she never seems to have a problem."

They'd actually reached the area behind the barn a few minutes ago and had stopped in the middle of a cluster of modest, but well-tended mobile homes. There were no streets, they weren't needed, but a network of well-worn paths separated the approximately two dozen singlewide homes.

"This is where most of us live. Most of the barn has been converted into office spaces for those of us that work remotely. Veronica handles the admin from her office up at the house and a couple people work up there with her. Most of the others work here on the ranch, feeding us, selling livestock, and even making some things we sell at the local market. There are also guest quarters there, that's where you and Jimmy will be for now."

"The entire ranch is a little more than 650 acres. There's another barn down the road a bit that still does what a barn is supposed to." It was pretty obvious that Kim only had a surface knowledge of what a barn was for, but then Winnie probably knew even less.

There really wasn't that much to see, and Winnie still couldn't really get her head around the whole blowjob thing, then caught herself thinking that and laughed unexpectedly. "What?" prompted Kim.

"Oh, I was just thinking I couldn't get my head around the sex here, and realized how funny that was, uh, considering," Winnie admitted, hoping she hadn't offended Kim even as the words tumbled out. Fortunately, Kim chuckled along with her.

"Yeah, we laugh about stuff too. The thing is, it isn't a big deal, even if it is important to us. I don't know if that makes sense, but really, once you've been here a while, the actual sharing just isn't that big a deal. What is a big deal is how awesome it is having such a tight Community without all the fear and mistrust between neighbors that you have in the outside world."

Winnie nodded, it made sense she supposed. If you were going to insist that oral sex was basically just a friendly thing you did with neighbors, it wouldn't be much different than a wave across the street on the outside. Getting to that point was another thing, Winnie thought to herself. But this line of thought brought up another question, "So, if it's not a big deal, then what, do you just go up to a guy and unzip his pants?"

Kim gave her a smile, "Well, it is a bit bigger deal than that. Most of us prefer some privacy and even if it isn't making love, it is a pretty intimate thing. You'll see it sometimes, again, because it isn't something anyone is ashamed of, but outside of special celebrations of the Community, it isn't usually a public thing."

"Celebrations of Community?" asked Winnie.

"Well, the sharing of the seeds of our community is a huge part of what makes us such an awesome place to live. No one is forced to be here, we're happy here and we like to celebrate that. Golden, who is the one that realized what was wrong with the outside society and helped us build what we have always leads our celebrations. It is an honor to share with Golden at the celebration."

Wow! Winnie was speechless. She was imagining a group of dancing and chanting revelers surrounding Golden as some woman gave him a blowjob, but it was too silly to believe.

"Ah, our hour is already almost up, we should head back to the house to see Golden."

Winnie wasn't sure that she'd be able to look the man in the eye after just imagining what she had, but Kim had already begun striding back toward the house. As soon as they'd rounded the barn, she saw Jimmy and Darby coming up the road from wherever they'd gone. Jimmy looked shell-shocked and he was looking at her as if to gauge how she might be reacting to everything. Hoping to be encouraging, she shot him a smile, but that seemed to just confuse him more. Winnie instantly shifted her face into a neutral state and suddenly wished she could be alone with Jimmy to talk things over.

Golden and Veronica met them on the porch, which Winnie hoped indicated that this wasn't going to take long. "I hope you enjoyed the tour; I trust your guides were informative," boomed Golden as they drew close. Both Winnie and Jimmy nodded in response. "Great!" he continued, switching eye contact between the two of them. "Is there anything you want to ask me then?"

Winnie replied, "I don't think so, I'd just really like to try and digest all of this and talk with Jimmy, if that's OK?" From the corner of eye, Winnie could see Jimmy nod emphatically.

"Oh, I'm sure you both need some time to think about everything you've been told and all you've seen. Kim will take you back to the barn and show you your room. You'll have privacy there and can think and talk all you want until this evening. We're having a potluck tonight to introduce you to everyone. Tomorow you can spend the day exploring and talking with everyone before we have a special Community Celebration where we'd be honored to have you and Jimmy be our esteemed guests."

Golden's gestures made it clear that "our" included himself and Veronica, his eyes also met with Winnie's briefly, seeking confirmation that she understood exactly how "honored" she could expect to be. Winnie felt her face flush and she looked away, to see Veronica smiling at her.

"Um, yeah, that sounds swell," said Jimmy awkwardly, still seemingly in a bit of shock.

"Great, we'll see you this evening then. Of course, after you get settled, you're free to wander around, meet people, and explore, just try and be back about six, alright?" Golden and Veronica both turned and walked back into the house with Darby following.

Kim took them back to a modest, but fully functional studio-style apartment in the barn and left them there with the promise that she'd be back to check on them a bit before six, but if they needed her, she'd be up at the house most of the afternoon.

Once Kim had left and they felt they were alone, Jimmy turned to Winnie and blurted out, "These people are crazy!" His eyes were a bit wild, thought Winnie, and the veins in his neck were extended.

"I know, but what got you so worked up?" she asked.

"Darby took me down to a big henhouse where there were some women feeding the birds, getting eggs, and stuff. He said I should understand about sharing, and then he called that girl from the van, Martha, no, Marla over and asked her if he could 'share' with her. Then she gave him a blowjob right there while he was talking to me telling me about the ranch's economy!"

Winnie looked at him with amazement, "Really?"

"Yeah, then when he was done, he asked if I would like to share with Marla, or one of the other women there!"

"Well, did you?" asked Winnie, attempting to be as casual as possible, both to calm him down a bit, and to let him know that she wouldn't go crazy if he had.

"No, of course not!" he replied emphatically, but noticeably less excitedly. "To be honest, it crossed my mind, but it was too weird!" He smiled wryly at his own admission.

Winnie smiled, "yeah, I don't think I could do it if someone just threw it out there like that." She carefully hadn't dismissed the philosophy behind this place, she wanted to find out more about Jimmy's perspective and what he thought.

"The people we met all seemed so nice, relaxed, and well, happy. Was it the same where you went?" she added.

Jimmy noted her careful wording and then thought a bit about the people they'd met on their walk. "Yeah, now that you mention it, everyone seemed really 'chill'—friendly and happy. Kind of like everyone was on vacation."

"Yeah!" agreed Winnie, "but not just on vacation, but on a great vacation with good friends or even family." Now that she thought about it, she realized just how rare it was to ever see people react to each other the way everyone here seemed to. For a big part of her childhood, she'd been the outsider—the one who watched the others and studied their interactions, hoping she'd fit in someday, somewhere. It was a habit she'd never really lost, but she'd been preoccupied today with asking Kim about the outrageous customs of this odd community.

Jimmy nodded. "They must be drugged or something," he said half seriously. "And what was all that stuff about your birthmark? That you're special?"

Winnie cocked her head and frowned. "Are you saying I'm not special?" she asked. Jimmy backtracked. "No, no, of course you're special Winnie," he said. "All that stuff about your birthmark being a powerful talisman and that you were touched by the hand of god . . . I thought he said they weren't religious. It doesn't fit their narrative is all I'm saying." Jimmy couldn't help feeling suspicious that this Golden dude had special plans for Winnie; that he might use her and her birthmark to ramp things up to a heightened sexual level within the community.

"I was as confused as you about that," she admitted, although she couldn't help secretly feeling good that he'd singled her out as unique. ""Who knows, maybe they have killed jealousy and just found a way to build a better society," offered Winnie. She was actually amazed, not that she'd said it, but that she actually thought there might be truth there. It seemed weird, but then, not being weird didn't seem to be working that well for society at large. Maybe it wouldn't be so bad having a place where she could be happy and with family that wouldn't leave or pull her away from everything every few months; a place where instead of being a freak, she was special, like Golden had said.

Jimmy could almost see her thought process and his slight frown deepened. "Winnie, they expect the women here to perform oral sex basically on demand!"

"Well, they expect the men to be willing to return the favor too, and besides, they don't consider it cheating. It's no big deal to them really, but it seems to bring everyone together," Winnie hadn't expected to be arguing the cult's side to Jimmy, but the more she thought about it, the more curious she was, and the more attractive the social order of this place seemed.

"Really?" Evidently Darby hadn't explained the whole two-way street concept to Jimmy, but then Winnie realized that Kim hadn't brought it up until she'd been asked. Now Jimmy seemed tentative as he asked, "um, ah, did anything happen on your walk with Kim?"

"Nah, Kim told me that most of the time people prefer a little privacy, and that most of the women don't need or want a lot of 'sharing.'" Now it was Jetty's turn to frown a bit. "So, could you share with the women here, if it wasn't in the henhouse around everyone else?"

Jimmy started to swear that he would never, then seeing that Winnie was serious, considered for a few moments. "Well, yeah, sure I could. I've got to admit I got a little excited seeing that Marla woman sucking on Darby—I've never seen anything like that in real life. But I think I'd feel guilty afterward, and I don't know if I could get over that."

"Well, would you still feel guilty if you knew I was giving blowjobs while you were getting them?" she countered.

"Probably not, but then I don't know if I could ever get used to you giving blowjobs to all the guys."

"It was your idea that I do that to earn some money when we were trapped in the RV park," she reminded him.

"Yeah, but that was because I thought then that you didn't love me," he said.

"But I do love you, Jimmy!" she said, moving close enough to reach out to him. "No matter what, I'd still love you and you'd be the only one I'd make love to," she said as her arms went around his neck and she looked up into his eyes.

"I don't know about all this Winnie, but I love you too," he said before returning the embrace and kissing her deeply. The next thing either of them knew their clothes were scattered on the floor and they were on the bed, energetically making love.

Winnie slowly rose from sleep. She usually didn't fall asleep after sex, that was more Jimmy's thing, but for the second time in a row, she'd awoken after having sex to find Jimmy out of bed and gone. Whew! She thought to herself, talking about sex all day sure does make a person horny, even if they don't think it will. She'd been pleased, and a little surprised at how passionate and needful each of them had been. In some ways, it was like the first few times they'd made love, but with the bonus of now knowing exactly what to do to make the other go just a bit more crazy!

Just after getting dressed, Winnie began wondering where Jimmy had gone off to this time. It was a pretty good bet he wouldn't find a Snickers bar in a vending machine, but maybe he was out getting flowers again. Maybe, she thought, with only a touch of dismay, maybe he's out getting a blowjob? She'd just about decided that no other possibility could be true, and she should go looking for him when the door opened and Jimmy quietly stepped in, clutching a handful of wildflowers.

"You fell asleep and looked so peaceful. I didn't want to wake you, but I wanted to look around some more," he said, once Jetty had finished hugging and kissing on him. "It's almost 6:00, we should be thinking about getting ready for the party."

The potluck gathering was a confirmation of all the positives Winnie had already felt from the brief tour earlier. The small group really did feel like a closely knit family, with easy conversations, lots of laughter, and unforced camaraderie. She felt buoyed by the atmosphere and bounced from conversation to conversation and group to group.

Jimmy however seemed ill at ease. Always a bit more than slightly introverted, the casual intimacies and bewildering interpersonal connections felt threatening and reinforced his feelings of being an outsider. He politely answered questions, asked those he felt were expected, laughed at jokes, and complimented the food, but kept the core of himself carefully cataloging the gathering much as an anthropologist might observe a primitive tribe celebrating in the wilds.

Finally, as the night wound down and many of the community had left, Jimmy convinced Winnie to retire to their apartment. He couldn't help but notice that she seemed energized, whereas he felt deeply tired. Even back in the room, Winnie seemed oblivious to his exhaustion. It wasn't until his lack of response to her attempt to recreate the steamy session from the afternoon that she noted his troubled face.

"What's wrong?" Winnie was surprised and immediately felt guilt for not sensing his mood. "Did something happen at the potluck?"

"No, nothing happened. It just seems to be going too fast." Jimmy felt defeated and confused. He knew Winnie seemed quite taken with the community, but he wasn't and couldn't really articulate why.

"Well, things have been moving fast ever since I got the call from my dad," Winnie said. When Jimmy nodded glumly, she continued. "Really, we don't have a lot of choices. The RV is gone, the police and that Porshe guy are after us, and we're out of money." This brought another even more defeated nod from Jimmy.

Winnie decided to switch to focusing on any and all the positives. "At least here we have a chance to catch our breath. There's food, someplace to sleep, and we'd be hard to find. It might take a while to fit in, but you had to notice that as weird as the community is, it seems to work for them."

Indeed, it hadn't just been the potluck itself, or even the friendly welcome that had made Winnie almost giddy. It was noticing the differences in the community dynamics from every social gathering she'd experienced. The men were different. There seemed to be so much less macho posturing and the men seemed so relaxed.

The women were different as well. They seemed to interact so much more openly and freely. The undercurrent of potential romantic competition that marred so many female casual relationships was almost nonexistent. The community did seem truly strong and happy.

"Yeah, I noticed that too. It seems to work really well for them, I'm just not sure it's for us and the life we planned. I guess I'm afraid that if we stay, we'll never leave, at least not together."

Snuggling next to him on the bed, Winnie hugged him and said, "We can stay here, let things calm down for a while and try to find some options. When we can figure a way out, if you still want to go, of course I'll go with you."

With that, they both settled into their own thoughts as they waited for sleep. Winnie wondered how she could help Jimmy feel connected to the community and hoped he'd come around. It was strange, but she was thinking that she wanted to belong here and 'never leaving' didn't seem such a horrible idea. Jimmy's mind was busy thinking of options and how they'd get themselves back on the road.

They both awoke refreshed and ready to explore the community some more. The tension between them after the potluck and nighttime discussion was gone. A fruit and breads platter with honey, butter, and yogurt had been left outside the apartment. Despite being anxious to start the day, they couldn't help but savor the still warm breads and fresh fruit as they devoured nearly everything on the platter.

It was a gorgeous day. The bright Colorado sun balanced nicely with a cool breeze washing down from the mountains. It might get hot later, it might get chilly, it might even rain or snow, but it was close to perfect right now. Not surprising after the fairly late event the evening before, there didn't seem to be many people about. Some animal noises coming from around the corner caught Winnie's ear.

"I'm going to go look at the animals, seems only right if you're on a farm, want to come with me?" Winnie asked as she took a step in that direction.

"Hmm, I think I want to head up to the house and see if they can tell me what the guys do all day and how they make money to keep this place going. Let's meet back here for lunch about noon, OK?"

The large rambling shed around the corner was the source of the animal sounds. Heavy wooden shutters were open and the smells of hay and assorted manures were pungent but not unpleasant Winnie thought as she found a door and entered the roughly framed building.

Immediately, Winnie was reminded of the county fairs she'd attended as a child. A couple dozen pigs were penned in one end, with access to their own outside pen area. A smaller group of pens held an assortment of sheep and goats. Hutches for what Winnie assumed were rabbits or other small animals lined one wall. The other end of the sprawling building held stables and milking stalls. Among the wide hay-strewn aisles a handful of women and a guy or two were busy shoveling manure into wheelbarrows or emptying bags of feed in various troughs, dishes, and containers.

Winnie walked through the big barn looking at the animals and thinking that the place seemed remarkably clean and organized considering the cliché about pigpens. As she came to the end where the milking stations were, she found Kim, her guide from yesterday, milking a massive black and white cow that was slowly munching on some hay from a basket.

"Hey you! Come to check out the barn?" Kim was all smiles, evidently the potluck hadn't gone too late for her.

"Yup, figured I'm on a farm, might as well see what that's all about. So, how many cows do you have to milk and when do you get started?" asked Winnie as she stared in amazement at the thick spurts of milk being expertly coaxed from the cow.

"We have ten dairy cows that we milk twice a day and generally the first milking starts about dawn. Usually, there are two of us and we'd be done by now, but Becky didn't show up this morning, but I'm almost done."

"Whoa, so this cow makes this much milk twice a day?" Winnie was truly flabbergasted.

"Pretty much, yeah, close to six gallons a day. I've heard of some cows that can produce as much as 15 gallons, but our cows give us a total of between 50 and 60 gallons a day."

"That's a lot of milk for a couple dozen people!"

Kim laughed, "It is, but we use a lot to make cheese, butter, yogurt, and other things. We sell some of the cheese, extra butter, even some gallons of raw milk in our stand out by the highway. We don't make a lot of money on the cows, or the eggs either, but we get all we need to feed ourselves and a bit of cash left over."

As she finished her explanation, she released the cow's teats, stood, and with Winnie's help dumped the milk pail into a large stainless steel vat attached to plumbing and an array of humming machines. "Someone else will come handle the processing later, I'm done in here for now."

"So what's next?" asked Winnie, anxious to see and learn more about day-to-day life in the community.

"Well, I'm going to take a shower, then spend some time working online. It's not that interesting to watch, you should probably hang out with some of the other women, maybe by the chicken coops or in the hall."

"Working online? What do you do online?" Winnie was surprised that there was internet access. She'd been so focused on the totally foreign bucolic concept of farm life that she hadn't imagined there was a place here for modern high tech, much less online communication technology.

"Oh, lots of things. I'm mostly just a helpful gofer, answering emails and stuff, but most of us spend at least some time working online. A couple people specialize in it, doing consulting, web design and, of course, a couple have 'real jobs' working remotely for outside companies. The farm provides much of what we need, but we still need steady income to pay the bills and get things we can't grow or make."

Winnie digested that information as they walked toward the hall, another large structure near the chicken pens. As they neared the hall, Kim pointed to a door set into the tin wall at the near end. "Just go in and mingle. I'll catch up with you at the celebration tonight."

The inside of the hall was abuzz with activity. Men and women were clustered around different work areas. Some were working with big sacks of wool, there were a couple of women hunched over sewing machines, one woman was hand-dipping candles, and another was examining eggs, sorting and placing them into cartons. An old boombox set in the middle of the room was playing 60s pop music.

As she slowly made her way around the different work areas, Winnie was welcomed with smiles, greetings and waves, as if she were already a member of the family. Settling down in an empty chair near where a younger man was combing wool next to a woman slowly feeding wool into a spinning wheel, Winnie caught the eye of the man and could see him preparing to say something. Before he could get whatever he was going to say out, the woman admonished him. "Joe, you know there's a celebration tonight and Winnie is still our guest."

Although Winnie wasn't sure what that was all about, she noticed the sheepish, slightly embarrassed smile Joe gave the woman. "Boys, honestly!" The slightly older woman beamed brightly at Winnie. As Winnie struggled to recall the woman's name . . . Bernice?, Bridget? . . . another part of her mind put the pieces together. Joe had been about to ask her for oral sex! She immediately felt her face flush with embarrassment and all hope of recalling the woman's name was gone.

"Oh Betty!" Joe's good-natured laugh filled in one question, but didn't do much for Winnie's sudden awkwardness. "Everyone knows they'll join up, they're a perfect fit."

"You know the rules. Until the celebration, they're our guests. Anyway, you know there isn't any sharing on the day of a celebration." Joe nodded, but didn't look terribly contrite.

Now that the subject had been broached, Winnie couldn't help but ask the questions she'd been hoarding up about tonight's celebration. "What rules? What happens at the celebration if there isn't any sharing?"

Both Joe and Betty laughed before Betty explained. "We don't expect guests to share . . ."

Joe interrupted, "well, the women guests aren't asked to share."

Betty gave him a look, but continued. "Right. Female guests shouldn't share until they've been welcomed into the community. New couples are welcomed into the community at a celebration, like the one we'll have tonight."

Joe enthusiastically added, "and during the celebration there is plenty of sharing!"

It confirmed everything Winnie had suspected. Inside she was in turmoil, but she tried to hide her shock from the smiling couple. Nevertheless, Betty reached out and patted Winnie's arm. "It's a big step, but I know you'll be as happy here as we will be to have you."

Winnie smiled, only slightly reassured, and almost sleepwalked in a daze out of the hall hoping to find Jimmy and get a handle on her emotions.

Jimmy was sitting on a bench near where they'd agreed to meet. He seemed anxious and literally bursting with energy. Winnie was oblivious to that as she plopped down next to him and wrapped her arms around him and buried her face into his chest.

During lunch, Jimmy began by filling her in on his adventures this morning. Winnie reciprocated and found that just talking about the various economic and social structures they'd seen was calming her down. Jimmy was impressed by the communal structure they'd built here. Everything was owned by everyone, and all income was pooled. People rotated through committees and everyone was expected to work at least sometimes in every facet of the group's labors. Major economic decisions were voted on by the community, minor decisions by the committees.

Social agreements and disputes were handled by a permanent "leadership council" consisting of Golden and Veronica along with a couple selected quarterly by them as exemplary members.

Evidently, most of the economic model for the group was based off the original Oneida commune, along with key updates from the incorporation articles that resulted in the tableware company that still existed.

Their discussion ranged from the obvious manpower shortage and recruitment issues faced by the group. Jimmy explained that the group had goals and plans for more than 100 couples before they'd need to expand their real estate holdings. Recruitment was a major hurdle. They couldn't afford sensationalist coverage, and they were adamant about only considering committed couples. Internet discussions and groups were the obvious recruiting grounds, but there was the inherent contradiction with keeping a low profile and getting the word out.

It was pretty obvious to both why they had been welcomed so quickly and openly—the group needed them and Winnie and Jimmy needed a place to lay low. Finally, they got to the issue of how they might fit in. Winnie felt a bit guilty skirting the sex issue, and the entire celebration thing, but Jimmy didn't bring it up either. Jimmy mentioned that his writing and reporting experience could translate into steady freelance jobs online. Winnie hadn't thought about how photography might fit, she'd sold her camera, and there didn't seem to be a commercial aspect for photos in the community anyway. Still, she was enthused about learning the many crafts and jobs on the farm, as well as doing odd tasks online.

Feeling happy that Jimmy was giving the place a chance and seemed excited about the work and growth potential, Winnie was glad that the thorny issue of the celebration hadn't really come up. They'd deal with that when it did, she told herself, and almost believed it.

As they were finishing lunch, a couple of women came up and asked Winnie to come with them and help stock up the merchandise for the roadside produce and gift stand. Jimmy was hustled off to help in the slaughter and butchering of a steer.

Winnie lay on the bed in the apartment, too tired to get herself up for a shower. Her and others had loaded case after case of produce, heavy containers of ice-packed cheeses and butter, and bulky woven and sewn scarves, jackets, and whatnot into a shuttling pair of pickup trucks that were running up and down the dusty road toward the highway stand. When Jimmy dragged himself in, covered in absurd amounts of blood and more unsavory things, Winnie was torn between laughing and commiserating—laughing won. Jimmy gave her a wan smile before stripping down, wrapping a towel around himself, and heading off to shower.

"Well, I feel better. Ready for the party I guess!" he exclaimed after taking the time to scour his entire body nearly raw. Winnie had almost dozed off, still lying on the bed.

Winnie looked up at him, surprised at how casually he'd mentioned the "party". Then she realized that Jimmy must not know that Community celebrations featured Archibald Golden getting his dick sucked as part of the festivities.

As one of the guests of honor, she was pretty sure what she was expected to do to gain entry into the Community. True, that hadn't been explicitly said that her and Jimmy would be expected to participate, and she was pretty sure they'd be given a choice, but she had no idea what the alternatives would be. Would they just be shown the gate and expected to walk the miles to the highway? Would they be given a ride into town, straight to the police?

On top of all that, Winnie wasn't sure she was ready to leave this place. It had all been so fast, and as crazy as it seemed, she wondered if she and Jimmy could be as happy here as the rest of the Community appeared to be.

She almost told him, but then decided not to. She wasn't completely sure her assumptions were right, she rationalized. "Uh, Jimmy, remember that no matter what happens to us at this party, I love you and you're the only one I want to make love to," was what she said instead. Before Jimmy could respond, she pulled away and headed out the door saying, "Gotta hit the bathroom to freshen up for the big gala!" Jimmy, looked a little puzzled before shaking his clothes out and getting dressed.

Winnie was careful not to be finished until she heard Kim come up the stairs and knock on the apartment door next to the shared bathroom, and then she gave it a few more minutes so it wouldn't be obvious that she'd been waiting. She wasn't sure how Jimmy would react to things at the party, but then, she hadn't decided how she'd react yet either.

Kim seemed a bit extra buoyant when Winnie entered the room. "Jimmy just told me that you two had a great conversation this afternoon and were looking forward to the party!"

Winnie immediately saw that Kim had jumped to a hugely wrong conclusion. Although Winnie thought she knew roughly what was expected to occur, she was in fact much too nervous and conflicted to really be looking forward to the party. It was likely that it would go terribly wrong. She also knew that Jimmy probably was looking forward to the party, but only because he didn't know the expectations.

When he'd told Kim they were looking forward to it, she must have assumed Jimmy was fully on board. Getting down the stairs was dreamlike. Winnie's heart was hammering and her mind still wildly flipping from "I want to belong!" to "What if Jimmy doesn't understand?" mixed in with a huge dose of panic bells singing "how can you even think of giving a stranger a blowjob in front of an audience that includes the man you love?!?!"

As they approached the bottom of the stairs, Winnie noted that the auditorium/church area had been expanded, with the seating pushed apart down the middle. The partitions along the back had been removed to reveal a large open space with tables laden with food and drinks and flowers everywhere. It kind of reminded her of high school prom where they tried to convert the gym or cafeteria into something it could never be.

Darby, who she really hadn't had an opportunity to talk with, smoothly swooped in and took her arm as Kim led Jimmy away to introduce him to someone. Winnie couldn't meet his eyes, she couldn't help herself from thinking about him getting a blowjob and despite herself, wondering how long she'd be in the group before he'd come to her for sharing. Once that thought had come to her, she couldn't shake it and it spread to every man she was introduced to as they made their rounds.

It was totally surreal, making small talk as her mind raced and her heart continued to chatter. More than once she caught herself on the edge of hyperventilating and forced herself to take deep breaths. No one seemed to notice, or at least they pretended not to. What did penetrate her awareness, however, was just how friendly and kind the other women were, not only to her, but also around each other. The normal protocol for a party included a strong, invisible-to-men, tension between women as they decided which were competition or a threat to their relationships. It didn't seem to be here and Winnie, who wasn't good at female politics, was almost giddy at its absence. At that moment, her mind calmed. She was going to be part of this.

"Hello everyone! What a wonderful day to be part of a splendid Community so full of friends! Tonight, as always, we celebrate the ever-strengthening bonds between each of us." Golden's rich baritone held everyone's attention as conversations ceased immediately. "But this is even more special because tonight we have two guests, Jetty Jet and Jimmy, who have decided to be our honored guests." At that, despite Golden's presence, an excited buzz seemed to spread through the hall. Winnie was stuck on the odd phrasing . . . damn, I may have chosen to be honored, not so sure about Jimmy, she fretted.

Where was he anyway? He and Kim were nowhere to be seen. Maybe it wasn't supposed to be Veronica, who was up on the stage beside her husband. Maybe Kim would do the honors. Or, maybe Jimmy had found out and freaked out and Kim was trying to calm him down. All these could be it, but suddenly Winnie was unsure again. Without Jimmy here, in some ways it would be easier, but in others, especially dealing with guilt, it would be harder.

She didn't have long to think about it. Whatever you could say about these people, they didn't draw things out any longer than necessary. Golden called her to the stage, then looked around, presumably for Jimmy. After a few seconds, he shrugged and turned to Winnie as she arrived on the stage.

"Jetty Jet," he said, using the same volume he did when addressing everyone, "we're all glad to have met you and we're thrilled that we are going to have the opportunity to build links to you and Jimmy and strengthen our Community even beyond where it is now. I'm humbled and privileged to be the first to offer the seeds of our Community." It sounded like a ceremonial speech to Winnie and suddenly she wondered how many times he'd given it.

Obviously to most of the couples currently here, but surely there had been other couples that must have left after some time for a variety of reasons, and there must have been others who'd heard the speech, then backed out. Suddenly, she had so many questions, but this wasn't the place or the time to ask them, and, where the hell was Jimmy?

Golden backed away from the lectern toward his chair and beckoned for her to follow. As he did so, Veronica rose from her seat and swiftly pulled down the elastic-wasted pants Golden had been wearing just before he sat on the chair. Three things fought for primacy in Winnie's mind: really? Elastic slacks? Where would you even buy those? Did Veronica really just pull her husband's pants down and should I return her intense smile? And whoa! Archibald Golden was packing some serious equipment. She wanted to look away but couldn't.

Like so many things over the past few weeks, this didn't feel real. She didn't think about anything other than those three random thoughts, yet she found herself moving without deciding to. She opened her mouth and prepared to share the seed of this man as his wife smiled and whispered in her ear, "watch the teeth dear."

Soon, Golden moaned, bucked his hips a few times, and it was over. Incredulously, Winnie realized that the people were still there, they'd watched her do that, and now they were cheering for Christ's sake. As she let the rapidly deflating appendage slip from her mouth, Veronica grabbed her elbow and helped her stand. Before she could turn her around to face the insane bystanders, Winnie glimpsed Jimmy walking toward them from the house.

Seeing all the smiling, happy faces didn't make her as happy as she thought it should. She was one of them now, but what about Jimmy? She didn't have to wait long to find out as he bounded onto the stage. "Winnie, I'm sorry I missed it," he said loud enough for everyone to hear, "but I can explain. Will you listen to what I need to tell you in private?" As he asked her, he looked over at Golden, still sitting in his chair, immense flaccid penis still exposed, for permission. Golden nodded, but already Jimmy was leading Winnie down the stairs and up the dirt road a little way.

Taking her wrist, Jimmy looked back at the crowd, now merrily celebrating. With a hiss, he said, "C'mon!" and began running with her wrist now tightly squeezed in his hand. To avoid falling, Winnie involuntarily took two or three large strides, then found herself running to keep from being dragged by Jimmy. Almost to the house she saw the dark car parked to the side of the road, its engine was running, but the lights were off.

It was happening all so fast, and her mind was still reeling from what she'd done on that stage. She barely protested when Jimmy literally threw her in through the driver's side, then pushed her over as he got behind the wheel. There was no dramatic squeal of tires, they were on dirt after all, but the car did fishtail and spew significant amounts of dirt and gravel at the few men who'd seen them running and had given chase.

They were both breathing heavily still when Jimmy broke the silence. "Sorry honey, I know you think you found a home, one that you maybe never knew you wanted but it is a home for couples. We're still deciding what kind of couple we are. We aren't the couple we were. This—me and you, Winnie/Jetty— this is new. We need to let it develop, let it grow a bit."

"I promise, when we've discovered what this thing between us is, when we decide that we want to get married. If at that point, you want to come back, I'll come with you."

Winnie looked at him, not knowing how to react. Of all the possible reactions she had imagined Jimmy having, this wasn't even close. She was still looking at him when he turned his eyes from the road for a second, pointed to the corner of her mouth and said, "you've got a little community seed there."

Using the sleeve of her shirt, Winnie wiped the remnants of Archibald Golden's sperm from her lip. Once again, here they both were, in yet another vehicle, speeding away from the scene; this time, in a black Honda Civic. This was becoming a pattern with them of late. Winnie glanced over at Jimmy. He was focused intently on navigating the winding gravel road in front of them. Winnie twisted her body around in the seat to look behind them. In the widening distance between them and the Community, she could see a number of people scampering after them on the road, but then dropping back, and ultimately giving up pursuit. And in that moment, an odd sense of calm washed over her with the sudden and very significant realization that Jimmy had probably just saved her life. Not in the physical sense. She didn't feel that they were in any real danger. No, he just may have saved her from herself.

As the car's tires bucked and bounced over every pebble and crevice in the rough road, the jarring sensation made Winnie feel alive, aware, as if she had stirred from a dream or awakened from a spell; as though Jimmy had snapped his fingers and she had abruptly come to her senses. How could she have fallen for that whole Community seed nonsense anyway? Was she really that gullible? Thank god Jimmy had the presence of mind to see through Golden's con. Admittedly, the guy was charismatic, but it wasn't like her to be taken in so completely. And . . . she'd performed oral sex on him, in front of an audience! It made her feel nauseous now just thinking about it.

The dude was old enough to be her father, no, her grandfather . . . ew! And she did it in front of everyone; her thoughts jumped from one repellent thought to the next as she mentally beat herself up.

Jimmy looked over at Winnie, and based on the dismayed look on her face, he could tell the wheels were turning in her head. He could always tell when she was thinking extra hard. Her brow furrowed and she clenched her jaws together tightly. Jimmy was pretty sure he knew what she was thinking about. He needed to keep a steady grip on the wheel because of the roughness of the road, but they were far enough away from the Community now that he felt okay slowing down a bit. He reached over and touched her arm, but Winnie recoiled from his touch; she felt far too embarrassed and ashamed to return his gaze.

Jimmy withdrew his hand and placed it back on the steering wheel as they continued on in silence. He wouldn't press her. Winnie was clearly not ready to talk, Jimmy figured. And besides, they needed to get farther away from the Community, specifically, off this unpaved road and onto a public roadway where they could blend into traffic and disappear. Jimmy hadn't had a chance to mention it and Winnie hadn't asked, but he'd stolen the car from the compound. Although it didn't seem likely that Golden would call the cops and report the plates— they might be reticent about drawing unwanted attention to themselves—Jimmy wasn't sure if they should chance it. He'd taken some money from the house too, but it wasn't enough to get a replacement vehicle. He guessed they'd just have to make a go of it and hope they weren't on the cop's radar.

After a half hour or so of driving, they finally arrived at the end of the unpaved road. Because both he and Winnie had fallen asleep during the initial drive in, Jimmy had no idea how long it had taken them to reach the Community's compound. During their drive Winnie had dozed off but woke up when she heard Jimmy getting out of the stopped car. A large, chain-link fence with a heavy steel chain and padlock attached to it created a barrier between them and the outside world beyond it. Barbed wire fencing spread out from it on either side, so driving through it was not an option.

"Shit, Jimmy said as he opened up the car door and got out. "We are so screwed." Winnie looked out and saw the gate.

"Oh no," she groaned. "What if they're coming after us Jimmy?"

Winnie watched as Jimmy walked over and examined the fence and the lock, then stood for a good five minutes sizing up the padlock. He paced back and forth, scratching his chin and running his fingers through his hair as though deep in thought.

Looking at the fence and then back at the car, he wondered if the Honda Civic had enough power to crash through it. He'd seen it done once on an episode of a TV show called *Mythbusters*, a total man-fest in which two nerdy guys basically smash and destroy things and blow shit up, all in the name of science. But as he was pondering this, he happened to look up. "Oh crap," he said out loud. There was no time to think any more about whether it might work or not. He turned and sprinted back toward the Civic. "Get back in the car, Winnie!" he shouted.

Winnie hopped in, but not before catching a glimpse of what had startled Jimmy so. In the distance, she could barely make out a pickup truck coming down the road toward them. It was still far enough away, but it was kicking up a cloud of dust behind it and coming up fast. "What are you going to do Jimmy?" Winnie asked.

Jimmy looked over at her panic-stricken face and said, "Buckle your seatbelt and hold on tight honey," he said.

"What are we doing Jimmy?" What are . . ." her voice trailed away as Jimmy started the engine, twisted his body sideways, and backed the car down the road a few hundred yards. With both hands firmly gripping the wheel, he glanced over at her. "Ready?" he asked. Winnie nodded. Jimmy punched the gas pedal hard, sending them barreling full throttle toward the gate.

Winnie closed her eyes and instinctively bowed her head down between her legs. At about 50 mph, the car hit the gate and slammed through it, breaking the padlock on impact, but cracking the windshield and knocking the front bumper off completely. Fortunately, no cars were going by when they hit asphalt on the other side. Jimmy managed to keep the car under control and without slowing down, he made a wide arc to the right and they tore down the road and away from the pickup truck that was just now arriving at the smashed-up gate.

"WOOHOO!" Jimmy hollered with unbridled exuberance, lifting his hands off the wheel and raising his arms in the air as they sped away. "Oh my god Winnie" he said. "Did you see that? We did it!" Winnie had since lifted her head up and couldn't help being amused at Jimmy's display of pure, unadulterated man joy. "Did you see that? Did you see that?" he asked, grabbing her arm excitedly. "Yes, yes, I saw it," she said laughing. "That was awesome!" Jimmy was grinning from ear to ear like a schoolboy.

"Was that fucking awesome, or what?" He pounded on the steering wheel and woohooed a few more times before Winnie cautioned him to watch the road. "Let's get outta here," she said smiling at her fucking amazing boyfriend.

"Okay lady!" Jimmy said, grinning back at Winnie as they sped far and away from the confines of the Community.

They drove along in silence for a few miles before reaching I-25 south, which would take them all the way through Wyoming before veering west on I-90 in Montana toward Seeley Lake where the cabin was located. Although the car was pretty banged up, it actually drove a lot better than it looked, and even though the windshield was cracked, it wasn't bad enough to hinder visibility. The front bumper was gone, but it likely wouldn't warrant a ticket. Jimmy hoped the cops, if they hadn't been alerted to the stolen plates, would simply view it as just another old beat-up clunker.

Once they were out on the open highway, Winnie relaxed a bit, leaning back in the passenger seat and watching the slideshow of barren landscapes whooshing by. It felt good to be on the move again even though part of her would have liked to stay with the community, minus the weird community seed nonsense, of course. Some of the people were really nice. In fact, she'd felt an immediate connection to the group. Making friends had always been difficult for her, so coming that close to making real friends made Winnie sad.

"Jimmy?" she said.

Jimmy looked over at her. "Yeah, babe."

"I feel like talking about stuff now," she said, pushing herself upright from her slouched position in the seat and tilting her body in his direction.

"Now?" he asked.

"Yeah," she answered. She began hesitantly. "Well, first, I want to tell you thank you for what you did back there."

Jimmy nodded without responding. He figured he'd let her talk; throw everything out there that was on her mind before he interjected. He'd always been bad about interrupting her and he wanted to make a conscious effort to really listen, to hear what she thought and felt.

"I guess we should talk about what happened at the community," Winnie started. "I thought it might be what I wanted. It seemed like a place where I might fit in, with a community of people that cared about me and liked me and welcomed me."

Jimmy gave her a reassuring look. "I know," he said.

Winnie's lip started trembling and she began to cry. "I don't know how it happened," she sobbed. "I just got all caught up in it." She was trying not to cry, but once the faucet was turned on, there was no stopping it.

Jimmy reached out and gently touched her hand, but acknowledging how distressed she was, as soon as he came to an exit, he took it. There were no businesses here. It was just an off-ramp leading to some road to somewhere elsewhere, but it was a good place to pull the car over and talk. Jimmy stopped, killed the engine, and immediately reached out and wrapped his arms around Winnie, pulling her in close to him.

"I'm so sorry Jimmy," Winnie blubbered, burying her face deep in his neck. He could feel the warm drizzling stream of tears on his skin. Normally, weeping girls made him uncomfortable, but after everything they'd been through, holding her and feeling her close was probably the most real thing he'd ever experienced in his life. So filled with emotion, in

fact, he could feel tears welling up in his own eyes. He couldn't
remember the last time he'd cried, maybe when he was five
and his dog Odin died. It was strange, but at the same time,
purifying. Feeling Jimmy's tears on her cheek, Winnie looked up
and started to cry more. "Oh god Jimmy, now I've made you cry
too." She wiped the tears from his face and clung to him tighter.
They stayed that way for a while, wrapped tight around each
other, neither one wanting to let go.

Finally, Winnie pulled away and broke the spell. Lifting her
head off of Jimmy's chest she said, "Thank you for helping me
find Winnie."

Jimmy started to open his mouth to speak, but she put her
fingers to his lips. "All those things I thought I needed," she said,
"I have with you."

Jimmy smiled. "You're my best friend, Win," he said, "and I
love you, so much."

Suddenly overcome with an overpowering surge of emotion,
Jimmy clutched the back of Winnie's head and kissed her long
and deep. And she kissed back. He had never wanted anyone
as much as he wanted her right now. Who cared if it was the
middle of the day? Who cared if anyone came along? He didn't.
She didn't. He reached up inside her shirt, stroking the firm
muscles along her back. He knew that he had aroused something
in her as well when she pulled her shirt up over her head and
hurriedly took off her bra, arching her back and exposing her
breasts to his eagerly awaiting voracious tongue. He slipped his
fingers down into her pants and between her legs. She was more
than ready.

Clumsy within the confines of the small car Winnie managed
to slip out of her jeans and panties and Jimmy did likewise. In
a rush, he scooted over to the center of the seat and pulled a

very naked and very hot and aroused Winnie on top of him. Completely caught up in the moment and focused solely on each other, the world outside stopped, although if anyone had driven by they might have noticed a small earthquake rocking the black Honda Civic parked under the overpass. Hard, fast, sweaty, intense, it was the best sex they had ever had with each other— impromptu, unplanned, middle-of-the day, in a car on the side of the road, fierce, impassioned hot love.

"I wish we had cigarettes," Jimmy said afterward, catching his breath a little.

Winnie, who was slumped next to him in the seat, pushed the hair off her sweaty forehead. "Why?" she said breathlessly, "we don't smoke."

"I know." He smiled and closed his eyes dreamily. "It just seems like we could both use one after that."

The next thing he knew, Winnie was climbing back on top of him. "Let's do it again," she said with a sly grin.

It was dark when Jimmy pulled the car into a parking space at a Motel 6 off I-25 near Buffalo, Wyoming. In the roughly six or so hours, minus their brief steamy interlude under the overpass, since they'd stormed the gate in Colorado, they had put a good deal of distance between them and the Community. As far as Jimmy could surmise, no one had followed them or set the cops after them, which was great, but he was exhausted from driving. Winnie had offered to take the wheel, but they conceded that they could both use some rest. They'd be in Montana tomorrow and neither knew what they might encounter when they arrived at the cabin. Some downtime would allow them to decompress and be better prepared to deal with whatever awaited them there.

"Do we have money for this?" Winnie asked before getting out of the car. Jimmy made a face. "ehhhh . . . sorta . . . well .

.. yeah," he spluttered. With everything that had transpired today, he had completely forgotten about what happened at the Community, and Winnie hadn't asked.

"What does that mean exactly?" Winnie wanted to know.

"We have enough money to stay here tonight." He assured her as he opened he passenger door and got out. He leaned back in through the window and said, "I'll explain it all to you after we get a room."

Without her disguise Winnie decided to wait in the car while Jimmy went in to get the room. This would also be a true test of whether their plates were hot. If there was any sort of problem, Jimmy was prepared to jump back in the car and drive away. But the transaction went smoothly. The desk clerk, an elderly man wearing a camouflage cap and a plaid shirt, took the cash and barely glanced at the paperwork before shoving it into a dusty file cabinet and handing Jimmy the key to room 112.

"Ground floor, around back," the clerk said, motioning in that direction.

"Thank you, sir," Jimmy said, saluting as he headed out through the office's sliding glass door and back to the car. "It's around back," he told Winnie as he backed the Honda out of the parking space. The room was clean, but nothing special, as most of these chain motels tended to be. Neither had anything in the way of suitcases or, well, anything so it was basically opening the door and crashing. Jimmy unlocked the door to their room, but before Winnie could go in, he turned around and scooped her up in his arms.

Surprised, she actually squealed. "What are you doing Jimmy?"

"I'm sweeping you off your feet, that's what." Jimmy said.

"Oh, okay," she said giggling. Once in the room, he pushed the door shut with his foot, and then pretended to trip tossing her onto the double bed.

"You are such a goof!" she exclaimed, as he dived onto the bed beside her.

He rolled over onto his back and put his hands behind his head. "Ahhh," he sighed. "Yis is the yife!"

Winnie snuggled up next to him with her head resting on his chest. Using her free hand she traced her fingers down his belly on a slow march to his crotch. "Now that we have a real bed . . ."

Jimmy turned over to face her on his side and rose up on one arm. "Let's talk first."

"Oh boo," Winnie play pouted. "Okay, let's talk," she said, "and then I'm hopping in the shower."

Jimmy didn't want Winnie to think he was a criminal, but he hoped she'd understand that he did what he did to get her away from that place.

"Okay," he slowly began. "When you were . . . uh… preoccupied in the barn . . ." Winnie frowned at that. "I snuck out and went up to the main house," he continued. "I wanted to see if I could find keys to a vehicle, and I did. It was super easy. They had about half a dozen keys hanging up on a key holder in the kitchen."

"How did you know which one to take?" Winnie asked.

"I scoped out the farm the day before and I noticed there were quite a few vehicles, you know, farm trucks and the like," he said, "but also besides the minivan that we came to the farm in, there were about four other cars. I saw the Honda Civic and figured it was newer and probably in better shape."

"Okay, so you took the keys, and then what happened?" Winnie asked.

Jimmy sighed. "Just as I was reaching for the key, Kim walked in and wanted to know what I was doing."

Winnie's mouth formed a giant "O." "Oh man, busted. What did you tell her?"

"I didn't really tell her anything," Jimmy said. "I tied her up."

Winnie sat up. "You what?" she asked.

"You heard right," Jimmy said. "I tied her up and put duct tape on her mouth so she couldn't scream."

Winnie was stunned. "Oh wow," she said. "I knew obviously that you stole the car, but I can't believe you tied her up."

"That's not all," Jimmy said.

"There's more?" Winnie asked.

"I took some money, too," Jimmy blurted. "I went through Kim's wallet. She had about $240 in cash, so I grabbed it and left the house. I knew we had to get out of there quick before the meeting was over and someone found Kim at the house." He paused before saying, "I got there right at the end of . . . well . . . you know." He waited to see her reaction, but her face was a blank slate. He couldn't read her nonreaction.

"Okay, so what I did though, Winnie," he said, "is I wrote a note."

"A note?"

He pretended like he was writing on a piece of paper. "I wrote an apology note. I told them we were really sorry, but we had to go and that we'd send them the money I took and money for the car as soon as we could."

Winnie looked at him incredulously. "You left an IOU?" she asked.

"Yeah, yeah, that's it. That's exactly what I did," Jimmy said. Winnie didn't seem mad, but he couldn't tell for sure. Winnie was funny. She vacillated between wearing every raw emotion on her sleeve one minute or clamming up and building up a nearly impenetrable wall around herself the next. He thought he'd done the right thing. He wasn't a bad guy. He hoped Winnie would see that too. All he could think to do was to slink down and give her his best, aw shucks, hangdog face. That seemed to work sometimes.

Winnie shook her head, looked away, and when she looked back, she was smiling at him. She put her arms around his neck and kissed him. "I'll say this, you're not much of an outlaw, but you're the best boyfriend ever."

Relieved, Jimmy relaxed and kissed her back. "Do you have any idea how much it's gonna cost to replace that car?" she asked as she withdrew from him and headed toward the bathroom for a shower.

"Plenty," he called out to her. "It's gonna cost plenty," he said rolling back onto the bed and closing his weary eyes.

Twenty minutes later Winnie emerged from the bathroom a new woman, or at least a much cleaner one. Her wet hair wrapped in a turban, she removed the other towel that was wrapped around her body and slipped into bed naked cuddling behind Jimmy in big spoon fashion.

"Jimmy," she whispered into his ear. "Jimmy," she said again. Jimmy stirred and mumbled something indecipherable in his sleep. Well shit, Winnie thought. It was certainly the waste of a good bed, but she would let Jimmy sleep. It had been a very long horrifying and wonderful day for both of them. It blew her away . . . oops, scratch that. It was hard to believe that she had started the evening giving Archibald Golden a blowjob in front of a captive audience; she'd went on a Mr. Toad's Wild Ride with Jimmy that had sent them careening through a padlocked gate; and driven down miles and miles of endless highway to an exit in the middle of nowhere where they had parked and had a mind-blowing sexual encounter . . . twice—undeniably, the best sex they had ever had in the history of their relationship. Yep, quite an interesting day they'd had. But now, despite the bad beginning, Winnie couldn't help smiling a secret, shy smile. She felt guilty thinking about Dallas, but he really was her only basis for comparison. She had been fond of Dallas, sure, but their encounter didn't even come close to what she and Jimmy had experienced yesterday on the road. Dallas had awakened her sleeping desire, but Jimmy gave it substance and import. She felt giddy now thinking about it. To think, all these years they had taken their relationship for granted. Sex was something you did once a week, like mopping the kitchen or cleaning the tub, rather than something you needed and craved and actually looked forward to.

Winnie glanced over at Jimmy's sleeping form and felt a newfound sense of love and longing stirring within her. She never knew how much she wanted him until she did. This was new and different and exciting and nice. She pressed her body up next to his, closed her eyes, and fell right to sleep.

Winnie awoke to Jimmy brushing her hair away from her forehead. He sat down on the bed next to her and wrapped her hand around a cup. "What's this?" she asked sleepily. "Coffee," Jimmy said. Winnie sat up and rubbed her eyes. "What time is it? Is it morning already?" When her eyes focused, she looked around the room. It looked dark.

"It's still early," Jimmy said, "but I think we should hit the road. As soon as you drink your coffee, get dressed and we'll go."

"Are you bossing me around Jimmy?" Winnie playfully chided him as she pulled the sheet off revealing her naked body underneath. Jimmy's eyes widened. If he'd been a cartoon character, his eyes would have popped out of his head and steam would have come out of his ears. "Yowza!" Grabbing the coffee cup from her hand and placing it on the side table, he leaned her back against the pillows and started kissing her mouth and her eyes and her ears. "Mmmm," Jimmy crooned in her ear, as he fumbled with his zipper, finally managing to extricate his legs from his pants.

"Are you sure?" Winnie asked good-humoredly as she helped him tug his shirt up and over his head and then wrapped her legs tightly around his waist. "Because I can get dressed and we can be on the road in like five minutes."

Jimmy smiled. "What road?"

Following the multiple aforementioned delights of the morning, Winnie and Jimmy found a local thrift shop to purchase a change of clothes for each of them, an ice chest, and to pick up a new wig for Winnie—this time it was a lovely chartreuse. And Jimmy picked out a beat-up pair of cowboy boots. "Cowboy boots, really?" asked Winnie, surprised. "You don't strike me as the cowboy type".

"Yeah, in case we run into rattlesnakes."

They gassed up the Honda Civic and loaded up on water and snacks for the final leg of their journey, a seven-and-a-half-hour drive to a cabin somewhere near Seeley Lake, Montana.

Around 11 a.m., the pair headed out of Buffalo, Wyoming, traveling northeast on I-90. . . Cue Tom Petty and the Heartbreakers—Jimmy and Winnie . . . *into the great wide open*

. . . as they passed through what would become long patches of nothingness; signs with the names of towns that provided no services; passing mesas, rock formations, herds of cattle, desert sagebrush and copious road kill, and slow-moving trains meandering along a railway in the middle of nowhere. It was times like this that Winnie missed having her camera. It felt like a piece of her was missing.

It felt great to put Colorado and all the adventures they'd had there behind them. It felt even better whenever he looked over at a relaxed and smiling Winnie. Funny, he thought to himself, but I don't think I really appreciated her until I lost her and had to win her back. Never would have guessed that the best thing for our relationship might be her sleeping with another guy and almost joining a sex cult. Actually, Jimmy realized, it wasn't just their relationship that had improved, he felt better about himself than he ever had and so did Winnie.

Maybe he just needed a reason to really grow up, and maybe a big part of why he and Winnie seemed better off than ever was because he'd finally started living rather than just letting life happen. Whatever it was, it was working.

"So, we've been going like crazy and we really haven't talked about our plans when we get to the cabin," said Winnie after turning off the radio when it started to lose the Casper signal.

Jimmy let out a big sigh. It had been at the edge of his mind for days, but there had always been obstacles and other issues in the way. The first couple days in the RV, it had all been about trying to negotiate their own relationship, well, and get the hell away from the guy in the Porsche and Hooker, Oklahoma. Then it was figuring out how to get gas and food to continue the trip.

Then there'd been the craziness of the community. But now, with nothing but six or seven more hours of highway between them and the cabin, it was certainly time to think about what they were doing.

"Well, your mom must know something about what is going on," Jimmy said, letting Winnie know he didn't really have a clue.

"Yeah, but something doesn't feel right. Why did she leave pretty much the same time as me?"

"Your Dad must have warned her too," replied Jimmy, thinking that made perfect sense.

"Maybe, but I don't think so. They weren't exactly on good terms and even if he did warn her, I doubt she'd believe him or care. But even if I'm wrong, if she's in hiding, why go to the cabin, it isn't really a secret place, we lived there for almost a year when I was in fourth grade. Besides, even Mom would know better than to answer her cell phone when I called her from that burner phone."

Jimmy thought about it for a minute, and then nodded. "You're right. You told me that you guys moved a lot when you were little, sometimes skipping town. Avoiding bill collectors isn't the same as hiding from the mob, but she must have learned that much. But if your dad didn't warn her, and she's not really hiding, then why did she take off, and why go to the cabin?"

"The only thing I can think is that she knew I was running, and she thought I might go there," said Winnie, frowning as she tried to piece it together. "Maybe the mob found her and told her a story like they told you, hoping she'd lead them to me."

"That makes sense," said Jimmy after considering it. "But, that means that the mob is probably waiting there, maybe even the Porsche guy."

"Yep, but we don't even know really why they want me. The only thing that makes sense is they want to use me to force my dad not to testify against their boss," said Winnie. "They can't get to him directly, but if he knows they have me, he wouldn't take any chances. They'd have to keep me safe until after the trial, then there'd be no reason to keep me anymore."

"But, Winnie, we saw that guy who shot Dallas. I saw those fake cops too. Your mom must have seen some of them too, maybe even the same ones. They may not need you after your dad refuses to testify, but they can't just let us go because we can identify them."

"Damn, you're right," said Winnie, realizing that the promised safety of the cabin and her mom's presence was just another illusion. "But we can't just leave Missy there." As much as she hated to admit it, bad mother or not, she still had feelings for Missy and she didn't want to see her hurt. "If we don't show up in their trap soon, they'll just come looking for us on their own or set up another trap. We've got to figure out a way to warn her and get her out of there."

"Well, you could call her again," said Jimmy, knowing better than to argue the point. Winnie and her mom had a complicated relationship. In many ways, Winnie was more protective of her mother than her mother was of her. "Just don't tell her exactly where we are or what road we're on, they might be listening."

Winnie was fumbling for the phone. She felt like an idiot, how could she not have thought to call her mother before now? She'd actually forgotten about the thing. "Dammit, the battery is dead!"

"Don't you have the charger?" asked Jimmy. After a few moments digging through her purse, Winnie found it and managed to plug it into the cigarette lighter.

After 15 more miles, the phone finally had enough juice to boot up, but out here, the bargain carrier wasn't picking up a signal. "Doesn't matter, we'll be getting close to Billings soon and we'll get a signal there I'm sure," said Jimmy when he could see Winnie becoming frantic. "Wait, maybe even when we get to Billings, we might not want to call," added Jimmy.

"You think they might be listening into her cell phone calls?" asked Winnie, a little incredulously.

"Um, maybe," said Jimmy half-heartedly. What he was really thinking is that they may have Missy captive, or maybe she was in on it. "It doesn't really matter. We've been on the road for days, we'll be there in a few hours and we can get everything figured out."

The relaxed, happy vibe of early this morning was gone as if from another lifetime. They passed through Billings, Bozeman, and Helena and became more tense as they approached the last few miles. Winnie had told Jimmy what she remembered about Seeley Lake. It wasn't that much. There'd been a few hundred people in the area; you couldn't even really call it a town except in the summer when a few thousand fishermen and campers would cause the population to swell. She remembered that it was beautiful—lots of trees and mountains and a crystal-clear lake, and one store with a post office. Now, according to the Wikipedia entry Winnie had found using the phone's Internet, there were almost 2,000 people living in the area and it had become a true town, even if it was still almost entirely dependent on the tourists.

Finally, after a few false alarms and only a little backtracking, Winnie was able to find the lightly graveled access road that led up to the cabin. There was still only a single mailbox out at the turn-off. The town may have grown, but the cabin was still pretty remote.

"Pull over here," said Winnie as they came to a wide spot in the road. "This is the last place to turnaround until you get to the cabin. It's about a half mile I think, around the bend there and behind that hill," she said, pointing at the rough pine-covered outline that Jimmy could just make out against the slightly less black of the sky.

"OK, you stay back once we get close. Let me go find out what's up. If you hear me yell, don't even try and understand, just turn around, run and get in the car and drive to town. Do you have a cell signal?" Jimmy was in full commando mode and Winnie wanted to tease him, but one look at his face told her that he was in no mood for anything but agreement.

"Wow, yeah, they've got coverage out here, but we knew that, remember, we called Missy." Winnie didn't bother acknowledging the rest of Jimmy's instructions. She had no intention of running away if he started screaming. She would, she decided, call 911, and then see if she could help him.

For about the hundredth time, she wondered if they'd made the right decision, avoiding the cops until they could find out whom they could trust. It seemed simple at first; the cops wouldn't believe her, and she'd be an easy target for anyone trying to hurt her. Now, the cops might just make things worse, not so much for her and Jimmy, but for Missy. Jimmy hadn't said anything, but Winnie was a realist when it came to her mother, and she'd had the same thoughts—she could be with the bad guys, either as a prisoner, or maybe just to get back at dad.

Time for thinking about it was gone. They'd come around a corner and the lights from the cabin were spilling out, highlighting the area in front. There was a big SUV and there it was, the shiny red Porsche sitting in front. "So much for Missy not knowing anything," Winnie thought grimly.

"OK, find a good place to hide around here, I'm going in," said Jimmy, his voice hoarse with tension.

Winnie found a good-sized pine tree with ample brush around the base and slid in where she could peek at the cabin, but not be easily seen. She saw Jimmy walk right up to the door and knock. Incredibly, a man inside could be heard saying, "What the fuck!" just seconds before the door swung open and the person who opened it was Missy!

"Jimmy!?!?" she finally managed to get out, before moving around him and looking all around the driveway, obviously expecting to see her daughter. Before she could ask, Winnie saw the Porsche-driving man from the diner come to the door, take a look at Jimmy, and grab him by the arm.

"Where's the girl!" he bellowed. Winnie watched as Jimmy tried to shrug his shoulders and mumbled something. She almost didn't register the swinging fist, but the smack of knuckles on jawbone made it unavoidable. Jimmy's knees simply folded. If the big man hadn't still been grasping his arm, Winnie knew that Jimmy would be down flat on the ground. Instead, the man pulled Jimmy, like a rag doll, into the cabin and called to someone else, "Tie this asshole up and if he so much as looks funny, kill him!" he commanded the unseen other. "I'm going to find that bitch."

Missy seemed to finally have gotten over her shock because she screamed, "What are you doing? You said you weren't going to hurt them!" Winnie felt her stomach drop. So, she knew all about it, all they had to do was promise not to hurt her daughter and she'd been willing to lure her in. Missy didn't trust the police, but damn, she'd turn her only daughter over to a friggen mobster?

Winnie pulled in tighter to the tree as the man came out, striding down the driveway. This plan had gone all to hell, but then, it wasn't much of a plan to begin with. Once the man was well past her, as quietly as she could muster Winnie felt around on the ground for something she could potentially use as a weapon, or the very least, to defend herself. Fortunately, close by, she found a baseball bat-sized limb that had fallen onto the ground. It wasn't much, those guys almost certainly had guns, but somehow, having a club clenched in her fist made her feel primal and not quite so scared, not to mention the fact that this guy in particular, Porsche Man, had killed Dallas, and over the course of this odyssey she had built up more than a little pent up anger toward the asshole that was responsible.

A few minutes later, Winnie figured he'd probably reached the car and was on his way back, but before she could see him, the beam of a flashlight swept first one side of the road, then the other. Carefully, she squeezed around the trunk of the tree. Someone might be able to see her crouching in the brush if they pointed a flashlight from the house, but she was pretty sure Porsche guy wouldn't see her from the road. But, even if he didn't find her, she was still screwed she knew.

If the burly man had been as quick with his mind as he was with a fist, he'd have simply threatened Jimmy and she'd have given herself up. In fact, he'd probably realize his mistake any moment. With that in mind, Winnie thought of a trick she'd seen on more than a couple TV shows. It always worked for them.

Reaching down to the ground again she picked up a rock. As the man drew close, she flung the rock a bit deeper into the woods behind her. For a few tense seconds she waited, afraid he'd seen a bit of movement when she'd thrown the rock, or maybe he'd seen the same shows she had. After a few tense moments holding her breath, she heard him noisily step into the brush and point his flashlight deeper into the woods, away from her, where the rock had landed.

Holding her breath again, she waited until he'd taken a step past her hiding spot, and she pounced! The thick branch made a sickening crack as it collided with the lower part of the man's skull. Even though the branch had broken, it had done its job and the big man pitched face down with little more than a grunt. Amazed that she'd pulled it off, Winnie kicked him, but he didn't react.

Grabbing the flashlight, she played it over him. A lot of blood was oozing from of a two-inch gash where she'd hit him, but the thing that caught her eye was the gun he was still holding onto in his other hand. Wrestling it from his unresponsive fingers she tossed it toward the road. Thinking furiously, she finally undid his shoelaces and quickly tied his hands behind his back and then tied his ankles together. Pulling off his shoes, she took his socks and stuffed them in his mouth.

As she was scrambling out of the brush, Winnie decided that she should have kept the gun. Fortunately, it was lying right on the side of the road. She wasn't sure if she could even fire it, much less hit a person, but it had the same fortifying effect as the now broken club.

Cautiously, she approached the cabin and peeked in a window. Through the dirt smeared pane she could barely make out Jimmy sitting in a chair. It looked like there was a trickle of blood flowing from his lip, but he seemed otherwise all right. There was Missy with her back to Winnie yelling at some man that Winnie couldn't see clearly through her mother. Then, much like the blow that put Jimmy down, the man backhanded Missy, knocking her across the room. When he turned, she got a good look at him, and recognized him as a man named Clayton. He'd been the latest "uncle" as her mom insisted on calling them.

"Fucking bitch! Say one more word and you'll wish I'd just hit you once." Missy lay against the wall whimpering as blood poured from her nose. Clayton went over and sat on the hearth of the big fireplace and turned to Jimmy. "And you, you better hope Walter finds your little girlfriend soon, otherwise we might need to convince her to come on in."

Winnie looked around the room and suddenly remembered as a child playing with the firewood box. There was a firewood shed attached to the cabin and a box in there that opened into the house. During a storm and a heavy snow, you could get firewood without having to go outside, well, if you'd remembered to stock the box beforehand. It had a latch, but it had been long broken when she was a child. She couldn't tell from looking in the window, but she just hoped that no one had bothered to fix it over the years.

Not sure where to put the gun, Winnie stuck it in the front pocket of her hoodie. She worked her way around the cabin and cautiously slipped her body into the woodshed. It was mostly empty, but there were a few big-ish pieces that would work nicely as clubs, even better than the one she'd found earlier. The little half door was right next to the hearth. If the latch was still broken and if Clayton was still sitting there, and with a little luck and the element of surprise on her side Winnie might be able to get one good whack. It was a four-part plan. Again, not much of a plan, but it was all she had.

Tensing up, she burst into the door, and it slammed open! Although everything was happening at a frantic pace, a corner of her mind calmly noted "one down," as her body flew out of the door, she saw Clayton, just where he'd been "two down." His eyes were almost comically bugged out and his jaw was practically on his chest "three down" and she was starting to feel a surge of confidence until her feet got tangled up in the door as it rebounded, trying to close.

She found herself sprawled roughly at Clayton's feet. Partly out of frustration, but mostly because she didn't have any other ideas, she swung her improvised club as hard as she could at his shins. "Fuck!" he screamed, but Winnie knew that she hadn't been able to deliver the elusive "shin kill shot" and she'd lost control of the club on impact. She couldn't even try and stand up, that would have brought her up right in front of him, so she rolled away, hoping that she'd at least broken one of his legs.

Maybe she had, but it didn't really matter. He jumped quickly to his feet and half fell, half dove to land on top of her as she was rolling. His elbow caught her just beside her right breast and she heard more than felt her ribs crack. Then, he raised a fist and punched at her nose. Instinctively, she turned her head a bit so that the blow landed mostly on her cheekbone. This she felt every bit as much as she heard. Her eyes were watering up and now it seemed that everything stopped as his fist readied to come down again.

In that freeze-frame eternity, Winnie saw something black and beaklike streak overhead and crash into her tormentor's head. Then, rather than a fist, she felt the much gentler impact of a limp body collapsing on top of her. It took a second to realize what had happened. Missy, still whimpering over her bloody nose and split lip, stood above her, in her hands an iron fireplace poker that grossly held a chunk of Clayton's scalp.

Taking a deep, but incredibly painful breath, Winnie managed to roll the unconscious man off her and stand up. "Missy," she gasped with the last of that breath as she fell into an embrace with her mother.

"Oh Winnie! I didn't know!" Missy sobbed.

Winnie did what she always did, she bit back her own anger and comforted Missy. You were going to turn me over to these assholes and I'm supposed to make you feel better? That was what was hammering through her mind, but that was also quite possibly the first time Missy had called her honey, softening her anger so that what came out was "I know mom, it's going to be ok."

"Oh, Jimmy! Mom, I've got to untie Jimmy!" It took two more brain-searing breaths just to get near Jimmy. Dropping on one knee, she began to untie his feet, when Jimmy began squirming wildly. Damn, she thought, I should have removed the gag first, but then she heard a loud bang and the cabin seemed to shake.

Turning toward the source, Winnie froze. Clayton, struggling to hold up the pistol, had it trained for a second shot. Although his face was literally drenched in blood and Winnie could tell that his eyes weren't able to focus quite right, from this distance, he didn't need to be very accurate to be deadly. Fortunately, his hands were shaking, compounding his trouble aiming and his blood-slicked fingers had come off the trigger.

A surge of adrenaline she didn't think she still had brought her back across the room and she kicked the gun from his hands, and for good measure, she kicked him in the side of the head. He exhaled abruptly, and then farted wetly and fetidly. Winnie immediately knew, he was dead.

Feeling suddenly every bit as hurt and exhausted as she was, she began to turn once again to help Jimmy get loose when she noticed her mother on the floor. A pool of thick red blood was pooling into a halo around her head. The shot had gone in just under her chin.

In a daze, Winnie made it to Jimmy. She didn't remember undoing anything, only falling into him as he murmured, "I'm so sorry Winnie" over and over. They may have been there a minute and Jimmy may have said that ten times, or they could have been there for an hour and Jimmy may have said he was sorry thousands of times. Winnie didn't care, as long as she didn't have to turn around and look, she could just be in Jimmy's arms and nothing bad had to be acknowledged.

But she did have to look. Missy stared up at the ceiling, unblinking and unreal looking, like a gruesome lifelike full-size doll; a replica of a human. Every detail correct, but no one would mistake her for a person—the person who'd once been Ruth, had once been Missy, who was her mother, wasn't here any longer.

Although she wanted more time to let all of this sink in, Winnie realized that wasn't possible. And despite her injuries, she managed to say, "We've got to get the Porsche guy, he's tied up in the woods," said Winnie, jealously hoarding her breath between agonizing gasps for air.

"Yeah. Get him in here and find out exactly what all this shit was about!" said Jimmy with a determination that made Winnie wonder just what her boyfriend might be capable of.

Gingerly, they went out the door, Jimmy doing his best to hold her up without touching her ribs. He was oblivious to his own hugely swollen face. Idly, Winnie speculated that his jaw was probably broken.

They didn't have to get all the way to Winnie's original hiding place to see that Porsche man wasn't there. The brush was rolled flat and there was plenty of blood on the leaves and sticks. There were even pieces of broken shoelaces, but no gangster.

"He can't be far, but we've got to make sure he can't get in his car or the cabin, he's probably got a gun somewhere around here," Jimmy said. That reminded Winnie and she pulled the pistol from the small of her back.

"Like this one?" she said. "I don't think I can use this, you should have it," she said, handing it over to a dubious Jimmy. Jimmy looked it over, and then slid it into his waistband before bending over and choosing a limb that he could use as a club. Here they were, in the woods, battling gangsters, and their choice of weapon was a crude tree branch. Somehow, the gun seemed an appropriate backup plan.

"He may have intended to get medieval on our asses," Jimmy said, "but we're going old-school stone age!" Despite Jimmy's weak attempt at humor in this desperate situation, his eyes shown with something cold, and Winnie wasn't really sure that Jimmy would be content to just merely capture the Porsche guy. Winnie realized that she might not be able to control herself either. But first, they had to find the guy.

Turns out, finding him wasn't hard at all. They hadn't walked more than a couple dozen yards when he dropped out of a tree right onto Winnie. Before Jimmy could react, the man had stood up, with his beefy forearm across Winnie's neck and his other hand wrapped over her head and grasping her jawline. "OK asshole, I know you've got my gun. Slowly, very slowly, take it out of your waistband and put it on the ground. If you try and fuck with me, I'll break her neck, then I'll take you apart so fast you won't know what hit you."

Stunned, Jimmy reached back and brought the gun forward very slowly then knelt down and placed it on the ground. "OK, now back up asswipe." Jimmy started to take a step back, and then saw Winnie raise her eyebrows just before she simultaneously twisted hard, driving an elbow into the man's side and stomping as hard as she could on the instep of his foot. She slid free from the surprised man only a split second before Jimmy delivered a massive blow from the club to his shoulder and glancing off the side of his head. It wasn't enough to put the guy down, but it dazed him, no doubt adding to the trauma Winnie had inflicted earlier. Before he could recover, Winnie grabbed her club and swung hard into his other side. Jimmy's solid hit to the man's hip sent him to the ground.

With Winnie standing over the man, club upraised, ready to bring it down on the guy's head, Jimmy noticed that neither arm looked quite right, and realized that they were both probably broken. As if confirming this, the guy tried to grab Winnie's leg, but only groaned in pain as a white shard of bone suddenly jabbed out of his forearm. Still, Jimmy's adrenalin was in high gear. Seeing what this bastard had almost done to Winnie, weeks of pent up anger exploded inside him—anger at Dallas and the truckers—one that had tried to rape her and another that had exposed himself; at Archibald Golden; at her dad for getting her into this mess, at her mother for giving her a shitty childhood, at himself for not protecting her sooner, and at the piece of shit Porsche man here who tried to hurt her. Adding insult to injury, he raised one cowboy booted foot in the air and landed a devastating blow to Walter's groin.

"Why'd you do that? He's down," Winnie cried, shocked at his brutality. "I bought these boots in case I ran into any snakes," he shrugged, "and I saw a snake." Jimmy picked up the gun, shoved it back in his pants, and removed his belt. "If he so much as breathes hard, end him with your club Winnie," he said before using the belt to cinch the mangled arms together. Despite the instructions, the man cried with pain, grunted, and then seemed to pass out for a minute. Winnie followed closely behind wondering what had happened to that mild-mannered reporter she'd once dated.

"She's right behind you and we all know that one more shot to the head just may be all it takes, so come along nicely and maybe we won't break anything else," commanded Jimmy, tugging on the end of the belt, leading the broken man toward the cabin.

Walking into the cabin, the Porsche guy took a look at his partner and the golf-ball sized hole in his skull, still oozing blood and a bit of brain. If possible, his face turned an even more sickly white and he looked at Jimmy with no little bit of fear.

Using the rope and belts that had bound him so recently, Jimmy carefully hobbled and attached their captive securely to a heavy chair. The man was obviously going into shock, but they weren't taking any chances. Motioning Winnie over, he retreated to the doorway where they could whisper without being overheard. "Get the recorder on the phone going, but don't let him see it."

Winnie walked back in, past the man and went into the bathroom, coming out a few seconds later, but staying behind where he'd been tied up, out of sight. Jimmy had seen plenty of cop shows, but he really had no idea how to wring a confession out of a real person. Fortunately, he didn't have to do a thing.

"You two think you are scot-free now, but you're fucked," he spat as Jimmy approached him.

"Why's that? Do you heal super-fast, or what?" Jimmy asked him, hoping he'd keep talking.

"Cause we're just the caretakers. We're just supposed to hold you here until the real icemen come. There's no sneaking up on those guys. Hell, you won't even see them coming." Jimmy could tell that he was telling the truth, he knew that help was on the way, and he believed that the men coming were more deadly than he was. Jimmy felt a knot in his stomach. Clubs weren't going to make a difference if he and Winnie had to deal with professional hit men.

"So, why do you guys even care about us? We know nothing about the mob and haven't done anything." Jimmy asked.

"Hah!" laughed the prisoner, "Your bitch has been marked since the day her old man turned rat. The organization doesn't tolerate rats."

"Don't call her a bitch!" Jimmy barked, arching back and starting to lift his leg ready to kick him again. "She had nothing to do with it. Her dad left when she was a little kid."

Porsche guy nodded his head back, but continued, "Don't matter! Fucking snitches gotta pay, and the best way to make them pay is to hurt their family. Best thing is, it reminds anyone else thinking of turning snitch that it isn't such a good idea."

"But, why now? Her Dad left almost 20 years ago." Jimmy asked, calmer, realizing he needed to keep his cool so he could keep the guy talking for the recording.

"Don't know why they didn't whack her and her mom right away, maybe they were waiting until the trial. Anyway, Big "G" took off and the trial never happened. Probably by the time they got everything running smoothly again, they'd lost track of the girl or they had other fish to fry."

"OK, but why fry those fish now?"

"Easy. Big G got nabbed in Greece? and they're bringing him back here for trial."

"Really? You guys care about a guy that cut and ran away 20 years ago?"

"Nah, not really, but Big G isn't the point. Hell, half the bosses would kill him themselves if they could. The point is sending the message. Rats get killed and their brats get killed."

"So, you followed me to Oklahoma so you could kill Winnie and send a message?"

"Nah, I ain't an iceman, I don't do contract work. I was just supposed to pick her up. We'd use her to send a message to her daddy, let him know that he didn't want to work with the feds. Then the guys from Portland were going to come and do the job. They're still coming, and they're going to do that job." Incredibly, beaten and bound, the guy's confidence was astounding and growing as he explained what was going to happen.

"So, was Winnie's mom working for you guys?" Jimmy knew that this could upset Winnie, but he thought she needed to know one way or another, but more importantly, he needed to establish for the recording as much as he could.

"That stupid cunt?" Winnie winced at the word. Missy was a lot of things, but she wasn't a cunt. It was all she could do to keep from bonking this guy on the side of his head again with her stick, but she resisted for the same reason Jimmy did, to get as much information out of him as they could while he was being recorded.

"Everyone knew she didn't mean shit to her old man, but we knew she might be able to bring the girl in. She thought we were just going to have a nice little chat, maybe some tea and cookies," the man snorted in disgust. "She thought Clayton liked her, but he was just waiting 'til the job was over and the boys from

Portland could take care of her. But then, you two fuckers went and killed him."

Jimmy couldn't help himself, "Nope, it wasn't us. Missy did it when your buddy tried to hurt Winnie; she clocked him with the poker. But before he died, he shot her."

"Meh, didn't think the old bitch had it in her." Jimmy could tell that the man really didn't care that much about his "friend" and next to nothing about Winnie's mom. In a way, it was fascinating talking to someone with no apparent conscience. However, he could see Winnie's face contorted in pain and rage just behind the chair.

"Yeah, like you didn't think a girl could knock you the fuck out with a stick, right?" Jimmy taunted, disgusted. Now it was the Porsche man's turn to be enraged. Jimmy figured he had enough, and probably wasn't going to get any more from the guy anyway. Nodding to Winnie, he moved back out of easy earshot. "Did you get all that?"

Winnie was working on the phone and then Jimmy heard the start of the conversation and Winnie smiled and nodded, "Got it!"

"We need to get the police up here. And we should get out of here ourselves in case those guys from Portland get here first," Jimmy said.

"Is it OK to leave him here?" asked Winnie.

"Yeah, he's not going anywhere, not with his arms so busted up. Hell, I'm surprised he's even conscious after the beating we gave him."

Jimmy started to push Winnie out of the cabin, but she brushed him aside, instead turning back around to face Porsche man. Despite her injuries, Winnie picked up the poker her mother had used to save her life and brought it down hard on the man's kneecap. "That's for Dallas," she said, leaving Walter, aka the Porsche Man whimpering like a little girl on the cabin floor as she now allowed Jimmy to usher her out of the cabin and closing the door behind them. Jimmy offered a weak smile. He was certainly no fan of Dallas, but he knew how good it must have felt for her to be able to unleash her anger upon the person responsible for her friend's death.

Outside, Winnie dialed 9-1-1. Jimmy was surprised to notice that dawn was well underway. The Porsche, earlier just a sexy shadowy outline now showed blood red and was slowly brightening as the sun continued to rise. On impulse, he strode over and checked the doors. It was open.

There wasn't much inside, a bunch of fast-food wrappers, an unfolded map, and some sunglasses. Jimmy found the control to pop the trunk and released it. Inside, was a large duffel bag sitting square in the middle of the small trunk. Unzipping it partially, Jimmy could see it was packed with cash. Damn! There must be hundreds of thousands of dollars in there!

Just then Winnie stepped over. "OK, the cops will be here soon, I told them we were going to hide until they get here . . . what is that?" Winnie's eyes popped open at the sight of the bag full of cash.

"This is payment for all the trouble these assholes have put you through . . . and for killing your friend Dallas," said Jimmy as he rezipped the bag and tossed it over his shoulder. "Let's find a place to hide."

They walked past the cabin, and then Jimmy ducked into the woodshed and popped back out with a shovel he'd found. Taking it slow, because Winnie simply couldn't get enough breath to walk more than a few steps at a time, they finally got high enough on the hillside that Jimmy thought they'd be safe, but still be able to see any cars that arrived. He helped Winnie get as comfortable as possible, then moved a bit further up the hill. He quickly dug a shallow hole and buried the satchel, making sure to cover it with a smattering of leaves and sticks to camouflage it.

Returning to Winnie, Jimmy noticed that she was very pale, and her face was shiny from perspiration. He knew enough first-aid to recognize that she was probably in mild shock. Broken ribs, witnessing the murder of your mother, hitmen coming to kill you, he supposed it would be amazing if she weren't in shock.

With a few minutes of nothing to do but wait, Jimmy began replaying all the events of the long night. How stupid it had been to walk right up to the door. In retrospect, they should have left as soon as they saw the Porsche, called the cops, and waited. Even after, he should have had Winnie call the cops as soon as she'd set him free, before they went to search for Porsche man.

Dammit, too many things had happened, too fast. In the back of his mind, Jimmy had assumed that once they called the cops a whole fleet of squad cars would arrive moments later. That's how it worked on television shows, hell, that was pretty much what happened in Southern California. However, this was remote Montana, the nearest real city was a good hour, maybe an hour and a half away. There probably wasn't more than a single sheriff's patrol on duty at what, 6:30 on a Sunday morning. Dammit, why hadn't they called earlier?

Only about 15 minutes had passed, but it seemed like hours. Winnie was shivering and giving little gasps of pain every few breaths. Jimmy was almost ready to go back to the cabin and grab a blanket when they heard the crunch of tires on gravel. A few seconds later they saw that it wasn't the cops unless the sheriff's patrol here used late model corvettes.

The men inside must have noted the car parked down the road because they got out of the sports car with their guns drawn, cautiously approaching the cabin. One man went to a window and peered in while the other stood next to the door. The window man nodded, and the doorman quickly opened it and took a step inside. Then, seconds later, the other man followed him inside.

"Damn, where are the cops!" said Jimmy, only realizing when Winnie looked up at him that he'd spoken aloud. "Babe, call 9-1-1 again and tell them that the bad guys are HERE and they have guns, but try and keep your voice down."

He could hear Winnie murmuring to the dispatcher as he pulled the gun from his waistband. He had no illusions; it would be a miracle if he hit anything. Hell, he didn't know if it had a safety, if it was on, or even if the gun was loaded. Gingerly, he began examining the weapon. Okay, that must be the safety switch, he decided when he saw the small red rectangle and could get it to disappear and reappear by moving it. There are surely bullets in it, no one had fired it and Jimmy assumed that no bad guy would be carrying an unloaded gun. He had no idea how to check though. There might be a single bullet, maybe six, or maybe this was one of those guns that held 10 shots—he had no clue and really hoped it didn't turn out to matter. So much for the whole good guy with a gun argument if the if turns out the good guy doesn't know what the hell he's doing!

Winnie finished her call and looked over at him with frightened eyes locked on the dark metal in his hand. Just then, the two men came out of the cabin, followed by Porsche man, limping badly and with both arms hanging dead at his sides. As the two hit men swept their gaze across the forestland around the cabin, Porsche man made his way to the car. After saying something to them, one of the men came over and opened the car door for him and popped the trunk. A few seconds later, he slammed the trunk closed and hit the defenseless man along the head, almost knocking him down.

Jimmy couldn't hear anything they said clearly, but both men resumed their examination of the surroundings while Porsche man stumbled back to the porch and let himself sink onto a chair where he could watch the parking area. Using hand signs and nods, the hit men set off, one taking the left side of the road, the other on the right. With relief, Jimmy noted that they were working their way down, toward where they'd parked the car.

"Damn! If I'd have been thinking, we could have gotten down to the car right away and been gone before they even got here," he berated himself mentally, then realized that even if they'd done that, there was a good chance they'd have run into them on the narrow driveway anyway. When were the cops going to get here? It wouldn't take those guys long to make it down to the car and back, and it wouldn't be much longer before they thought to search in this direction. The Porsche guy must have told them how beat up Winnie was and that they couldn't have gotten very far.

"Crap!" muttered Winnie, alerting Jimmy to the fact that indeed, the men were working their way back toward the cabin. They'd just come back onto the driveway and were gesturing in Jimmy and Winnie's general direction when a green Crown Victoria came barreling around the bend of the driveway followed closely by a black and white SUV. Both vehicles slid to a stop, turned sideways presenting their passenger sides to the cabin.

Caught in the open, the two hit men had time to scramble behind the Porsche just as the officers in each vehicle were getting out and taking positions behind their respective front fenders. "Put your hands up!" bellowed one of the cops in a shaky voice. In the back of his mind, Jimmy noted that real cops, unlike the ones on television, weren't immune to fear and adrenaline overload.

Porsche man, on the porch, had stood up and was shouting out a warning to his accomplices as the cops arrived and now it appeared he was trying to raise his hands in surrender, but instead, they only moved ineffectually and unfortunately for him, suspiciously enough that a rifle shot rang out from the SUV and Porsche man dropped.

Almost immediately the hit men began firing from either end of the Porsche. The cops returned fire. It seemed that the deafening roar of firearms echoing through the forest went on forever, but Jimmy knew that there couldn't have been more than a few dozen shots fired. No pistol had unlimited ammo, and even the rifles of the police had to be reloaded. Jimmy watched as both cops switched to their handguns and emptied those clips. There was a pause, and he watched the officers putting fresh clips into their service pistols.

At some point, the return fire from the Porsche had stopped. The silence seemed unreal and went on for way too long before finally the cop behind the SUV shouted, in a somewhat calmer voice this time, "Drop your weapons and come out from behind the vehicle!" From their vantage point, Jimmy and Winnie could see only the feet of one of the hit men; the cabin blocked everything else. Those feet didn't move.

After another agonizingly long silence, the cop behind the Crown Vic began scuttling off to the side, obviously trying to get an angle to see if the shooters were still alive. Just as he was almost to the brush on the edge of the driveway, a shot came from Porsche??? and the officer fell into the brush. Immediately, the SUV officer returned fire, and then a moment later the wounded officer in the brush fired a couple quick shots. Once the SUV officer had once again emptied his pistol, Jimmy saw him grab and reload his rifle just as his partner called out, "They're down!" Still, neither officer made a move toward the car, but the SUV policeman began talking into his radio.

Seconds later, startling them both, Winnie's phone rang. "This is the Seeley Lake dispatcher. What is your current situation?" Winnie started to answer, but her voice cracked, and she gasped for breath between her now pronounced shivering. She held the phone out to Jimmy.

"We need an ambulance! My girlfriend is hurt. One of the cops got shot, I think. They killed her mother. There are dead gangsters everywhere. We're hiding in the woods!" It came out in a flood of words, faster than any morning DJ could possibly speak, and Jimmy felt like crying all of a sudden.

"Sir, sir? Ambulances are on the way. Are you in immediate danger, are there still suspects that you know of in the area?" The dispatcher was like the ones you see on TV, calm and all business. Jimmy was able to collect himself a bit.

"Good. No, I think that was all of them. What should we do?"

"Sir are you armed?" asked the calm woman.

"Ah, um, yes. We have one of the gangster's guns, but I'm not sure how to even use it," Jimmy replied, momentarily panicked that they might expect him to use the gun.

"That's alright sir. The officers have the situation under control. Place the gun on the ground. Are you and your companion capable of walking?"

Slightly chagrined at his misunderstanding about the gun, Jimmy tried to gather himself once again and took a look at Winnie. She'd obviously heard the dispatcher because she nodded her head tentatively and said, "I think I can."

"Yes, we can walk I think, but probably not very far. I think my girlfriend has broken limbs and is in shock," Jimmy finally managed to answer.

"OK then. Leave the gun on the ground and walk to the officers. Can you put your hands up where they can see them?"

"I, I can, but I'm not sure she can," Jimmy replied, worried that the wrong answer might somehow disqualify them from help. My God, he thought to himself, I'm losing it! Of course, the good guys will help us, won't they? With a groan and whimpering, Winnie was already rising out of the brush. Jimmy quickly followed and put an arm around her to steady her. The other went up in an attempt to follow directions.

"The officers see you. Make your way down to them," said the dispatcher, for the first time Jimmy heard the composed training of the dispatcher broken by a touch of humanity and emotion.

Both officers were now by the Porsche. The SUV officer was still talking into his radio, still had his pistol drawn and was watching intently as they made their way slowly and carefully down the hill toward him. The other officer sat with his back against the Porsche, next to the prone body of one of the hit men. His pistol was sitting in his lap, and he had one hand covering a wound in his upper shoulder.

Before they even made it to the policemen, an ambulance, lights flashing and siren wailing came around the corner and came to a stop near the police cars. The paramedics scrambled first to the injured policeman, helping him to his feet and one helped walk him back to the ambulance. Seconds later another ambulance arrived along with two other cars that screamed "government fleet vehicle."

The next thing Jimmy knew, he and Winnie were swarmed by medics while police and men in suits examined the interior of the cabin, the Porsche man's body on the porch, and two dead hit men. The paramedics started to lead Winnie away, but she stalled and with effort called out, "I want to stay with Jimmy!"

Once they'd determined that his injuries were not a priority, the medics gave Jimmy an ice pack to help with the painful swelling of his jaw but left him pretty much alone. Now he moved back toward Winnie. "Honey, you need to get to a hospital. I'm sure they'll bring me right behind you." Jimmy didn't want to be separated either, but he knew that Winnie was hurt more than she'd admit.

Reluctantly, Winnie nodded, and then painfully raised her arms in an effort to hug him. Jimmy resisted hugging her in return because he didn't want to hurt her more, but despite the awful pain it caused in his jaw, he gave her a little peck on the cheek. Noticing both his restraint in the hug and the pain of the kiss, Winnie smiled crookedly at him and vowed, "We'll do that better once you get to the hospital!" He did his best to return the smile and wondered just how gruesome the effect was.

With Winnie gone off in the ambulance with the injured officer, Jimmy seemed to have nothing to do. A stream of cars continued to flood into the now crowded clearing that was the defacto parking lot of the cabin. Jimmy wondered just how the ambulance would be able to navigate out the narrow road with so much traffic and cars parked on the sides.

A small army of people with cameras, fingerprint artists, forensic teams, and coroners had shown up and were swarming everywhere. Finally, someone brought a couple chairs out from inside the cabin. One of the men in a suit and tie offered Jimmy a chair and he and his partner took seats opposite him.

"I'm agent Crow, and this is agent Baker. We're with the FBI and we'd like to ask you a few questions if you're up to it." Although it was technically a question, Jimmy had seen both men talking to the medic that had examined him earlier. He nodded. The truth was, he was anxious to tell someone about this entire mess.

Removing the phone from his pocket, Jimmy smiled, or tried to, "We got the dead guy on the porch to explain lots of it; we recorded it!" he said triumphantly. The two agents looked at each other, then looked back at Jimmy, returning his grin.

Winnie was just beginning to drift away again when the nurse—Sophie it read on her badge—entered the room and checked her pulse for about the gazillionth time. It was so true what they said about hospitals, she'd discovered, that you don't go there to get any rest. She had barely slept more than 30 minutes at a time since first arriving early this morning. Everything was a blur; nurses and doctors probing here, poking there, and severe pain whenever she coughed or moved her upper body in the slightest. Heck, breathing hurt. Mercifully, the ER doc had injected her with some powerful narcotics that knocked her out for a good while.

When she awoke later on in the hospital room, she noticed that she was hooked up to two IVs, one probably for dehydration, the other must be some mighty powerful, kick-ass painkiller, because the pain had been knocked out too, much to her relief. A heavy belt-like bandage girded her chest, and evidently, she had injured her right arm because it was bandaged up too and held in place at her side with a cloth sling. She must have done that back at the cabin when she was wielding that substantial tree limb as weapon of choice. Yet, despite the good drugs, she felt sore all over, and tired, exceedingly tired. More tired than she'd ever felt in her life, and for sure some of that might be mental fatigue and trauma. Her mind flashed on her mother's crumpled body on the cabin floor. She was sure she would have to deal with that sooner or later, but now all she wanted to do, goddammit, was sleep.

"How are you feeling," Sophie asked as she lifted her hand and pinched her wrist between her fingers.

"Thirsty," was all Winnie could intone.

"I bet you are," the nurse said. When she finished checking her pulse, she filled up a cup with ice chips and handed it to Winnie.

"This'll help," she said.

Surprisingly, it did. As tired as she was, crunching the ice between her jaws and feeling the soothing coldness rushing down her dry throat was the best thing that had happened all day. Giving up on sleep, Winnie reached over and picked up the remote control for the TV that was nestled down beside her in the folds of the blankets. She watched Ellen DeGeneres dance for a while until her eyes involuntarily closed and she fell dead asleep, still holding the cup with the ice chips in her hand.

Except for a single light coming from the TV the room was dark when Winnie woke up again. Had she actually slept? It seemed like she had, and she felt markedly better. A tray of food sat untouched on the bed table beside her. Evidently someone had brought it in, but had the common decency not to disturb her, which was good, because she was starving! She pulled it over close and started devouring its contents—Yankee pot roast, a spinach salad, mashed potatoes, and carrot spice cake—for hospital food it wasn't so bad.

Shortly after, as she was finishing off the last bite of the carrot cake, a new shift nurse bustled into the room.

"You were hungry, I see," she said cheerfully.

"I'm Lily," she said pointing to her badge, "and I'll be checking in on you tonight, if that's okay."

Winnie nodded without speaking. It was funny that Lily was asking for her permission now after various hospital staff had spent the entire day checking in on her without ever once asking if it was okay. Lily took her vitals and helped her get up and go to the bathroom and she was comfortably ensconced back in bed when Jimmy showed up. She was never so happy to see anyone in her life.

"Jimmy!" she cried, stretching out her one good arm in a welcoming gesture.

"ohhh," she lamented when he got up close. "Your poor face," she said as she gently touched his jaw. The angry bruises lining it and his swollen cheek made him look like he'd stepped out of the ring with Mike Tyson. Jimmy attempted a weak smile, but it was difficult.

"Is it broken?" Winnie asked.

Jimmy shook his head no. Talking was painful, but he managed to ask, "How are you? Are you okay?" which came out sounding like hoo aw woo aw woo okay.

Before she could answer a local newscast came on the overhead TV.

"Turn it up," Jimmy said trying hard to avoid moving his lips.

Winnie quickly unfolded the remote from the bedding and turned up the volume so they could hear.

". . . And we go live now to Monica Gonzales, who is reporting from the scene."

The newscast cut to a live feed of a swarm of news crews and police combing the area around the Seeley Lake cabin. "I'm here now at the scene where earlier today a deadly shootout occurred involving local law enforcement, FBI agents, and several suspects believed to be members of a national organized crime group. Early this morning, dispatchers received a call from a couple hiding near the Seeley Lake cabin. When police arrived, three men engaged them in gunfire and were killed at the scene. One of the police officers was shot but will recover from his wounds. Inside the remote cabin, authorities discovered the bodies of a man and a woman, who have not yet been identified. The woman that made the 9-1-1 call sustained injuries that required hospitalization. Her male companion, also injured, is cooperating with the police to piece together what led up to the events that transpired today. Monica Gonzales, reporting from Seeley Lake."

Jimmy turned and looked excitedly at Winnie. "They didn't say anything about the money. Maybe they didn't find it!"

"What about the car Jimmy? Do they know it is stolen; do they know we had it? Did you at least drive it out of there?"

"It's still there, I think. They wouldn't let me drive," he said. "I wanted to go, but the EMT guys gave me some pain meds and then told me I couldn't drive. The cops took me back to the station, and then they dropped me off here.

"Wait a minute," Winnie said. "So what happened after I left? They questioned you?"

He could see that Winnie was getting upset, twisting, and pushing herself up, and he didn't want her to move around too much and hurt her ribs more. His jaw was beginning to throb, but he'd have to power through the pain to explain all this to her.

"Winnie," he said, placing his arm across her and gently easing her back down against the mattress. "Take it easy. It's okay. It is."

"But . . . but . . ."

He placed his fingers against her lips to shush her. "Seriously, Jimmy, are you shushing me?" she said.

"I am," he said. "Just lie back. Be quiet now for a sec and let me explain what happened. Quit being so . . .

"So what?" she asked.

"So . . . Jetty Jet-Jetty," he blurted.

That made Winnie giggle, which made Jimmy laugh too. The pain meds were wearing off and laughing exacerbated the soreness in her ribs. Jimmy's jaw was killing him, but the fact that they were both laughing was a pretty good sign.

Jimmy explained how after she had been taken away in the ambulance, the two FBI guys had approached him and taken him aside to ask him a few questions; how he'd handed over the phone with the recording she'd made of Porsche man, and after listening to it, they'd said this was all the evidence they needed, and he was free to go. "They said if they needed anything more, they'd be in touch," Jimmy finished.

"That's it?" Winnie asked. Jimmy nodded, "Yep," he said, except it came out more like "theppp."

"And the money? What about the money?" she whispered, a look of worry crossing her face.

Even behind his bloated cheeks and fat lip, she could see that Jimmy wasn't able to hide his own anxiety.

"Well . . ." he hedged.

"Well what?" Winnie pressed.

"Well, I'll have to go back and dig it up where we buried it," he finally said.

"Oh jeez," Winnie said, rolling her eyes at Jimmy and carelessly tossing her good arm in the air. "Even if it is still there, how long before we can even manage to get back up there? It's a crime scene. It could be weeks or months before we can safely go up there again."

Jimmy pushed her arm back down. "Stop that," he said, "you'll hurt yourself," as he patted her hand like a father would pat the hand of a stubborn child. "Soon as you're released, we'll get a ride up there and pick up the car," he said. "And if nobody is around, I'll go dig it up; if not, we'll just have to wait a while longer, until the coast is clear."

Winnie returned one of her trademark exasperated glares and Jimmy shrugged.

"Oh look," Jimmy said, cleverly changing the subject, "an old episode of *Star Trek: The Next Generation*. Let's watch!"

On Tuesday morning, five days after being admitted, the orderly wheeled Winnie through the automatic hospital doors and out to the sidewalk. "I'll be right back," he said, locking the wheels of the wheelchair and leaving her alone to wait for Jimmy. Minutes ticked by, five, 10, 15 minutes . . . where was he? Winnie thought. The orderly returned a few minutes later to check on her. "Your ride still not here?" he inquired.

"Nope," she answered. She was starting to wonder if there'd been a problem with getting the car. He had told her not to worry, he'd get it taken care of, but maybe it wasn't there. What if someone had turned it in as stolen? What if he'd gotten caught digging up the money? Just as a thousand "what ifs" began to reverberate through her head, a luxury van she did not recognize pulled up to the curb in front of her.

"Hey pretty lady," Jimmy called out as he came round to her on the sidewalk. "Ready to go?" Winnie wasn't quite sure how to respond to this Jimmy—the one standing before her now dressed from head to toe in clothes she'd never seen before—jeans, a shiny new pair of cowboy boots, tan corduroy jacket, and perched on his head, a spiffy, way too hipstery bowler hat, which he whisked dramatically from his head, dipping in a ceremonial bow before her. "M'lady," he said with much flair, "your chariot awaits."

"Okay," Winnie said, "Where's Jimmy? What have you done with him?"

Jimmy winked conspiratorially. "I'll tell you if you get in my van."

Winnie smiled and let Jimmy help her out of the wheelchair and ease up and into the front seat of the tall van where he buckled her in snuggly. Her arm was still in a sling and her midsection bandaged up tightly. The doctor said it would take around four weeks to fully heal.

Jimmy hopped into the driver's side and closed the door. "Ready?" he asked her. "Yes," she said, "but first, I think you should probably tell me about the sweet new ensemble and this van."

"This ensemble?" he asked innocently pointing at his clothes. Winnie nodded. "And this van here?" he asked as he made a grand sweep of the dash.

"Yes," Winnie said, "this one."

"I traded the sex-cult car for it," Jimmy said matter of fact.

"You traded the cult car?"

"Yes, well sorta. I actually sold it to a mechanic who didn't care much about a title." he said as he started up the engine and pulled away from the hospital's curb. She had to admit, the van was super nice inside, leather, lots of room, air conditioning—much improved over the old Mini Wini RV Snake had loaned them back in Oklahoma in what now seemed like about a million years ago.

Apparently, while Winnie was convalescing in the hospital Jimmy had taken a taxi up to the cabin. The car was still parked on the side of the road where they'd left it, and incredibly, not a living soul around, allowing Jimmy to walk straight up the small hill where he and Winnie had hid, unearth the satchel with the money in it and drive away, nobody the wiser. Winnie couldn't believe it. For once in this whole fucked up, crazy saga, something had actually gone right.

Jimmy parked the van in front of the Missoula post office and pulled an envelope from the glove compartment. "What's that?" Winnie asked.

"This," he said, "is a $10,000 traveler's check addressed to Mr. Archibald Golden."

From there, Jimmy drove to a nearby RV park, their home away from home for the next four weeks while Winnie's ribs healed.

One evening as they sat together in the cozy van watching TV, Winnie sat up from her prone position, putting the weight of her body on one elbow. Since her release from the hospital, she had been quiet, distant. Their conversations were mostly superficial ones: What should they have for dinner? Should they eat out tonight? Was she comfortable? Did she want a blanket? Jimmy knew she had a lot of emotional issues to deal with and he hadn't pressured her. He figured she'd talk when she was ready.

"I think I'm fixed now," she announced.

"Oh really?" Jimmy said. "What makes you so sure? You're getting around much better, but not good enough to travel, I don't think."

"I mean mentally," she explained.

"I've been thinking a lot about my mother," she continued. "About Missy."

Jimmy nodded. "I know. I figured."

Winnie expelled a deep sigh as if to signal the unburdening to come. "I'm not sad," she began. "I won't miss her. She was not a good person."

Winnie's voice was becoming higher pitched, angry. "She was neglectful and self-centered. She was always leaving me places or forgetting about me. One time, she was supposed to pick me up from school, but never showed up. My teacher had to drive me home, but she wasn't there, and the door was locked. I sat outside in the cold, like freezing 35 degrees cold, until she finally showed up after the bar closed. Most of the time she forgot to feed me. She never took me to the doctor or the dentist. Sometimes she made me stay home from school because she said she was 'sick' and I needed to stay and take care of her."

"And she was embarrassed of this," Winnie said, pointing to her birthmark. That was the absolute worst most unforgiveable part of Winnie's story, Jimmy thought.

Winnie paused, drifting away momentarily, seemingly lost in a sea of bad memories. But then she began again after taking what seemed like a big, deep calming, Zen breath. "But one time she sewed a dress for me," she said wistfully. I remember it was for a Christmas pageant at school. It was frilly and it was pink and I looked just like a princess."

Jimmy remained still, letting her work through her recollections—the good and the bad. He knew her childhood had been unpleasant, she had told him before, but he hadn't really known how devastating it really was for her. Winnie looked over at Jimmy finally and said, "Well, that was a long time ago. One act of selflessness certainly doesn't change a lifetime of pain and neglect."

"Are you going to be okay though?" Jimmy asked, concerned that maybe she hadn't fully dealt with her mother's death.

Still sore, Winnie eased herself slowly up off the small couch and walked over to the refrigerator. Pulling a bottled water out, she took a big swig, and turned to Jimmy. "You know, I always felt like a motherless child anyway, and now that I am one, instead of it hurting, it feels fucking liberating. Does that make me a bad person?"

Jimmy shook his head no and smiled. Winnie was back. "I wanted to feel something," she continued. "I really tried to, but all I've been feeling is relief, relief that I no longer have to feel responsible for her or sorry for her or guilty anymore. I can be me now, and get on with my goddamn life, and even though it seems like I shouldn't, I feel better," she said, "inside." She laid her hand against her chest and patted her heart. Jimmy reached out, covering her hand with his and squeezing it.

"You know the doctor in the hospital told me they have ways of removing port wine stain birthmarks now with something called a pulsed-dye laser," Winnie said.

"Oh yeah," Jimmy said. "So are you thinking about maybe having it done?"

Winnie shook her head. "Nope. I've decided that for better or worse, it has shaped who I am." She leaned in next to Jimmy and said, "And you know, Archibald Golden was right, I am fucking special!

"Indeed you are," Jimmy said tenderly wrapping his arms around her in a loving embrace. "And as far as I'm concerned, you can be Winnie or Jetty Jet, whoever the hell you want to be just so long as you let me tag along for the ride."

Three months later.

Perched atop the washing machine in a coin-operated laundromat somewhere in Oregon, Winnie, dressed in T-shirt and shorts and baseball cap, swings her left foot back and forth, drumming a slow, rhythmic beat against the sides of it with her cowboy boot—a nervous habit.

In the several hours spent waiting for the clothes to cycle through she has already taken at least 100 photos with her new camera—images of lint in a variety of interesting shapes and sizes, patterns in the ceiling that sometimes look like cats, other times skulls, depending on the angle; the fascinating way the light filters in through the window blinds, and multiple shots of the inside of the clothes dryer. She is thinking about going out on the sidewalk now and doing some street photography when Jimmy breezes in.

Clothes done yet, babe?" he asks leaning over to give her upturned cheek a quick peck.

"Almost," Winnie answers without looking away from her smart phone.

"I want to get going soon," he says.

Having traded in the fancy van last week for a late model pickup and an old trailer, the provisional plan is to travel the country writing blogs, taking pictures of birds and waterfalls and tumbleweeds and bugs, exploring forests and caves and lakes and mesas, living happily ever after, basically.

"I brought you something," Jimmy says, pulling a Snickers bar out of his pocket and tossing it over to her. Winnie catches it and flashes him a knowing smile.

"So, Winnie, where do you wanna go first?" Jimmy asks.

She cogitates for a minute on that. "Mmm, I haven't seen Mt. Rushmore yet, but I think first I'd like to see the Grand Canyon," she answers in between bites of the candy bar. "Last time we went through the desert I was without a camera."

"Oh Right," Jimmy says.

"Let's not go to Colorado though."

Jimmy nods in agreement. "Yeah . . . no, let's not go there.

About the Author

K.J. Kolsen lives on a 10-acre farm in Deadwood, Oregon with his pet goat Gladys and two dogs—Muffy McFattypants and Spike.

COMING SOON from

 GladEye
Press

The Risk of Being Ridiculous: A Historical Novel of Love and Revolution
Guy Maynard
Join 19-year-old Ben Tucker for a passionate, lyrical six-week ride through confrontation and confusion, courts and cops, parties and politics, school and the streets, Weathermen and women's liberation, acid and activism, revolution and reaction.

Look for Maynard's second book coming soon.

Faith, Hope, and Dying
Patricia Brown
The fifth book in the Coastal Coffee Club Mystery series follows Eleanor as she investigates infidelity, murder, and long-buried secrets in the sleepy seaside town of Sand Beach.

Visit www.gladeyepress.com for fantastic deals on all GladEye Press titles.

Follow us on Facebook: https://www.facebook.com/GladEyePress/

GladEye titles can be ordered from your local book store and Amazon.com.

More Books from GladEye Press

The Time Tourists
The Yesterday Girl
Sharleen Nelson
Follow the adventures and missteps of time-traveling PI Imogen Oliver as she recovers lost items and unearths long-buried stories and secrets from the past in this exciting series!

Tripping the Field: An Existential Crisis of Ungodly Proportions
Ian Jaydid
Empiricist scientist, Professor Michael Huxley tumbles, stumbles, strides, and crawls through the jungles of South America, the mountains of Tibet, and the backwoods of Colorado in search of enlightenment and the hope of saving the world from a religious cult that has discovered a dark shortcut to the power of quantum realities.

The Midnight Show: bohemians, byways, and bonfires
Camille Cole
During the early days of Oregon's famous Country Fair, the Midnight Show was a stage shared by icons of the counterculture, lovers, children and family, and those of us finding our way through.

Teaching in Alaska
What I Learned in the Bush
Julie Bolkan
Among the first outsiders to live and work with the Yup'ik in their small villages, this book tells Julie's story of how she survived culture clashes, isolation, weather, and struggles with honey buckets—a candid and often funny account of one gussock woman's 12 years in the Alaskan bush.

All GladEye titles are available for purchase at www.gladeyepress.com, in book stores, and from Amazon.com

Dying to Win
Patricia Brown
Even a bucolic beach town has its skeletons. When the newly wed husband of the area's richest heiress mysteriously disappears, Eleanor and her friends find themselves entangled in dark secrets involving bullies, racists, murder, anonymous love letters, and more!

Under A Dying Moon
Patricia Brown
When a young girl washes up on the beach, there is no doubt murder is once again the topic in town. Two more brutal murders bring the town to the edge of panic. Are the newly arrived young swing-ers involved or the cute retired couple? And what is the deal with the gnomes scattered around town?

Dying for Diamonds
Patricia Brown
When a mean-spirited mystery writer visiting her sleepy coastal town is murdered, Eleanor Penrose, her retired detective friend Angus, the coffee club ladies, and Feathers, the irascible African grey parrot, work to solve the puzzles without becoming the mur-derer's next victims.

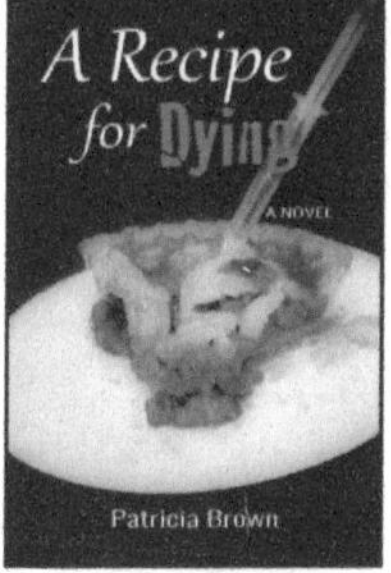

A Recipe for Dying
Patricia Brown
The old people are dying in the small coastal town of Waterton, but no one seems to notice—after all, that's what old folk do, isn't it? Eleanor and her delightful assortment of friends, most whom are getting up in age, set out to discover what is going on. Is it a series of mercy killings, or murder, and is their investigation putting them in danger?